STELLA GI

THE SNOW-

CW01499194

STELLA Dorothea Gibbons was bo... ... ...
was educated first at home, then the North London Collegiate
School for Girls, and finally at University College, London,
where she did a two-year course on journalism.

Her first job, in 1923, was as cable decoder for British United
Press. For the next decade she worked as a London journalist
for various publications, including the *Evening Standard* and
The Lady.

Her first published book was a volume of poems in 1930. This
was followed by the classic comic novel *Cold Comfort Farm*
(1932) which remains her best-known work. In 1933 she met
and married Allan Webb, an actor and singer, the marriage
lasting until the latter's death in 1959.

From 1934 until 1970, Stella Gibbons published more than
twenty further novels, in addition to short stories and poetry,
and there were two further posthumously-published full-
length works of fiction. She was a fellow of the Royal Society of
Literature, and was awarded a *Femina Vie-Heureuse* prize in
1933 for *Cold Comfort Farm*.

Stella Gibbons died on 19 December 1989 at home in London.

FICTION BY STELLA GIBBONS

Novels

Cold Comfort Farm (1932)
Bassett (1934)
Enbury Heath (1935)
Miss Linsey and Pa (1936)
Nightingale Wood (1938)
My American (1939)
The Rich House (1941)
Ticky (1943)
Westwood (1946)
The Matchmaker (1949)
Conference at Cold Comfort Farm (1949)
The Swiss Summer (1951)*
Fort of the Bear (1953)
The Shadow of a Sorcerer (1955)
Here Be Dragons (1956)
White Sand and Grey Sand (1958)
A Pink Front Door (1959)*
The Weather at Tregulla (1962)*
The Wolves Were in the Sledge (1964)
The Charmers (1965)
Starlight (1967)
The Snow-Woman (1969)*
The Woods in Winter (1970)*
The Yellow Houses (written c.1973, published 2016)
Pure Juliet (written c.1980, published 2016)

* *published by Furrowed Middlebrow and Dean Street Press*

Story Collections

Roaring Tower and Other Stories (1937)
Christmas at Cold Comfort Farm (1940)
Beside the Pearly Water (1954)

Children's Fiction

The Untidy Gnome (1935)

STELLA GIBBONS

THE SNOW-WOMAN

With an introduction by
Elizabeth Crawford

DEAN STREET PRESS

A Furrowed Middlebrow Book
FM62

Published by Dean Street Press 2021

Copyright © 1969 The Estate of Stella Gibbons

Introduction © 2021 Elizabeth Crawford

First published in 1969 by Hodder & Stoughton

Cover by DSP
Shows detail from an illustration by Leslie Wood. The publisher
thanks the artist's estate and the archives of Manchester Metropolitan
University

ISBN 978 1 913527 79 2

www.deanstreetpress.co.uk

To

CHARLES OLIVER

Introduction

Of *The Snow-Woman*, a new novel from Stella Gibbons, the reviewer in the *Sunday Times* (18 May 1969) commented, 'The astringent pessimism which underlay the exuberant parody of *Cold Comfort Farm* is also characteristic of Stella Gibbons's latest monster, the septuagenarian Maude Barrington, a rich Englishwoman who has hated nearly everybody since her three brothers died in the first world war'. That 'exuberant parody' cast a long shadow over the subsequent twenty-three novels that Stella Gibbons published in her lifetime; early success had been both a blessing and a burden. 'That Book', as she came to call it, had been a great popular success, had received rave reviews on both sides of the Atlantic, and in 1933 had won the *Prix Étranger* of the *Prix Femina-Vie Heureuse*, much to the disgust of Virginia Woolf, a previous winner. An excoriating parody of the 'Loam and Lovechild School of Fiction', as represented in the works of authors such as Thomas Hardy, Mary Webb, Sheila Kaye-Smith, and even D.H. Lawrence, *Cold Comfort Farm* was also for Stella Gibbons an exorcism of her early family life. There really had been 'something nasty in the woodshed'.

Stella Dorothea Gibbons was born at 21 Malden Crescent, Kentish Town, London, on 5 January 1902, the eldest child and only daughter of [Charles James Preston] Telford Gibbons (1869-1926) and his wife, Maude (1877-1926). Her mother was gentle and much-loved but her father, a doctor, although admired by his patients, was feared at home. His ill-temper, drunkenness, affairs with family maids and governesses, violence, and, above all, the histrionics in which, while upsetting others, Stella thought he derived real pleasure, were the dominating factors of her childhood and youth. She was educated at home until the age of thirteen and was subsequently a pupil at North London Collegiate School. The change came after her governess attempted suicide when Telford Gibbons lost interest in their affair. Apparently, it was Stella who had discovered the unconscious woman.

Knowing it was essential to earn her own living, in September 1921 Stella enrolled on a two-year University of London course, studying for a Diploma in Journalism, and in 1924 eventually found work with a news service, the British United Press. She was still living at home when in 1926 her mother died suddenly. No longer feeling obliged to stay in the house she hated, she moved out into a rented room in Hampstead. Then, barely five months later, her father died, leaving his small estate to Stella's younger brother, who squandered it within a year. As a responsible elder sister, Stella found a new home to share with her brothers, 'Vale Cottage' in the Vale of Health, a cluster of old houses close to Hampstead Heath. These Hampstead years were to provide a rich source of material. Not only the topography of the area but friends and acquaintances are woven into future novels. One young man in particular, Walter Beck, a naturalised German to whom she was for a time engaged, reappears in various guises.

In 1926 Stella's life was fraught not only with the death of her parents and the assumption of responsibility for her brothers, but also with her dismissal from the BUP after a grievous error when converting the franc into sterling, a miscalculation then sent round the world. However, she soon found new employment on the London *Evening Standard*, first as secretary to the editor and then as a writer of 'women's interest' articles for the paper. By 1928 she had her own by-line and, because the *Evening Standard* was championing the revival of interest in the work of Mary Webb, was deputed to précis her novel *The Golden Arrow* and, as a consequence, read other similarly lush rural romances submitted to the paper. This at a time when her own romance was ending unhappily. In 1930 she was once more sacked, passing from the *Evening Standard* to a new position as editorial assistant on *The Lady*. Here her duties involved book reviewing and it was the experience of skimming through quantities of second-rate novels that, combined with her Mary Webb experience, led to the creation of *Cold Comfort Farm*, published by Longmans in 1932.

In 1929 Stella had met Allan Webb, an Oxford graduate a few years her junior, now a student at the Webber-Douglas School of Singing. They were soon secretly engaged, but it was only in 1933 that they married, royalties from *Cold Comfort Farm* affording them some financial security. Two years later their only child, a daughter, was born and was, in turn, eventually to give Stella two grandsons, on whom she doted. In 1936 the family moved to 19 Oakeshott Avenue, Highgate, within the gated Holly Lodge estate, where Stella was to live for the rest of her life.

For the next forty years, in war and peace, Stella Gibbons continued to publish a stream of novels, as well as several volumes of poetry and short stories. Written nearly ten years into widowhood, *The Snow-Woman* (1969) is characterised as 'an exercise in self-mockery' by her biographer, her nephew Reggie Oliver. He comments that she gave to Maude Barrington, the 'Snow-Woman' of the title, 'many of her own prejudices and foibles – her passion for order and obscure Victorian novels, her hatred of modernity, [and] her occasional haughtiness', relating Maude's coldness to Stella's own 'emotional stasis' following the death of her husband. Stella has no qualms in dropping more material clues linking herself to Maude. For instance, Maude's home is, like Stella's, in Highgate, the great-aunt who bequeathed her the sofa ('covered in dark green repp') upon which the catalystic event of the novel takes place, is given Stella's own second name, 'Dorothea', the family doctor of Maude's childhood is 'Dr. Gibbons', Maude's school was North London Collegiate, and Maude's sojourn in France, where much of the novel is enticingly set, draws on Stella's last visit there in 1966. In one amusingly self-reverential sentence Stella allows Maude to declare '...it's like there always having been Starkadders at Cold Comfort', alluding to one of the best-known lines from 'That Book'. *The Snow-Woman* gives plenty of scope to the note of 'astringent pessimism' on which the *Sunday Times* reviewer commented, as Stella takes side swipes at, for instance, modern art, modern interior design ('as impersonal as a window-display at "Habitat's"'), and 'the small breaches made in the wall of conventional matters' that 'widen – widen – and in will pour the waters of Chaos and down we shall finally go'. Yet *The Snow-Woman*, like many of Stella's novels, has the charm of a fairy tale, as the icy splinter in Maude's heart melts with the revelation that, despite her brothers' deaths, her family was not expunged.

After Allan's death in 1959 Stella never remarried. Although avoiding literary and artistic society, she did hold a monthly 'salon' at home, attracting a variety of guests, young and old, eminent, unknown and, sometimes, odd. She continued to publish novels until 1970 and even after that wrote two more that she declined to submit to her publisher. As Reggie Oliver wrote in *Out of the Woodshed* (1998), 'She no longer felt able to deal with the anguish and anxiety of exposing her work to a publisher's editor, or to the critics.' She need not have feared; both novels have subsequently been published.

Stella Gibbons died on 19 December 1989, quietly at home, and is buried across the road in Highgate Cemetery, alongside her husband.

Elizabeth Crawford

CHAPTER 1

THE dry, gloomy afternoon had been refreshed by a shower. On my way back from the village at three, the pavements were gleaming under the March wind and the air was moist. The change did not last; when I looked out over London later on, lowering clouds were again suspended above the dark roof of the city.

That afternoon, five years ago, Lionel Crozier was coming to have tea with me.

Although we had kept up a fairly regular correspondence I had not seen him for nearly ten years. After the war—the second war—he had gone back to live in France, with Charles Handel, the art critic and historian, visiting England only occasionally on his journeys all over the world as Charles's emissary.

I was not entirely pleased at the prospect of seeing Lionel again, and perhaps my ambivalent attitude expressed itself in slight nervousness: I told Millie, my maid, to show him straight into the back drawing-room as soon as he arrived.

She glanced at me in a little surprise, for I had repeated aloud an order that had settled, over the years, into a household custom, but she only said:

'I'm making my coconut kisses, miss; Mr. Crozier always did like them. There was just enough coconut left. I did wonder if it would fill up my dozen, but we was all right.'

I smiled at her, noticing in her returning smile the remnants of the fragile prettiness which had been hers when she first came to us, as scullery-maid, in 1913.

'I'd best be getting on with them, miss; they're ever so indigestible eaten hot, and I'd like them to cool right down.'

She went out of the room. I can recall that prettiness perfectly in memory; it had been so delicate, with its crown of ash-blonde hair and its wild-flower skin. Poor Millie, I thought, sitting by the window in my back drawing-room that afternoon and looking out over my spectacular view of London; poor Millie. No strength of character.

Was Millie a little nervous too? She did not usually talk to me about her cooking, knowing that, unless some culinary experiment should fail noticeably, it does not interest me.

I expected that she would 'have a word', as she calls it, with Lionel when he arrived, and I was not surprised to hear, after his ring and her light step crossing the hall to answer it, the sound of their voices, in chat, in the hall.

But I was surprised to hear a third voice join in; younger and rather loud; a young woman's.

My slight testiness increased to annoyance: had Lionel retained that irritating fault of an over-prolonged youth, his habit of bringing strangers, uninvited, to call on his old friends?

The question was partly answered when he walked into the room, wearing, in spite of being in his early sixties, clothes that even I could recognize as being in the extreme of contemporary male fashion, and followed by a young woman in the last stages of a pregnancy so obvious as to appear exaggerated.

I was, I confess, exceedingly annoyed. Modesty did not enter into my irritation, except on behalf of the girl herself—I wished, for her own sake, that she could have realized how unpleasing her appearance was in the eyes of a septuagenarian—but social considerations did. And why, why, I asked myself, must she wear a kind of Greek tunic ending above her knees, made of black stuff and divided into four sections by lines of a crude pink?

Lionel advanced with hands held out.

'Maudie darling,' he cried, 'how divine to see you again! and not changed in the smallest detail except for your hair. Which I adore, at first sight. I simply adore. It's like that frost you sprinkle on things at Christmas.'

I had to let my hands be taken and pressed, and felt relief that no attempt was made to kiss them. Silly, disloyal Lionel knew quite well when to stop, though he seldom put the knowledge to use.

I smiled and observed that he did not seem to have changed, either, and then I looked over his shoulder at the young woman.

'Oh, of course'—and he turned his eyes away from my face, on which they had been fixed with a spoony expression—'darling, this is Teddie, Teddie Parker, this is Miss Barrington, who's known me since I was a very bad little boy indeed.'

She took a few steps towards me, slowly, because of her weight and size, and half put out her hand and mumbled 'Good-afternoon' from behind a hanging mass of hair that, in its colour, reminded me of the sovereigns and half sovereigns I used to see when *I* was a very little girl indeed, peeping from the purses of the grown-ups. These particular sovereigns had been in circulation long enough, I noticed, to become dingy.

'Get that weight off your feet, dear girl,' bustled Lionel, pressing her into the largest chair. She slowly settled herself into it and leant back, while I averted my eyes from her. My anger with Lionel was increasing.

He was now rapturizing at the window. 'Even the view! Just the same! No—no—it isn't, though. All those bony white things sticking up.'

'There has been a great deal of building in the last five years,' I pointed out. 'Do sit down, Lionel, and will you ring the bell for tea, please.'

I knew perfectly well that I spoke to him as if he were still thirteen, but how else could I speak? If he were not still thirteen, he was seventeen, and a tiresome seventeen at that.

But he lingered; presumably in order to sweep round dramatically as Millie came in with the tray. 'Do I smell coconut?' he cried. 'Yes, I do—it is—they are—my own, my so-well-remembered and so long missed coconut kisses!'

Millie was smiling. Her eyes were fixed on the tray as she manoeuvred it skilfully and at last set it down, with its load of silver, on the walnut table which she keeps properly polished.

As it touched the wood she just lifted her eyes for an instant and allowed the smile to dwell on Lionel's face,

The correctness of her manner gratified me, for an instant, in the midst of my irritation. She had benefited from the excellent domestic training at home, and had not forgotten it during those years that she had been away from us.

I caught her eye, and she went out of the room immediately.

I began to pour the tea.

The young woman was fussing. While I put more water into the pot from the spirit-kettle which I prefer to an electric one, and then awaited an opportunity to offer them bread and butter, I caught mutters about not wanting anything, accompanied by various repudiating gestures, and this was followed by a low question from Lionel, 'Do you feel all right, child?' which she answered by a violent jerk of her head. Finally he left her to peck at a piece of bread and butter undisturbed.

'How is Charles?' I enquired when he had asked if I would let him begin on the cakes at once, which he did.

'Oh, it's so sad, Maude. He's getting old . . . Charles! One can hardly believe it. Just in these last few months. Crumbling and decaying under our very eyes. It makes us all so dreadfully sad.'

'I really can't believe he's become old as quickly as that, Lionel . . .' I said. 'His nervous energy and health have always been unusually good, surely, and only last week I was reading an article by him in *The Apollonian* on the provenance of those two Courbets there has been so much discussion about . . . I thought it very good. He seems to be writing better than ever.'

'Oh, he can still do his stuff, all right,' said Lionel, staring at me gloomily with an expression that seemed to hint at some unspoken difficulty. 'That's . . . just the trouble.'

Fond as I was of Charles Handel, I did not wish to discuss any problems that might be troubling him in his old age. He was well-supported and cared for by a wife and a circle of devoted friends.

I also rather doubted if he had any difficulties; Lionel has always relished mystification and hinting; Jock and Harry and Edward used to tease him about it. They were all great teases.

Lionel's own life has been full of broken friendships and the treacherous and ungrateful behaviour of those he considers himself to have 'taken up and done *everything* for, but everything'. I concluded that the girl sitting silently in the background was yet another of these.

'How long is it since you've seen Charles?' he went on, rousing himself from his morose contemplation of my view. 'I was trying to think, on our way here.'

'Nearly twenty years. He dined here on the evening before he went back to France.'

'And you've never seen Belair?'

'No. I was to go there for a visit, you may remember, and then my father and mother—'

'Took so long a-dying, didn't they. Poor Maudie . . . ten years, wasn't it? First your father and then . . . did you know Charles has given me a house?'

'No.' I could say no more; I was recovering from his comment on my parents' deaths. I managed, however, to keep my eyes fixed on him in attention.

'Yes, the one he built on that meadow just below Belair, where the gentians used to grow. Gave it me before I left this time for America. It appears he has left it me in his Will, but he wanted me to have it before he dies—which he thinks he may do any day now. It's the latest bee in his bonnet,' he ended irritably, and suddenly became silent.

One of his lifelong habits has been his inability to appear interested in any conversation for longer than some minutes. After his first silly gush of welcome and gossip there is a gradual failing in attention to what one is saying, and then this bored silence falls.

I began to feel it was time that I addressed a remark to the young woman, who had been sitting at my tea-table for nearly half an hour, with less attention being paid to her than is often given to a dog.

Accordingly, at the end of a conversation about the garden at Lionel's house, Les Gentianes, and his good fortune in having secured the services of a gardener living in the village, I leant towards her, asking whether she knew France at all. (She might; her class seemed to get about everywhere nowadays.)

My question received, in answer, a silent movement of the head which might have been negative, and a mutter from Lionel—'Do let her be, ducky.'

There have been many occasions when I have longed to order Lionel out of the room. This was one. There he sat, wearing a boldly-striped suit of youthful cut, and from the curious way in which his hair was trimmed, to the rose in his buttonhole, he seemed to me pathetic. Irritating, too, but chiefly pathetic.

Old monkeys please nobody, as George Moore once wrote. But some of them still try.

The girl made no further sound or movement and he resumed the conversation, keeping it—skilfully, I must admit—skirting around names and situations which I should have preferred to avoid discussing. One particularly pointed allusion to his unhappy sister Frances finally convinced me that his precise object in coming was to anger and embarrass me.

I had not spoken Frances Crozier's name aloud for many years.

Seeing that I was not going to be drawn into questioning him about her, he went on to talk about the trip to America, from which he was on his way home to France.

'I spent a week getting Salter Blake to give up American Primitives,' he informed me, and I said 'Indeed?', not knowing who Salter Blake might be, or, indeed, what Lionel meant.

'An *entire week*,' he went on impressively, 'sitting up till four in the morning, night after night after night. I have never *conceived* such drinking!'

I observed that it must have been very bad for their livers.

'Oh, Salter's liver melted some years ago . . . you see, he had his doubts about the Mods. He's always collected American Primitives.'

Mods. is Lionel's name for contemporary painters and their work. He does not mean by it the young people who used to riot at seaside towns some years ago.

'American Primitives are scarce, of course . . . but there's still just a chance of picking up a terrific bargain; a wooden square from some top storey room in a shack buried away in Maine . . . (Maine's a big county) . . . with Mom or Pop or Junior on it, painted round 1840, for a song. But you can't buy the Mods for a song. *They* don't starve in attics, they can hang out for the prices they want, and Blake's a mean old dog. Said he wasn't going to pay that money for something looking as if the painter'd upset the pot and paddled in it.'

'Why should he, after all, Lionel?' I leant forward, ostensibly to help myself to a lady-finger biscuit, but actually to observe the girl. She had been stirring uneasily, and her cheek, visible between her falling hair, was gleaming with sweat.

'Sally MacGloire's things actually are painted like that,' added Lionel. 'Nice little colourist, too.'

'Surely one buys a picture because one likes it?' I went on, not knowing fully what I was saying, for I was becoming increasingly apprehensive about my younger guest.

'One buys as an investment, Maude. You are . . . out of touch, aren't you?'

'Instead of diamonds—I see. But . . . did . . . you . . .' (she seemed to be bracing her body against her chair, as if resisting a spasm of some kind) '. . . succeed in persuading him, then? Surely, with . . . Charles's authority and advice behind . . . you . . .' I broke off.

'Oh, yes—probably at the cost of my liver. Charles's authority and advice, yes . . . Blake bought two Maxwells and a Heck and promised to consider a Teremkezi. Charles is pleased with me.'

I heard the words and meant to make some congratulatory comment, but I never made it. The state of the girl was now such that I must speak. Leaning forward while Lionel was actually still talking, and interrupting him in a manner that would ordinarily have been inconceivable to me:

'I am afraid you are not feeling at all well,' I said to her.

CHAPTER 2

LIONEL turned quickly, exclaiming, 'Oh my God.'

Glancing from her face to his, I detected his expression before he could control it, and I thought: *He planned this, he hoped it would happen. I will never forgive him.* Foolish words; at my age, one knows that such vows can fade. But I, too, was having to control myself. I turned again to the girl, who said loudly, almost shouted, 'I should think you could see, couldn't you?'

'Now stay quiet; keep still,' I told her. 'Mr. Crozier will help you on to the sofa and I will telephone . . . how much time have we, do you think?'

She shook back her hair, and gasped out, 'I don't know . . . it's coming ever so quickly . . .' and the words ended in what seemed to me an appalling sound.

It reminded me of the bellowing of a cow, which I had heard throughout a seemingly interminable night, while I was staying with some friends in the country. It did not seem to be uttered by human vocal chords.

'Where are you booked in?' I urged her, when it ceased. Lionel had his hand on her shoulder and was gently kneading it and looking distressed—as if that were any help.

She shook her head distractedly, and Lionel, teetering in an irritating way on his heels, said in a disturbed tone:

'The trouble is, she isn't booked in anywhere.'

Then I did stare.

'Do you mean to tell me'—I turned on the pallid, sweating young creature—'that there's no bed for you to go to—you aren't under any doctor?'

She began to say something—I think it was a protest—when another spasm seized her, and, bending her head, she gripped the sides of the chair.

'Of course she's under a doctor,' snapped Lionel. 'She was going to have it at home, only now she's walked out of her home, she's left her husband.' He rubbed one finger agitatedly below one eye, with his mouth open.

Before I could speak she got clumsily up from the chair and staggered over to my sofa (a legacy from Great-aunt Dorothea, and covered in dark green repp) and sank on to it, keeping her frightened eyes, visible between the masses of her hair, fixed upon his face.

I crossed the room without another word; to the door; without looking at either of them again.

From the corner of my eye I just saw him bending over, and heard him say something—I don't know what—and then, actually, I saw him put his hand upon her grotesque tunic, as if to begin rolling it up or removing it, and I shut the door on the unbeliev-able sight.

Millie was hurrying across the hall, looking shocked and white. She had lost her head, as she invariably does in a crisis.

'Oh, miss—what's the matter?—it's the baby, isn't it?—I heard her—oh, miss—' She was making confused, useless gestures with her hands, and her large eyes were staring at me in fear. 'Oh, miss—please—'

'There is no "please" about it. Go in there,' and I re-opened the door, 'and help. You know something about such matters, don't you? I am going up to Mrs. Halliwell's.'

'Oh, miss—please—you don't know—'

'Don't waste time. In you go.'

I did not raise my voice nor did I glance into the room, but stood holding the door ajar. Millie went past me, lowering her head as if she were hurrying into a storm, and I shut the door.

Going briskly up to my room I packed a nightgown and other requirements, put on my coat and hat, picked up my book from the bedside table and went downstairs and out of the house. I heard voices, and then another—I can only call it a bellow—as I passed through the hall, and I believe that Lionel came hurrying out towards the telephone, but I shut the door without looking at him.

I walked quickly up the sloping path of my front garden, noti-cing that the Poetaz narcissis were going to be unusually fine this year; the buds stood thick in the moist foliage and one or two were already in bloom. I prefer flowers while they are in bud, I think; the promise is unspoiled.

I walked up the hill to the row of old white cottages where Tessa Halliwell lives. She was the friend living nearest to me (yes, I suppose, even at that time, I looked on Tessa as a friend) and I did not want the fatigue of going over to Hampstead or down into London with my case of night things, because I was exhausted by my anger, as well as annoyingly tired, as usual, at the end of the day.

I derived something from Tessa's friendship, though we had, then, nothing in common. I suppose I was lonelier than I knew.

I could admire her unfailing energy and her good-nature, sloppy though the latter is, and I did; the fact that she is a fool, and not a lady, I had almost grown to overlook, in the five years we had known one another. I knew with what relish and amusement she would hear the tale I would have to tell.

One of the large pink lampshades she affects could be seen glowing between the undrawn curtains of her small drawing-room as I approached. Those houses are too small, of course. I could not endure to be shut up in such a box. But Tessa is well content with hers, because the rooms are suited by the clutter that she likes.

As I opened the small iron gate which shuts off her four square feet of paving and flower-filled tubs from the road, I saw her move into the lamplight, against the background of the pieces of Indian and Chinese embroidery, and the fans and little dark pictures and oddments picked up in junk shops that she likes to hang on her strawberry-pink walls.

Tessa, as usual at that time in the late afternoon, was wearing one of her Oriental coats, or robes, all of them in what I should not hesitate to call an advanced stage of decay. Loose gold threads hang from them and catch in things as she passes, and the silk that covers the wadding of the sleeves is rubbed and worn. She explains the retention of these things long after they should have been thrown away by saying that she has owned them so long that they are 'not clothes, any more, but people'.

I have found it impossible, in my association with Tessa, to avoid some contagion from her fantasies. Of course I remain untouched by them inwardly, but, in order to keep on good terms with her—and I cannot endure her occasional scolding fits—I have had, to a certain extent, to talk her language. My parents would not believe their ears, could they hear me referring to one of Tessa's robes as 'the Persian Person'.

She caught sight of me through the window and at once began to gesticulate and make mouths. I drew closer, looking in, and saw that a dangling thread from the hem of her robe had become temporarily entangled with the flex of one of the lamps, a standard which, as she pulled impatiently at the obstacle, tottered behind her and threatened to fall on her.

I too gestured, warningly, and pointed over her shoulder, and at length she turned round, grasped the lamp just as it fell forward, and, having disentangled herself, finally appeared at the front door. She was laughing, as usual.

'Oh . . . it's grand to see someone. I phoned five people and everybody was out—come on in, love, don't just stand there—oh dear, when I saw you waving about and frowning at me I suddenly thought of those concert-party turns where the kids point at the ghost behind the comic's back and yell . . . and then I started to laugh and I couldn't stop . . . what's that for?' she interrupted herself, pointing at my suitcase. 'You running away from home? I thought you had an old flame coming to tea?'

Tessa would say this type of thing, and I had ceased to protest. I stepped into the warm little hall and she shut the door behind me.

'I am running away from home,' I said.

'You are?' Tessa almost stood on tiptoe, in a pair of slippers sharing, even to the dangling gold threads, many of the disadvantages of her People, and stared up at me through her extraordinary glasses, part of what she likes to call 'my spectacle wardrobe'. 'Is it Millie? What's up?'

'Nothing. It isn't Millie . . . Lionel Crozier, the man who was coming to tea with me . . .' I broke off, too angry and—upset, suddenly, to say any more.

'Oh—was-he-in-love-with-you-umpteen-years-ago?' Tessa cried, her eyes and mouth and even her nose, expressing curiosity and enjoyment.

'No, of course not, why must you always assume . . . ?'

I sat down on a chair covered with rubbed, grubby silk uninvited by Tessa, who does occasionally overlook such details, and kept quiet for a moment, with bent head. I was angry and shaken and disturbed. When I had recovered, I said:

'He has always been a malicious, twisted creature. My parents were sorry for him; he came of a bad stock and an unhappy home; he was perpetually in and out of our house . . . a kind of refuge, I suppose. This afternoon (I had not seen him for ten years), he walked into the room followed by a very young girl, not yet twenty, I should think, in the last stage of pregnancy. After about half an hour, during which she said not a single word, but looked more and more ill, she . . . started labour, and is in it at this moment, I presume. On Great-Aunt Dorothea's sofa.'

I paused, for, as I had expected, Tessa had begun to laugh. She laughed loudly and with an air of helpless amusement, and I sat and watched her and reflected that her temperament was a fortunate one. Then, abruptly, she ceased, wiping her eyes with a paper handkerchief which she dragged from a packet on the table.

'Oh my poor old dear! The last person, the very last person, in the entire whole world it should happen to! Great-Aunt Dorothea—oh dear, I *am* sorry, really, it must have been horrible for you . . . but'—suddenly opening her eyes very wide—'he isn't coping alone, surely?'

'Millie is there,' I said, 'I believe she once helped her sister in a confinement.'

'I suppose you couldn't manage to call it a birth, dear?'

'A birth, then,' I said, without irritation.

'But a First Baby!' proclaimed Tessa, returning to the field of excitement. 'There's always a risk with a first. I know I nearly died with Mike.'

'The young woman looked unusually healthy to me.'

'Well, Maude, I know you aren't like most people, but honestly . . .' Off she went.

'There . . . I'm a bitch,' she declared at last, having so to speak run down. 'When you're all nervy and shocked. Here,' and she darted to a cupboard and began fumbling.

'You certainly aren't that,' I assured her.

'Yes I am,' insisted Tessa, slopping brandy into a glass. 'I ought to have realized how shattering it was for you—all over your beautiful sofa—and frightening too. After all, you—'

She broke off and went muttering into the kitchen; she would make some coffee, she said.

She had been going to say that unmarried women do find such situations frightening, and had broken off the sentence because she didn't want to hurt me. But I am not easily hurt. Easily bored, I fear, yes; and easily irritated because of my blood-pressure, but not easily hint. And touchiness is among the vulgar faults.

Tessa always resorts to the cooking stove when the ordinary routine of life is deflected by a crisis, and coffee is her great resource. Clattering away at her coffee-making, she now called out: 'Come and talk to me.'

'Where were you rushing off to, then?' she went on, looking up from the saucepan of milk, 'with your little bag and all?'

'I was coming to ask you to put me up for the night,' I said, standing in the doorway and taking a sip of brandy.

'Well do *come in*, don't *loom* over me, I cannot bear being *loomed* over. Of course, love to have you, you know that, if you don't mind the spare room bed being propped up with a book, the blasted castor came off this morning while I was doing something or other . . . but are you actually going to leave them to it until tomorrow morning?'

'Yes.'

'I don't know how you *can*. I'm dying to know who she is and why he brought her along . . .'

'I don't care who she is or why he brought her, Tessa. I am only exceedingly annoyed with Lionel.'

'Lionel's him, is it? . . . and you've known him for umpteen years, you say?'

'Since I was eight and he was born . . . I am certain the whole thing is one of his peculiar jokes. He enjoys upsetting people and annoying them. He lives in France with Charles Handel, the art historian.'

'Oh, a couple of queers,' said Tessa, pushing past me with a tray. 'Do budge, love.'

I let the remark pass. I have deliberately shut my mind to this subject: I know what friendship between men can mean, and such talk seems to degrade it. Aberrations are a subject for the specialist.

I followed her back into the drawing-room, where she was now fussing at the window. 'Blast these things—they're *everlastingly* . . .'

'There are too many runners on the rail,' I said, when I had watched her for a moment. 'One has caught in the last hook.'

'Well, you might give me a hand!' cried Tessa, rounding upon me, 'Sitting there . . .'

'Now calm down,' I said, 'and I will do it.'

I like dealing with these little domestic problems; they are a challenge. I advanced upon the recalcitrant curtains and in less than one moment I had disentangled the runners and hooks and drawn the pair neatly together.

'Congrats!' exclaimed Tessa, making a face, and we smiled at one another as I sat down.

'Sure you won't have some?' she asked, beginning on the coffee.

'Quite sure, thank you. I had tea less than an hour ago. Why are you drinking coffee at half-past five in the evening?'

'Oh, well, you know me. I can always drink coffee. But actually there is a perfectly—good—reason for drinking it, this evening. You see I went out to—'

I forget how her tale ended. Its point was that she had not lunched until five, and the coffee was following her late meal. 'So for once,' concluded Tessa, 'I'm being quite *formal*.'

A little clock on her mantelshelf struck six, with a whirring silvery note. I seemed to have been in Tessa's house for a long time.

CHAPTER 3

'DON'T take any notice of that, it's fast,' Tessa answered, as if I had spoken; she does not like her guests to look at the clock. I suppose no hostess does, but Tessa dislikes it more than most. 'Tell me about Lionel? What's his *background*?'

Bad, I thought. It was the first thing I had learned, when I was eight, about the family which had moved into the house across the quiet road lying off Highgate Village where we lived.

Mr. and Mrs. Crozier regularly and loudly quarrelled, an almost unbelievable habit in the eyes of my parents, who never disagreed. They had also begun to owe money to the local trades-people from the first week that they moved in (I am afraid this fact was picked up by myself and Harry, my youngest brother, from the gossip of our maids, who repeated what was related to them by the milkman). Isobel and Frances, the little girls, wore dirty frocks and had buttons off their boots. It was all utterly unlike what we were accustomed to at home.

A sickly baby boy arrived in the household some weeks after the family had moved in. This was Lionel, who almost from birth settled into that routine of illness after illness which was to make his infancy and babyhood one long ailment. We grew accustomed to the sight of Dr. Gibbons's hired victoria outside Lyndon House with old Ford, the coachman, on the box, resignedly slapping his shoulders against the bitter wind or sweating through the summer in his thick uniform. 'Lionel must be ill again,' I would think, coming in from school, 'poor little boy.'

My parents did not forbid us to talk to the Crozier girls. But we three girls did attend the same school, the North London Collegiate, and took the tram together down to the foot of Highgate Hill, and then walked along Fortess and Kentish Town Roads to Patshull Road, and part of the way home again, every day, and I must admit that I found the lively and precocious Frances and Isobel, but more particularly Frances, a perpetual source of entertainment, and that when Jock and Edward came home for the holidays they too were fascinated by them and by the life in Lyndon House.

Perhaps it was the contrast with life at home, where the grown-ups were the important ones and we were kept firmly in a junior world. I believe the fascination was largely unrealized, and it was well mingled, at least on Edward's part, as he grew older, with contempt.

But even our youngest, Harry, felt it: the charm of Frances's rippling talk, with its vein of wildest fantasy, silencing, while he listened, his own flow of complaints during our daily walk to school. (He attended the youngest class there, for some years before going to his prep. school.) But I did not mean to disinter these memories of more than fifty years ago for the entertainment of Tessa.

'I am still at a loss to understand fully *why* he should have done such a thing,' I said, turning the subject. 'He has always been fond of malicious practical jokes, but surely, at our ages, I should have thought—'

'Oh, darling, you'd never understand,' Tessa interrupted. 'It was sheer naughtiness. And your being so set in your little ways, and all tidy and cosy with your Millie and everything—you're the perfect victim . . . *you* know, you see something all laid out *just so* and looking *too* perfect and you just long and *long* to poke your tiny finger in. *I* understand it perfectly. Like that woman who put her finger through that famous picture in that exhibition—it was in the papers—you remember.'

'I remember thinking that she must be unbalanced,' I said.

'Oh no, darling, it was quite natural. *I* understand it perfectly. Life would be even duller than it is if none of us ever did anything unbalanced,' Tessa said, her merry little eyes peering at me through her scarlet-rimmed spectacles. 'Now *I* can't understand how you can bear to sit there not knowing what's going on at home.'

'I intend to show him how angry I am,' I explained—and then, as I spoke, I felt that my anger was no longer there. In former years I could keep up a steady white-heat of justifiable wrath; the 'righteous wrath' of the Old Testament. But, abruptly, this particular anger against Lionel seemed to have flickered down and almost vanished. I was learning the bitter truth that, in old age, everything that nourishes one's willpower fails.

Tessa broke the silence with the observation that I 'gave her the shivers sometimes'. I made no reply.

'D'you s'pose he's the father?' she asked in a moment.

'I am inclined to think not. He has many faults, but I have never suspected the fathering of bastards to be among them.'

'Was he ever married?' she pursued.

'I believe not. No, I am certain he wasn't.'

Tessa's comment was that 'it stood out a mile', and then she asked if they shared a flat or a house or what?

'Charles and Lionel? Charles lives in the house he built after the war at St. Benoit, a village near Grenoble, with his wife and son and daughter-in-law, and Lionel used to live there too, but I understand that he now has a house of his own nearby.'

'Oh, Charles has a *wife*? Why couldn't you say so at first?'

'Because I assumed that *you* might have assumed that he had one.'

'You know,' Tessa said irrelevantly, having treated me to a long stare through the spectacles, 'it beats me—you're so clever about music and that sort of thing and in other ways you're as green as *that*.' She pointed to a cushion from which, inevitably, the fringe was coming off, and the telephone bell rang.

'I know who that is!' she cried, sparkling, and hurried to the instrument.

I could not help gathering that the caller was a man, and, as she seemed to have more to say to him than he did to her and the conversation was prolonged (which did not surprise me), I went into the kitchen and occupied myself with washing the coffee-cups, removing, in the course of my task, some stains of an earlier date than those incurred that evening. I do not wash up at home, and no doubt I was unskilful. Certainly, I disliked what I was doing.

Tessa was hurrying out to me, having disposed of her caller with a chorus of assurances and farewells when once more the bell rang.

'This time I feel it's for *you*. I am a wee bit psychic you know,' she cried, hurrying back again.

'Told you so! It's Millie,' she said triumphantly, holding out the receiver, 'I'm dying to hear—do hurry.'

'Yes, Millie?' I said, not hurrying.

'Oh, miss'—her tone was very subdued, I was gratified to hear—'it's all over and it's a lovely little boy. Eight pounds. Mr. Crozier phoned a minute ago. And his mum, miss'—Millie's voice began to thicken—'he's all right too. Both doing well.'

Tessa was rising up and down in her battered slippers with curiosity and excitement. 'Which—is—it?' she mouthed.

'Is the sofa much damaged?' I asked, and I heard Millie and Tessa give simultaneous gasps.

There was a pause. 'A bit, miss,' came Millie's voice, quavering now. 'Not badly, I'd say. I—I have moved it out into the hall, miss. Gave it a wipe over . . . and it'll be all ready to go off to be cleaned—if we can get them to come tomorrow, that is. We know what they are . . . d-d-don't we?'

'That was right,' I said. 'I shall be home in five minutes. Will you start my omelette, please.' A pause, and sounds with which I was familiar. 'Now, Millie,' I instructed her. 'don't cry, please.'

'I'm sorry, miss—I'm sorry—only—it's my nerves—'

'I don't want to hear about them. Millie. *Millie*. Steady, please.'

A pause; and then she said, 'Yes, miss. I'm all right now.'

'Good. I shall be leaving at once.' I hung up the receiver.

'Maude Barrington, you're *inhuman*!' Tessa blazed at me. 'It would serve you right if that poor little tart had *died* on your blasted Aunt Dorothea's sofa! What's a tatty old bit of walnut compared with a real live, kicking, breathing human baby . . . which is it?'

'Babies usually are human,' I observed, smiling at her as I put on my coat. 'It's a boy.'

Tessa flung off sideways, interrupting herself in the middle of a remark about my being a monster to exclaim, 'Oh, good—a boy—I adore boys. Always have. I cried like a drain with sheer disappointment when Gemma was born.' Gemma is one of Tessa's luckless children.

'Yes, well, everything appears to be more or less over,' I said, moving towards the door. 'Thank you for offering to have me at such short notice.'

I hoped that I could now get out of the front door, but no. Tessa began again. She moved across the room after me.

'Sure you wouldn't like me to come with you? Won't you be lonely—with the sofa all ruined, and Millie upset and everything?'

'Lonely?' I paused, looking at her.

'Yes, lonely. I suppose you know what the word means?' I have read of people 'flinging' sentences across a room, and this is what Tessa did.

I paused, as if considering. I felt that I must keep Tessa, and everyone else, at a distance that evening; an even greater distance than usual. I was upset, very upset, and annoyed with myself for being so. A deliberate sentence about my loneliness or otherwise would widen the distance between us . . . and then, suddenly, I could not be bothered. I just said, 'Oh, no, I shan't be lonely, but thanks all the same. Good-night,' and opened the front door.

'I'll call you in the morning,' Tessa shouted after me, 'I'm dying to hear all about it. Elevenish.' She waved and shut the door.

The chilly air of the spring night touched my face. A breath of scent came from some white hyacinths in a window box belonging to one of Tessa's neighbours. I walked home at my usual brisk pace, but I had to compel myself; I was exceedingly tired.

Millie has been trained not to begin chattering the instant she opens the door to me. But I did allow her to help me off with my coat, and while she was doing so I glanced towards the sofa, which she had pushed into the dimmest part of the hall. I could just discern, or thought that I could, some dark patches on the surface, and I had the ridiculous fancy that they would mark it for ever.

I looked away.

'I'll have supper now, please, Millie.' I went upstairs to wash my hands and tidy my hair.

The omelette was being brought into the dining-room as I sat down. Millie's face was swollen and her eyes were red and I could not bring myself to dismiss her without a word.

'You had better go to bed early,' I said. 'It has been a trying evening.'

'Yes, miss, I will. I am tired . . . it was ever such a nice place Mr. Crozier got her into, miss,' she went on, lingering, 'expensive. Somewhere up west.'

'Did Mr. Crozier tell you it was expensive?' I answered, beginning slowly to eat; I did not really want anything.

'Yes, miss. Said it would cost him a packet—it was kind of him, I thought myself, paying all that out for someone . . .' Millie's voice died off and she looked round the room, as if trying to collect her thoughts, while I unwillingly re-entertained Tessa's suspicions about the child's paternity. 'But he didn't say much. Just called out "Wish me luck as you wave me good-bye" as they went off in the ambulance. Made the men smile, that did . . .' Her still-pretty lips twitched. 'They were nice men, miss. Elderly, and careful about the place.'

She lingered yet, looking at me with an air of having something further to say . . . but I was too tired to give her manner much thought.

'Good-night, Millie,' I said.

But she lingered yet.

'What is it?' I said, with impatience: I was in that humiliating condition when the presence of another human being is painful.

'I don't know whether you'll want to hear, miss.' Millie can be insolent: it goes, I have noticed, with prettiness, and the habit lingers on into old age.

'If you have anything to say, say it, please, and go.' I pushed away my plate.

'The young—the girl—the—she sent you a message, miss,' Millie said, and her voice, I noticed, was no longer subdued.

I turned in my chair to stare. 'A *message*?'

'Yes, miss. Mr. Crozier told me over the telephone.'

'Well, what was it?'

'She said "Tell the lady I'm sorry I had my son on her sofa,"' Millie said.

I did not speak for a moment. Then I said, 'I think that was a "message" from Mr. Crozier. Good-night.'

And because we were two old women now, and because she had known Jock and Harry and Edward in our youth, I added, 'Sleep well.'

CHAPTER 4

I MYSELF slept as well as I usually do.

Sleep, for me, used to consist of six hours or so of light unconsciousness, easily disturbed and not particularly refreshing. But occasionally I dreamt, and I was ashamed to admit how much I looked forward to those dreams. Once in a fortnight, or perhaps in three weeks, there would be bright, happy dreams of youth with my brothers.

On this particular night, I dreamed. There was the usual sense in my spirit of mingled laughter and cheerful action: we were doing something: our onward movement through the light green leaves of those woods had a reason and a goal; we were not just rambling. The boys were in their delightful young prime, as always in these dreams, and I had my plait of fair hair again.

I awoke to a rainy morning and the harsh light of March.

After breakfast I went to the drawing-room to practise the accompaniment to a song by Duparc, but my attack on it was occasionally disturbed, I admit, by the memory of the girl's message.

'Tell the lady I'm sorry I had my son on her sofa.'

I was not so sure, now, that this was a final piece of insolence from Lionel. It did not seem to me to bear his stamp. He talks in almost as sloppy a way as Tessa; slang, over-emphasis and vulgarity have always spoiled, for me, whatever he is saying. But this little sentence had neatness and alliteration and balance; even the touch of mockery in her use of *the lady*, suggesting the jeering whine of a gipsy, had a kind of—yes, it was charm. It contrasted so abruptly with the raw fact stated in the words that followed. And then the final return to convention in the slightly prim, Victorian word *sofa*: yes, there was style here. It was a tiny novel, in twelve words, and it had not been written by Lionel Crozier.

Perhaps my ear for such details is an extension of my ear for music.

I was still exceedingly annoyed with Lionel: it has never been difficult for me to feel annoyed with him; it has been a perennial feeling throughout our lifetimes. But for the girl who composed that sentence I began to feel some indulgence. Probably her world was a narrow, if violent one. She would not know what things were an outrage and what were not.

My full attention was not given, that morning, to Duparc's setting of 'L'invitation au voyage'. When, after I had been at the piano for about an hour, the telephone bell rang, some relief was mingled with my customary irritation at its clamour.

'If that is Mrs. Halliwell, tell her I will telephone her later,' I told Millie when she came into the room.

'No, miss . . . it's Mr. Crozier. I did say I'd tell you. Oh miss, he's had such a business finding her husband . . . up all night . . .'

As I went to the telephone I was thinking that there were times when a cliché could be useful. 'Spare me these details,' is what I would have liked to have said to Millie.

But Lionel should have got his foolish self back to France and then written to me, if he wanted to apologize.

'Maudie?' began his light tenor, speaking, I presumed, from his hotel down in London. 'I'm sorry to interrupt your practising . . . you keep it up, then? You aren't still playing accompaniments, are you?' *At your age* vibrated, unspoken, in his tone. He, like Millie on the previous evening, also sounded subdued, I was pleased to hear.

'I am not yet eighty, Lionel. I frequently play accompaniments for my friends and, more occasionally now, professionally.' I paused. I was not going to give him any help.

'Oh . . . er . . . good. I say, I *do* want to say I'm sorry about what happened yesterday. You must let me pay for any . . . er . . . damage to heirlooms, and so forth.'

'Thank you. I don't think that will be necessary.'

'Oh. Well . . . er . . . it was bad of me, I know,' he said, quickly and irritably, 'and now I've said that, and said I'm sorry, could we just put the whole damned business out of our minds? I've been up all night, tooling round the Thames Basin looking for Teddie's wretched little husband, and I feel half dead.'

'Very well. Let us put the whole damned business out of our minds, Lionel. *I* don't want to remember it, any more than you do.'

'Thank God for that . . . I've got other things on my mind. Something I want to talk to you about. Can you lunch this morning?'

This was unexpected. I did not particularly want to see Lionel again, and, also, I knew that Millie had already been out to shop and was preparing some elaborate Italian mess for my luncheon, whether in celebration of the arrival of Mrs. Parker's son or as a peace offering for the added annoyance from her own uncontrolled behaviour yesterday, I did not know.

Still, Millie's feelings were a familiar story, and an elderly man's lifelong habit of malice is not helped by setting the figure of yet another offended old friend in his background. What was really causing my hesitation was that remark about having something he wanted to talk to me about.

My content, such as it is, has been built up with much thought and determination over the years. In proportion to the effort it has cost me is my dislike and fear of anything which threatens it, especially dislike and fear of the problems and the people who perform their dervish-dance around Lionel Crozier.

'Well, can you or can't you?' demanded Lionel impatiently, as I did not answer. 'Sorry, but I really do feel like hell, I didn't get to bed till four.'

I decided that I would go. I did not care for the prospect of eating my way through Millie's luncheon, with her beaming sentimentally over me as she hovered in and out with the steaming food. But I would steer the conversation away from Mrs. Parker, and I would of course avoid asking Lionel what he wanted to talk to me about.

'Thank you—I am sorry, too; I was just thinking . . . I'll come. That would be,' and I told the lie clearly, 'very nice.'

Social lies are the only kind which I condone.

When we had arranged where we were to meet and at what time, I went to tell Millie.

'Oh, miss! All that lovely chicken and the peppers. *I* can't never eat it all.'

'I sincerely hope you won't try,' I advised her, and was nearly at my bedroom door when she called up to me:

'Did he say anything more about the—the young girl, miss?'

'He spent most of the night looking for her husband, so I understand.'

'Yes, miss, I heard that. Mr. Crozier told me that. I only meant—anything more about her and the little baby?'

'No.'

I was going into my room, reflecting that Millie and Lionel seemed to take a disproportionate interest in the young woman, when she called up again:

'And her temperature, miss? It went up, he said. Nothing more about that? not how high it was nor anything?'

'No, Millie.'

She turned away, saying to herself aloud, in the irritating way she sometimes does, 'Psychological, that was—that going up like that—her husband not being there to see the little baby and everything.' I heard the sentence distinctly, in the morning quiet of the hall.

Everything, indeed. My admiration for Mrs. Parker's message was not strong enough to affect my decision that she was a nuisance.

When I go into London I wear black. Once, it was an expression of my grief. Now I know that it suits me, and in the knowledge there is something of ambivalence and pain. However, I am accustomed to pain, in many forms, and I know how to manage it.

Passing Tessa's cottage, I saw her struggling with the curtains again. I was naturally, having smiled, going by without stopping when she made a gesture expressing delight and slid up the window.

'Hullo, love! Where are you off to? I was just going to call you. How's the little mother?' she shouted. I paused.

'I don't know, I'm afraid,' I lied, out of sheer irritation, beginning to put a tighter roll on my lilac silk umbrella; I would certainly be there for some moments and it fussed me to stand shouting in the street and doing nothing.

'Hasn't the boy-friend let you know?'

'He telephoned this morning,' I said; suppressing the information about the search for Mr. Parker, which I knew Tessa would have relished. 'Her temperature had gone up.'

'Sometimes does, after a confinement,' said Tessa in a satisfied voice, though why the fact should have pleased her I could not imagine. 'You off to lunch with him now? You look smashing, love, you really do.'

I think she meant it. I looked away in embarrassment from the admiring smile on her broad face.

'Thank you, it's nice of you to say so.'

'You ought to go out more, you know,' continued Tessa, leaning half out of the window while lighting a cigarette and plainly preparing to gossip, 'it does a woman good to dress up and show herself around. Have people look at her.'

This woman often appears in poor Tessa's conversation, and wears no disguise, being Tessa herself. I was aware of putting up a silent struggle against her opinions and advice.

'No doubt . . . Tessa, I must go. I shall be late.'

'Bye-bye then, love. Have a grand time. That hat's a smasher! See you soon.' She withdrew, puffing clouds of smoke over the curtains, with which she at once resumed her struggle.

Lionel had chosen for our lunching place a restaurant at the very summit of the newest hotel. After our meeting, at which he presented me (in expiation?) with a yellowish-green orchid that looked sickly against the black of my astrakhan collar, I really enjoyed our sweep upwards to the top storey of the place.

Lionel's face was the same colour as the orchid, and the shadows beneath his eyes were almost black. As the lift doors opened upon a very large, low, round room that seemed all windows and glaring white light, he winced.

'Very un-cosy,' he muttered as we followed a waiter to a table for two immediately beneath the windows. 'Edward the Seventh wouldn't have liked this at all, would he?'

'I like it,' I said, as we seated ourselves. I took an unhurried look around while he began the preliminary rites with the waiter: Lionel has ever been a food-fusser. I suppose it is the penalty of irregular and for all I know ill-cooked and even scanty meals in infancy and childhood: the Croziers were not well off. (Neither were we, but my father, a lecturer in the classics at London University, was an admirable manager of money, and my mother serenely guided its use in the house.)

'Now, what would you like? There seems to be—' Lionel suddenly let the over-sized menu card drop on to the table—'Let's not bother with all this, shall we? I've got this thing to talk to you about.' He looked up at the waiter. 'Steak—can you eat steak, Maude?—all right, two steaks and some salad and a bottle of the best champagne you've got—no, I don't *want* the wine waiter— oh, very well. That suit you?' to me.

Because of my lighter mood, caused by the energy and brightness in the streets and the suggestion of spring flowers everywhere and the March wind racing through the white sky, I would have preferred something lighter to eat.

But I knew, better, with Lionel in this mood (he never could control ill-temper after a bad night), than to state a preference.

'That will do very well for me,' I answered.

He did not comment, and soon we were unadventurously eating an excellent steak. I was a little put out at being asked if I could eat it. My teeth are my own: my father had admirable teeth, and they 'ran' in the family.

Lionel muttered over the champagne, which, indeed, was not good, but I could see that he was thinking all the time about something else. I feared it was that 'something' about which he wanted to talk to me.

Even inferior champagne has its exhilarating effect. I felt my spirits gently going up. I surveyed the greedy, hard faces of our fellow lunchers with detachment and even the unpleasing sound of their voices was blurred against my ear-drums. Lionel ate with his exhausted face lowered over his plate and made no attempt at conversation. But his manners are nothing new to me.

'Sorry I'm such bad company,' he said at last, pushing his plate away. 'I can't finish this—you gave me too much. I'm not an American.' This to the attentive waiter, who looked contemptuous and whirled away the plate. 'I told you I was up all night, didn't I? If I can't have my sleep I'm simply finished. I suppose it's age but I'm damned if I'll admit it.' He stopped, rubbing one finger vigorously below one eye. 'You got Teddie's message?' he went on. 'What did you think of it?'

It was not only the champagne that made me answer with truth—'I liked it.'

He glanced at me in surprise and, I saw, with pleasure. 'Did you? I'm glad. I'm . . . so glad.' He broke off and picked at the tablecloth, looking downwards, I watching him tranquilly. There was a silence. Above the sharp clatter of knives and voices I heard the wind whooming around our tower. Whooming. Dear Edward's word. Lionel spoke suddenly.

'I don't suppose you've ever felt you've bitten off more than you could chew, have you?'

I considered. 'No,' I said at last. 'I have had situations forced upon me which I have felt I was not going to be able to endure. But—'

'Never undertaken something you felt you couldn't carry out?'

I shook my head, and Lionel smiled suddenly, and said on a note of affection, 'Good old Maudie.'

'I have asked you not to shorten my name,' I said.

'Oh, yes, "the boys" were the only ones who were allowed to do that, weren't they? I'm sorry, I forgot. You Barringtons!' He laughed slightly.

That was an old expression. 'And you Croziers,' I replied gently, silencing him. (Childish; so childish.)

In a moment he said, again. 'You *must* make allowances, I'm not really with anything this morning. What I wanted to talk to you about was this—' He leant back in his chair and surveyed me, fiddling with the stem of his wine-glass. 'Will you come back to France with me?'

No doubt it was the champagne that prevented my feeling very surprised. I recalled afterwards, with some confusion, that I actually retorted 'Permanently?' and that Lionel laughed.

'No, not permanently. That wouldn't . . . work. But for a month, say? I could drive us down; I've got the car at Calais.'

By this time the proposal had penetrated to my intelligence in all its peculiarity. My answer to his question had been coquettish. I used not to be without coquetry, but I have always despised the touch of it in my own nature. I pulled myself together and spoke truthfully.

'I am exceedingly surprised, Lionel, and I'm sorry, but I can't help suspecting you of some hidden motive. You know as well as I do that we have never . . . got on.'

'After some fifty-seven years of not getting on, surely our differences can almost count as a harmony? We could put up with one another for a month or so. You'd stay with me, of course. But Charles would adore to see you, I know.'

'I would like to see Charles again,' I said thoughtfully.

'It's because he's getting old,' said Lionel, with a return to vigorous fretfulness, 'it's only taken hold of him these last months.

Wanting to see Wally Burne, wanting to see old Cecily, wanting to see—' He checked himself, and my touch of dreaminess left me.

I could think of more than one name whose owner Charles Handel might want to see whom I would not. I must be on my guard, as always, with Lionel. It was tiresome.

'Dear me, is Cecily still alive?' I observed.

'Oh, she won't die. She's one of the special lot . . . Well, will you come? You can bring your paints—ravishing places to sketch—and I've got a piano and a man and his wife to look after us; and *you'll* like those bloody reproving mountains.'

'Yes, I have always liked mountains . . . I suppose I must say that it is kind of you, Lionel.'

'Oh,' suddenly cried Lionel, as he clapped both hands, palm downwards, on the tablecloth, 'if only you knew just how ruddy kind of me it is!' He shook his head, as if disbelieving in his own magnanimity, and his face was alight with a kind of rueful glee.

This was not reassuring; it was even alarming. I shook off the last fumes of the champagne, and, having cautiously thanked him once more, said that I would think the matter over.

His glee, his table-slapping, his hints, need mean nothing more than the customary exhibition of Lionel Crozier at play. I could think the matter over, and I could say 'no'.

Lionel was to leave London at the end of the week. He said that he would give me three days to decide.

The next day was really uncomfortable: I detest indecision, in any form, and about this I was undecided. I would like to motor down through France, I would like to see great mountains once more, I would like very much to see Charles, whom I admired and respected. As usual, change, movement and society would improve my spirits. I could surely put up with Lionel's company for a month. In any case, our tête-à-tête would not be unbroken.

But I mistrusted him. The incident of young Mrs. Parker proved that he retained all his peculiar humour and youthful malice.

As Jock used to say, 'Something's up.' I felt so too, quite strongly.

In the end, I am sorry to say that impatience took over and made up my mind for me. After a day spent in weighing plainly-seen advantages against disadvantages seen less plainly (I excluded from these the strain of Lionel's society for four weeks) I suddenly thought: I really cannot bother any more with this shilly-shallying, and wrote to him accepting. I must risk walking into another of his spiteful little traps. I could look after myself.

My letter caught the four-thirty post. When I let myself into the hall on my return, Millie was just replacing the receiver of the telephone. Our eyes met: I do not know why, but meet they did.

'Wrong-number, miss,' she said, 'It's funny; that's the third this week.'

'Our exchange is notoriously bad; I suppose the plant is wearing out,' I said.

If Millie liked to receive or make telephone calls in my absence, I did not particularly mind. I only wished that she would not lie about them.

But Millie has always been a liar. Sometimes I excuse her by remembering that lies are a weak person's weapon of self-defence.

'I still think it's funny, miss. Might be some person watching the 'ouse.' She only drops aitches when she is guilty and feels nervous.

'I hope you won't encourage these fancies while I'm away, Millie. I'm going to France for a month. To stay with Mr. Crozier; he is driving us down.'

Before she could control herself, an expression of delight crossed her face—still a girl's face sometimes, in spite of her years. She is pleased, I thought, because she will have the house to herself, and can do as she likes, and I controlled a small, bitter impulse to tell her so. Then she said quickly: 'Nice change for you. You'll like that. When do you go, miss?'

I told her, and instructed her to get my suitcases from the boxroom and dust them, and then I went upstairs to my room and, in another moment of weakness, I pulled off my hat and chucked it on to the bed.

How tired I was of living with Millie! It was a daily battle, made up of the smallest incidents, and resentments, and fifty-year-old memories. But it would not end until one of us died.

Then, I presumed, the survivor might count herself the victor.

Both Tessa and Millie grated upon me so much that the prospect of leaving them behind for a month added to the growing enjoyment with which I prepared to go on holiday.

CHAPTER 5

'NOT feeling sick, are you?' asked Lionel.

'Not at all, thank you.'

The first stage of our journey, the crossing of the Channel and the collecting of the Jaguar from the garage at Calais, was successfully accomplished, and we were speeding along a road named N.1 on the excellent A.A. route guide, towards Boulogne. The straight highway was empty of traffic and its grey surface showed almost lilac-coloured in the evening light.

It ran between wide, quiet fields where young wheat and vegetables already stood high. Little woods of beech in that early leaf for which, I think, no better name than emerald has ever been used, bordered the road (though Charles Handel says that young leaves are the colour of a peridot). The grass looked fresh, in the light beginning to decline from the sky. It was a lonely road, and the quiet landscape and the late afternoon hush added their burden to the one I always carried.

France! My brothers' bodies lie there. Jock and Harry are buried in one of the smaller cemeteries in the north where the terrible battles of 1915-16 were fought. Edward, dearest to me of the three, is literally one with the French earth; he was blown to pieces in 1918, and no remains were ever traced.

So France, for me, means memories and pain. But it also means Order, perhaps my favourite among the qualities which are distinctively human; order in its splendid architecture, and in the undeviating roads built in the tradition of the Roman ones;

order, above all, in the French language. I love that country, and with my love there is pain. Ambivalence! always ambivalence.

'As you haven't uttered for an hour, I thought you might be,' Lionel said suddenly.

'Might be what?'

'Feeling sick.' He accelerated slightly and the purr deepened.

'I am never car-sick. If I had been, I shouldn't have accepted your invitation,' I said.

'Oh, well, that's all right, then . . . but chatter away if you want to. I don't like driving in silence myself, I start thinking . . . Let's dine as well as sleep, at Beauvais; we don't want to get comfortable and then have to stir ourselves up again, do we? (My God, how I do dislike fields brooding at you. If I hadn't a conscience already, they'd give me one . . .) There's a tricky bit in a couple of miles. Just give me the gen, will you. We want a place called . . .' and he gave me a name which I forget.

I found it, and together we worked out the details. I was sitting beside him, holding the Michelin *carte*, folded conveniently to display our way; this was to be my duty throughout our two-day journey. Lionel, who does not wear spectacles, was so good as to enquire, when he broke the news to me, whether I was 'up to' deciphering the small print and signs?

'Thank you; my eyes were tested three months ago and these,' tapping my spectacles case, 'are new.' I was irritated.

'Well, I had to know, Maude; women always lie about their sight.'

But apart from incidents like this we got on pretty well; I enjoyed the small challenge of following accurately the yellow lines by which the roads are marked on the *carte*, and I enjoyed, too, as an ex-driver, Lionel's first-class driving.

I have never been nervous of fast driving; I enjoy it; and I could understand his satisfaction in sweeping, for mile after mile, along these superb roads with never a traffic jam and only an occasional lorry or French over-taking car to remind us that the road was not our private property. It was too early in the season for there to be any English cars about, and I enjoyed that, too; one does not go to France to see the English.

Grey villages fled by in the last light. Lionel broke a silence of half an hour to ask me if I were asleep, and I laughed.

'Of course not . . . I'm just enjoying it.'

But when, about seven o'clock, we stopped at Beauvais, my enjoyment ended abruptly.

Lionel began muttering about where should we dine some five miles before we arrived; the word *gastronomique* occurred frequently. This restaurant was famed for one dish, that for another; at restaurant A there was a *chef* who was a character, and at restaurant B the cooking was done by an interesting family; restaurant C was madly expensive but perhaps the best of them all.

'Cannot we just get an omelette and a glass of local wine somewhere?' I suggested at length, as the Jaguar worked its way, slowly now, along the grey streets of Beauvais, filled with crowds coming home from their offices and places of business. 'Oh!' I broke off.

'What's the matter?' he demanded, also peering through the window, 'Oh, the cathedral—very fine, isn't it . . . no we can't just get an omelette and a bottle of wine somewhere, and there isn't any local wine, the nearest vines are two hundred miles away. What's the use of being in France if you don't eat superbly?'

'I was speaking generally about the wine, Lionel. Remember, we also have to find an hotel, and I expect that dining late suits you no better than it does me.'

I think he muttered *nonsense*, but I was now feeling exceedingly tired, and I decided to ignore everything but the cathedral, and allow him to fuss us on to our dinner and into our beds.

The cathedral had surprised me, soaring, as it does, above the background of commonplace roofs seen in a casual glance through the car window. It looked immense and pale, the afterlight giving a silvery glow to its stones. It is of the thirteenth century, but to me, I do not know why, it suggested an age even more remote, and Christianity in the days of Imperial Rome's decay.

Yet its long windows and blunted towers gave to me nothing of the Christian flame of faith belonging to that era of persecution: they only suggested the decline of Rome itself. People of my generation know how sad, how incredulous, Romans in their seventies must have felt in those times. The cathedral was exceedingly beautiful.

After nearly an hour's searching, scrutinizing and complaining, Lionel found us a quiet, elegant restaurant where, I suppose, the food was excellent. But if I had not been brought up to finish what is on my plate, I should have left most of it; I now only wanted to be in bed.

I could hardly believe it when, having finished his brandy and fussed me into finishing my own, he proposed that we should go for a walk. It was now very late, thanks to his fastidiousness about where we should dine.

'Sleepy, nonsense. Let's go and look at the cathedral,' and, to my surprise, he took my arm as we stepped out of the hotel into the quiet street.

There were still a few people about, but that peculiar atmosphere of restlessness and aimlessness felt in a small English town after nightfall was lacking: I suppose that the French, poorer yet better-fed and less in the thrall of America than our own working people, are content to sit at home and digest, after their last meal. Certainly, except for some gossipers and a few youngsters sky-larking around a big car at a corner, the streets were almost empty.

But not the expanse of waste ground on which the cathedral stood. There were half-visible ruins here, reminders of the bombing in the war, and in their shadows, below the moon-lit walls of the great place, the pale dresses of girls glimmered and there was the sound of scuffling, and the raw voices of boys and their laughter. Here, the splendour of the cathedral seemed completely sad. A rock, I thought, gazing up at the high, blanched stones; a rock, and the tide coming in to cover it, perhaps for ever.

'Depressing, isn't it,' yawned Lionel, shifting about from foot to foot. 'Shall we get back?'

No attitude in a companion could have been less encouraging to confidences, and I suppose it must have been my uneasiness, and the sadness welling up in my heart because I was in France again, that made me, impulsively, tell him my thoughts about the cathedral. Then, of course, I was annoyed with myself.

'Rocks are still there when the tide goes down—if we *must* pursue the simile at this time of night,' said he, seizing my arm again and marching me off, 'I didn't know you were a Christian, Maude. How long has this been going on?'

'It isn't going on. I am not a Christian.'

'Oh well, don't let's go into it now . . . I'm as tired as a dog.'

I had not intended to go into it. But I said nothing; the waste ground was rough and broken and I was glad of his arm. The sky was cloudy yet moon-silvered, and the air sweet; I supposed that the vast open country lying all around the town gave it this purity. Lionel contented himself with a grunt at intervals and we did not talk any more.

In the morning, he was his usual self. I assumed that our excellent dinner on the previous evening had soothed his natural malice and made his society at least bearable.

But now, as we again swooped along the almost deserted roads between more coppices of budding beech, he insisted on having a transistor at the back of the car switched on, making the most disagreeable noise imaginable, and when I did pay attention to what he was saying I found he was speculating upon the situation of young Mrs. Parker.

'I'll phone her when we get to Versailles,' he announced, then, mercifully, told me to turn off the transistor.

There did not seem to be anything to say in reply to his remark, but 'Oh,' so I said it.

'Poor kid,' he went on.

'Do look at those geese, Lionel—I'm sorry, I know you can't take your eyes off the road.'

'I'll tell her I'm phoning from Versailles, she may have heard of it.'

I confess that Tessa's speculations about the paternity of the child returned disagreeably to my mind.

What was their relationship, that he must telephone from France to Mrs. Parker? It was all most distasteful—and just as we were entering the beautiful Fôret de Marly, and the trees and glades, glowing in clear sunlight, looking, surely, their best. I felt too irritated to remain silent and observed, 'You are kind to take so much interest in her.'

I was not going to ask him why he did so, which I suspected that he wanted me to do.

'M . . . m . . . m . . .' said he gloomily, compressing his lips, 'I hope they'll stay together now. But the boy's hopelessly weak.'

A moment's reflection, unwillingly indulged in, convinced me that he could not mean 'my son'.

'The husband, you mean? Mr. Parker.'

'"Mr."! He's not twenty-one,' scoffed Lionel, 'poor little bastard.'

I could not summon up the slightest interest in these young people, and made a bid to change the subject by calling his attention to the increasing press of traffic.

'Bound to hit it, just here, where every other sign says "Paris". I wish we could have spent a day there. But there isn't time. I'm not joking—I really do think hours count—Charles may go at any moment. Ninety, you know.'

I did not wish that I could have spent a day in Paris with Lionel, and I said no more.

CHAPTER 6

SOME of its charm, the charm of Paris, I thought, has spilled over into Versailles, where we stopped to lunch. The very broad approach to the Palace, half avenue and half *place*, was dappled by the sunny shadows of big trees and lined by the smartest of shops and thronged with shoppers and pretty women—and the air seemed to sparkle in white and gold. I thought, looking up the crowded vista towards the Palace of the kings of France, that if all conception of kingship were to be swept from the earth, one could point to Versailles and say, 'This was royalty.'

We sat down to luncheon at a table covered by a starched white cloth, below a large looking-glass crowned with gilt leaves, in a big sunlit room.

Having seen me settled there with an exotic *apéritif* made from oranges and recommended by himself, Lionel hurried away to make his telephone call. I sat there, well content. Cheerful voices were uttering light, precise syllables around me, the dark drink tasted delicious, and if only a well-trained chauffeur had been driving me down through France to see my old friend, I should have felt comfortable.

But a Crozier was my driver.

'Not so bad,' he announced on his return, gulping at his *apéritif*, 'They went off with the boy this morning, back to Rothbury. I phoned the clinic, of course. No telephone at home.'

I made what I trusted was a suitable murmur, accompanied by a suitable expression.

'I think they'll be all right now,' he went on. 'She's had a shock. That poor little bastard—'

'The baby?'

'No, no, of course not, the husband—Ronnie.'

'Is he actually a bastard, Lionel, or are you merely calling him one?'

'No, of course he isn't a bastard, so far as I know, but he's the type that makes you call him one. No harm in him and not much else either. About a third of her weight. That's the trouble. Now, what shall we eat?'

He snatched up the menu—once more outsize—and began to consult it with an air I can only call voracious, and as I did not care what we ate because anything at this place was sure to be excellent, I mused on the young Parkers.

Their numbers were increasing. First, there had been the girl; then 'my son', born on Aunt Dorothea's sofa; and now this poor bastard, not yet twenty-one, the young father.

I derived much pleasure from the shady glades and superb trees of the Fôret de Fontainebleau, through which we drove after leaving the Seine valley behind us as we sped south. As I have already said, I enjoy motoring; I regretted, with an intensity I have sometimes felt to be petty, having to give up driving because of a tiresome heart condition. As a former driver, I could appreciate Lionel's skill and our unhampered advance, for mile after mile, along the fine Autoroute du Sud. Lionel presently turned to me with a smile.

'Like to take over for a bit?'

'I would, and you know it. But that would risk killing us at seventy miles an hour, and you know that too. Doctor McRae was quite emphatic with me.'

'I was joking . . . I don't want to die just yet, especially at seventy miles an hour. I don't know about you, but I hope and intend to die in my bed.'

'I shall die when I do, I suppose . . . The thing about death'—I said, after a moment in which I did not think about anything at all—'the thing about death . . . one has thoughts about it, and one faces it, and then one has no idea. No idea at all.'

'Other people's deaths, you mean.'

'Yes.'

'It's worse?' Lionel stated rather than asked, accelerating. The marvellous green and blue spring landscape streamed by.

'Much worse.' I said no more. We were both silent.

He knew that my life ended when Edward was killed; I suppose that everyone whom I had known since girlhood knew that. I had never spoken to any of them as I had just spoken to Lionel, and in the quiet that fell between us I glanced once at his sallow profile, in surprise that it should have been he to whom I offered this distillation from nearly fifty years of sorrow.

The next instant he said something that I could not believe I had heard.

'What?' I cried, turning on him.

'Arthur Courtney. You ought to have married him.'

'You are very kind,' I said bitingly. 'But I didn't love Arthur, and I suppose that even you can understand it would have been wrong to marry him?'

I was back, as if I had never been out of it, in the old familiar air in which I always talked with Lionel.

'You might have grown to love him, and a bit of rough and tumble in the ordinary world would have done you good, knocked some of the high-falutinness out of you.'

'I believe we have had this conversation before,' I said.

'Oh, surely . . . in fifty-seven years or so . . . I'm running out of gas.'

'Well, there are no petrol stations on the motorway. It says so here,' and I held up the route guide,

'We'll manage.' And we drove on in silence.

There was no hesitation about our choice of a dining place that day. As we approached Pont-sur-Yonne, gazing out across its river, as if from the Middle Ages, at the modern world scurrying past on the main road, I exclaimed, 'There—there,' like a child, and actually pointed.

It was a restaurant just across the bridge, raised above the road on a little eminence, with a courtyard shaded by a thick creeper already in leaf, and enough bright paintwork and discreet gilt lettering to make it cheerful. And the town—the little town with its rounded grey towers and ancient russet and silvery roofs, sitting there across the river! How would I have liked to wander through its streets! Lionel's expression, as he parked in a paved courtyard at the side of the place, was almost benign. He felt, I suppose, that the food here would be more than excellent.

That was the pleasantest dinner of our journey. There were some people at another table, whose chatter and laughter relieved the pensiveness imposed by the apparently slumbering town. Not a car, not a human figure, moved along the miniature streets visible from where we sat for more than an hour.

The host of this charming *relais* was a stout old man who exuded the materialist gaiety typical of France, he made his little dog dance for us, and spoke of his approaching death, possibly rather near to him, in his eightieth year, with the grotesque fancy that his spirit would 'become a sputnik' revolving in the skies.

I should have said that the first three quarters of an hour of dinner were pleasant. While we were drinking our coffee, and lingering because it was pleasant to sit in the evening light and feel ourselves poised on our hillock between the past and the present, I am blessed—it is not a polite expression but I must use it—if Lionel did not begin again upon those Parkers.

'I hope everything *will* be all right, now the child's arrived,' he said suddenly, not ceasing to watch the flow of the river.

'Ronnie's got a goodish job. Not tip-top but quite good. I suppose he brings home sixteen pounds a week—eighteen with overtime.'

I supposed that it was to Lionel's credit if he could continue to feel concern for his protégés in our present carefree circumstances. Also, I was mellowed by an excellent dinner.

'Is that so good, nowadays?' I asked. 'One has to remember the cost of everything, and the reduced value of money.'

'They've got a council house,' said Lionel, turning from the river. 'Two bedrooms, living-room, bathroom and loo. Bit of garden. Bearable if it wasn't for the houses in between . . . it would kill you or me in a week, but we haven't got to live in it. And she's a good little manager. They ought to be all right . . .'

'One would not suspect powers of management from her behaviour the other day,' I could not refrain from observing. 'And her appearance was not . . .'

Lionel instantly 'flared up', like some tiresome firework which has been temporarily quiescent.

'A kid can be a good manager in an Op-Art shift. I suppose that's what's upsetting you.'

'I thought it grotesquely inappropriate to her condition, certainly.'

'Well, she'd just rushed out of the house . . . she grabbed the first thing handy. You don't stop to pack a suitcase with piles of clean underclothing when you're nineteen and leaving your husband . . . probably she hasn't *got* piles of underclothing . . .' he gabbled.

'Really, Lionel, need we discuss Mrs. Parker's underclothing?'

He made one of his grotesque, violent gestures meant to express despair, and I resumed my study of the town across the river. But now I was no longer thinking about it.

Lionel intended me to ask him questions about these Parkers, and I was not going to do it. I supposed he had some grand notion of 'making me face reality'; he probably thought that I 'lived in an ivory tower', as the expression used to be (now, I believe, it is *escapist*). And I was just not going to let him succeed in his silly scheme. I lived as unmarried women of our class with money have always lived, and I felt no guilt about it. (I have implied that when I was young our means were moderate, but the death of an aunt of my mother's, at a great age, changed the situation considerably, in the year before my parents died.) But I was beginning to be really annoyed. Why could he not leave me to enjoy the town and the gliding river in peace?

'And I'll bet you've decided the child was born three months after marriage, too,' he went on, glaring.

'I haven't thought about it. I have been trying to keep to our agreement and put it out of my mind.' I paused. 'But—as you introduced the point—I *did* think there might be an irregularity of some kind.'

'I knew it!' He actually shook both hands in the air then smacked them, palm-downwards, on the table. 'Oh, how well I know you, Maude, like the back of this hand,' waving one of them at me.

If I had not decided, years ago, that his mother was a spineless creature who did little more than drift through her shiftless life, I could on occasion have wondered about Lionel's own paternity. He might have Italian or Spanish blood; he *is* so emotional and peculiar; quite un-English.

'They were married exactly a year ago,' he ended, looking slightly conscious under my cold stare and speaking more quietly.

'Don't you think we ought to be moving?' was all that I said, and glanced at my watch, the silver one given me by the boys on my twenty-first birthday. It is my dearest possession (apart, of course, from their letters from France) and I always wear it, hanging from its filigree bow, pinned to my dress. 'It is nearly nine o'clock.'

Lionel was now looking as miserable—the simile occurred to me—as a sick bird. He nodded, and beckoned to our gay old host for the bill.

We slept that night at a clean, but not especially interesting, hotel, in a town whose name I have forgotten.

CHAPTER 7

'LET'S stop for a drink, shall we?' he suggested abruptly, about six o'clock on the following evening, 'at the next village?'

It had been a pleasant, uneventful day. The roads, superb and uncrowded as ever, had taken us, down into Burgundy; there had been no mention of the Parkers, and our luncheon hours had passed swiftly. Gradually the ubiquitous beech thickets were being replaced by acacia, and we were making for Beaune. I had been thinking that we were both in better tempers—because we were interested in our travels and growing accustomed, I supposed, to one another's society.

'That would be nice,' I said.

In fact, I thought that the inevitable discussion about where we should dine would not be at all nice. But if both of us carped and were moody, all pleasure in this chequered journey would be at an end. I must be the adult of the party. 'A good idea,' I added.

Lionel disconcerted me by a laugh and a mutter of that 'Good old Maudie' which I found so offensive, and shortly we stopped at an ordinary little café, in the middle of an ordinary little village.

We chose our table from among the groups, painted orange, which stood on the pavement outside, and I went in to tidy myself while Lionel ordered our drinks: a Pernod for me, and for him one of his *mandarin curaçoa*, to which he had previously introduced me.

It had not grown much darker when I emerged, for this was April and the long evenings were beginning. There sat Lionel in the dying light, staring at nothing and looking strikingly smart and incongruous in the setting of the shabby red and grey village street which climbed up a short hill to a crossroads where the country began again. A group of elderly friends, local people apparently, sat laughing and gossiping at another table. The air smelled sweet, and it was quiet.

I settled myself opposite him and lifted my glass, prepared to break the silence in which he was glowering, with a little toast.

'Damn and blast England!' he burst out, slapping his palm down on the table. 'Takes me a week to come alive again every time I've been back there. How you can go on living there I *do* not know.'

'I suppose because it is my home,' I said, unobtrusively mopping from my skirt the Pernod which my start had caused me to spill.

'It's half dead, the atmosphere chokes me, and that appalling feeling, special to England, that every town and village is only leading on to somewhere else . . . and the advertisements—the advertisements . . .'

'Well, it isn't your home now,' I said, and perhaps the tone in which I added, 'Aren't you going to drink to the success of our holiday?' was slightly too coaxing, because he muttered, 'Oh, all right, nanny,' as he snatched up his glass and made a vague gesture towards me before drinking.

'Who was it who talked about a "spiritual home"?' he went on. 'Haldane, wasn't it?'

'Yes. He said it about Germany, and caused a lot of ill-feeling and suspicion about his sympathies in the First World War,' I replied readily, hoping to change the subject.

'I know what he meant . . . compare this little place,' he nodded round at the surrounding houses and the quiet high-road, 'with a typical English village nowadays, just *compare* it. When I remember the Home Counties when I was a boy—sheets of wild flowers, lonely lanes full of birds, hedges smothered in bryony in autumn and honeysuckle in June—'

'I always understood that such things gave you a conscience, Lionel,' I could not resist saying: it was unwise, but I did resent my stained skirt.

'They do *now*, of course. Forty years ago it was different,' he muttered, draining his glass. 'Debauched. That's what England is. In process of being debauched. One can't do anything, and it makes one hate her.'

'Not me,' I said.

'No—possibly not—well, we all know you're not like most of us—let's be getting along, shall we?—unless you'd like another?'

I shook my head and he got up from the table; heavily, I thought, and in spite of his light frame and his smart clothes; for a moment he seemed like a much older man. 'We'll sleep at Champforqueuil. There's a fifteenth-century château there you might like to see, and it'll take the last taste of England out of our mouths.'

I expected to hear next that there was a *relais* attached to it with a *cuisine* of international fame, but he said no more as we settled ourselves in the car, than that the hotel there was newish and 'quite presentable', and the food good.

I do not know why these depressing thoughts should have set me to thinking about Arthur Courtney. We drove away into the dusk, leaving that village to fall asleep under the hushed sky, and, almost at once, I was thinking about him.

He, Edward, Jock and I had spent a week together in Paris in 1913, under the eye—an eye regarded as just a little casual and 'fast', in that era—of Great-Aunt Dorothea. It was a clear, brown eye, small and sparkling, embattled behind a single eyeglass on a chain of blueish Egyptian beads, and its characteristic expression was an amused cynicism.

Europe was beginning her love affair with the Russian Ballet, and we four young people were as 'smitten' as everyone else. (That is, the boys and I were; I think that Arthur regarded the leaping and whirling as rather comic and a heaven-sent model for imitation, while the beauty passed him by.) My brothers gave me presents of Eastern scarves, starred and gauzy, to twist round my shoulders and about my head, and we could praise no colours but the rainbow ones of Bakst.

One night, on our way home from the theatre, our brains were still whirling with images of those bounding limbs and burning colours. Our mind's eyes were still printed with jade green and peacock blue and fuschia. We were all talking at once—ah, I can hear the voices now—recalling, admiring, praising: it was like a peripatetic hymn to the ballet rising through the midnight air as we loitered homeward arm-in-arm: arm-in-arm, Jock, Edward, Arthur and I.

At last, as if by one thought, and still talking at the tops of our voices, we stopped in a little *place* lit only by one old, dim lamp, and Edward began to try to show us how one of our idols had performed a certain movement. The others joined in, each endeavouring to illustrate some particular gyration, seriously at first, which made it all the funnier, and gradually in increasingly helpless laughter; bounding, leaping, flinging their arms out, with Jock attempting that difficult feat of dancing with bent knees and folded arms, and Arthur swarming up the lamp-post and hanging there, by one curled leg and arm and shouting 'À la lanterne! à la lanterne!' above the wildly gesticulating forms. I glided dreamily and pirouetted round the group, waving my scarf above my head and humming some theme from the ballet music.

All young people feel, consciously or unconsciously, that there has never been such laughter and delight as that peculiar to their own youth. This is a law of nature. But we—we who were under thirty in 1913—we were the archetypes. There never was before or ever would again be such gaiety, because never before or again would such a darkness fall.

But then my memory turned to my father's poem *Lightheart*, and instantly I switched away my thoughts.

It is in every popular anthology of verse published since 1919. I wish I did not know it by heart. In the years following Edward's death I used to awaken every morning with it repeating itself incessantly, mercilessly, in my inward ear. I believe now that the writing of it helped to save my father from a collapse of some kind—a loss of all sense of order in the universe, perhaps, and, with him, my mother was also saved; but I had never been able to forgive him for writing it.

I mused a little about Arthur; I could do so without pain, except when I recalled scenes in which he had been with the others; and once more I came to the sad conclusion that he had never lived up to his youthful promise. A solicitor in a London suburb! But Arthur's interest at twenty-two had been in divorce law. I *shall* always believe that Florence Formby was not the wife for our old friend, and that had he married a different kind of woman he could have realized his potentialities.

I aroused myself to see hints of a growing picturesqueness in the landscape through which we were passing. Forests bordered our road and stood far out on the dim plain, dark and distinct in the light of a rising moon, and for the first time I saw on the horizon the outline of mountains.

By seven o'clock we were bumping our way, in tricky clouded moonlight, through the outskirts of a tiny village lying off the main road; past bulging broken walls and ruined outhouses, over the surface of a lane that might have belonged to the Middle Ages.

'Up there,' Lionel said suddenly, with a jerk of his head, 'the château.'

I peered through the window into the silvery dusk. High above us, crowning a wooded hill, was a building whose roofs gleamed fairily in the moonlight, with towers soaring slim and dark against the moving clouds. Up, up they went, making one marvel that human hands could rear structures so slender and so tall. The names of Mélusine and Riquet with the Tuft drifted through my mind. I had more sense than to mention them to Lionel.

'Not my cup of tea,' was his comment, thrown off between muttered ejaculations over the condition of the road, 'I don't go for Disney architecture.'

I was wondering what it must be to look out over the moonlit landscape from a window in one of those towers, and I did not answer.

The evening was so warm that we dined by moonlight and candlelight in the courtyard of the hotel, under the budding trees. We were the only visitors, thus early in the season, and received smiling and undivided attention from the staff, who spoke another language than French.

'Greeks,' said Lionel, as we were drinking our coffee and watching what seemed to be an entire family having its staff supper at a table across the courtyard, small children included, 'That's what C.H. has done at Belair.'

'Imported Greeks, do you mean?'

'No—no, Italians. It's getting almost as difficult to get staff in France as it is in England, and besides, he decided it would lead to all kinds of bother with the village, gossip and feuds and so on, if he got his staff from there.'

'And of course there may still be some feeling against him because he ran away during the war,' I said.

Now, looking back, I still don't *fully* know why I said it. Even as I spoke, I knew that my words were provocative, and they led almost at once into the bitterest scene of our journey. But I have humbly tried—so far as *humbly* means anything to someone with a nature like mine—to seek out what prompted me to say what I did. And I have concluded that it was the sight of the Greek children at the table across the courtyard.

Light from the kitchen windows shone warmly on the family group, the small dark heads and gay little faces and the indulgent gesture of some mother or aunt as she agreed to peel an orange or pour out just one more sip of wine. I think, as I heard the tired, affectionate voices and saw the faint communal smile that was yet warm and comforting as the kitchen light, that I realized, yet again, how much I have missed.

I only know that as I spoke I felt, once more, that I was just a heap of pain that had existed for more than seventy years.

Lionel was looking across at me with the well-known expression.

'If you like to call it running away, well, yes,' he said.

'I don't *like* to call it running away, Lionel, but that was what it was. He did run away.'

I felt that it was my mask who was speaking, my dignified, decisive old mask. Behind her, the other old woman sat crying silently and watching the Greek children and thinking of her dead and of the living whom she had never borne.

'He was over seventy when war broke out. I suppose you'd have liked him to stay there and be deported or shot. We all know there's a death-or-glory tradition in your family.'

'Yes, there is. Both death and glory,' I said.

Silence followed. But not of the kind preluding the gradual subsidence of the contestants into a gentler mood. The air between us—I could almost feel it—seemed to be quivering. I was trembling, and the accelerated beating of my heart was shaking the soft material of my dress.

Lionel, so to speak, charged again.

'Do you still carry on with that morbid business of brooding over Edward's V.C. on his birthday?'

'I do. Not on his birthday, Lionel, on the day that he was blown to pieces.' I had not ceased to look at him immovably.

'Oh. Well . . .' and now he did look down, 'It's your life, of course. But there are times when you don't seem to belong to this century at all, you're like something out of the *Chanson de Roland.*'

'Thank you. That suits me very well,' I said.

The silence that followed my words did have a different quality: Lionel, I could feel, was in retreat.

He knew, of old, that he could win no contest in words with me, and in this case I did him the justice to imagine that he must feel some shame. Even his petty soul must feel it. I drank some coffee, keeping my unseeing gaze fixed on the Greek children who were now being given a last sweetmeat before being taken off to their beds. I heard their soft piping voices and watched the sleepy movements of their small limbs and still I was nothing but pain, pain; one mass of old, searing pain.

'Well,' Lionel began to rise from his chair, 'as I'm neither dead nor glorious I'm going to bed. How about you?'

'I shall sit here a little longer, I think. Good-night.' I did not look at him; I could not.

'Right, then. Good-night. I . . . good-night . . .' and he went off. I think some outburst may have been averted by my not looking at him, but I was not sure and I did not care.

CHAPTER 8

ON AWAKENING the next morning my first thought was, this is the last day that I shall have to endure the society of Lionel unrelieved by that of anyone else.

Lionel was markedly attentive at breakfast. I think he was relieved to find that I was not sulking. But any tendency I may have had towards *that* was knocked out of me, before I was twelve, by the boys. 'Don't *brood*,' authoritatively uttered, is a command with which I have been familiar.

We breakfasted in the garden, full in the sunlight, this time. The place was quiet, for the elder children had gone to school and a dark-eyed little creature of three or so, running about with a doll and a watering-can, did not disturb us. We lingered with our cigarettes. I looked up at the old trees, moving on towards their full strength of spring foliage, and studied the young ones planted by the proprietors of the place; they were spindly but healthy and full of promise. The air was already warm.

'I suppose . . . er . . . would you like to see the château?' asked Lionel at last, putting out his cigarette.

'Very much, if you think we have time.'

'Oh, yes. They aren't expecting us at any particular hour. And Charles has ignored all sense of time for years, deliberately. Damned annoying it can be, too.'

'Does he go to bed early?' I asked, as we left the low wall surrounding the hotel garden behind us, and began to walk along the road that wound gradually upwards towards the château.

'He does now. But only for the last month or so. I tell you . . . he's breaking up. No-one will face it, but he is.'

I thought it more sensible to change the subject, for Lionel's tone had been gloomy yet excited.

'Who is living there now?' I asked.

'Still the crowd . . . Mimi, Emil and Laurette—and Bunny, of course. And he still has visitors. From all over the world,' he ended on a sarcastic note.

'Bunny must be getting on.'

'God, we're *all* getting on,' he exclaimed, stopping in the middle of the road. 'Do you know the average age in Belair is sixty-three? I did a sum last night in bed.'

I could not help laughing. 'Really, Lionel, I should have thought that you would have been better employed in going to sleep.'

'I couldn't get to sleep. Yes, sixty-three. If it weren't for Laurette it would be higher. She was thirty last month. The baby of the set-up.'

'How old was she, nineteen, when she came to you?'

'Yes.'

'. . . Remember, I have had little news for ten years.' I reminded him, in excuse for my questions.

We were approaching the precincts of the château; some old buildings shaded by trees and standing on an enclosed slope, whose grassy incline led downwards to the drawbridge and moat: the great sparkling roofs and slender towers with their slit windows and the expanses of dressed pale stone now soared immediately above us.

I was wondering if it would be possible to climb a winding stone staircase inside one of those towers and find oneself, at the end of it, in a turret room. It has always been one of my minor secret wishes to live in a turret room. But, as we drew nearer to the gateway, Lionel muttered 'Damn—it's closed,' and I saw, on a notice attached to the portcullis, that the château was open to the public on every day except Wednesdays : that morning was a Wednesday.

'I'm sorry; bad staff-work.'

We lingered for a few moments, looking down into the moat. Tall seedlings of acacia and beech filled it, and birds darted and perched among the brilliant leaves. *Looking down* on birds in flight has always fascinated me, and I would have willingly stayed longer, breathing the scent of moss and dampness, which was all that remained of the water once protecting the place. The young trees embowered the thick lower walls, here half-veiling a small secret door, there wandering downwards in fresh green thickets. The guardians of the castle grounds had not made the mistake of giving to it a municipal neatness.

'Ready?' Lionel asked, when we had gazed and made our comments and I had asked him what it was that gave a coloured sheen to some of the roofs, and he had answered that his antipathy to what he called Disney architecture had prevented his studying the details of its tiling processes.

'Yes, thank you. Can we go back through the village? I should like to see it by daylight.'

'It's a dirty hole . . . I'm sorry you couldn't see the château.' So we turned away from Mélusine's castle and went down the hill.

Undeniably, the village was dirty. It had more muddy fore-yards, piles of animal manure, collapsing walls, crumbling stone staircases winding up ruinous cottages and small dark rooms with one tiny window than I had seen since a holiday in North Cornwall more than forty years ago. But the curtains at those windows were clean, and the buxom women who glanced at us incuriously as they went about their work, if they looked dour, also looked in a way content; calm, and completely one with their surroundings. They fitted into the scene like fingers into a well-fitting glove.

'It's beautiful,' I observed, as we re-entered the courtyard of the hotel once more, where the Jaguar, which had been refilled with petrol during our excursion, awaited us.

'It's *very* beautiful,' he agreed, with unexpected enthusiasm. 'You know that painting of Caneletto's—"The Stonemason's Yard"? It reminds me of that. There's the same beauty of roughness, and a kind of poetic disorder. The tones in the painting are all varied browns and in this place they're varied greys, but the feeling it gives one is the same. But I am sorry you couldn't see the château.'

He turned his attention to the car.

While he was getting us out on to the road, I was looking back over the years, as I was always doing at that time, and realizing that most of my capacity to appreciate the beauty of paintings I owe to Lionel.

I recalled many observations he had made, little pieces of casual criticism thrown off, during the years we have known one another, and each and every one—I knew now—had increased my appreciative powers.

He had known better, however, than to make such remarks to me about any picture painted after, say, 1870. I neither look at contemporary paintings nor wish to. And I am no beauty-worshipper, let it be said plainly; I look for courage and honour in the human creature and for some sort of kinship with the world of nature in works of art.

Then, as we settled ourselves into the car for the next stage of our journey, I congratulated myself—prematurely, as it almost instantly appeared—on having passed a pleasant morning.

'I wonder how Teddie and the brat are doing?' began Lionel, as if I had pressed a button.

When anything tedious occurred, Harry used to say, '. . . and I groaned in spirit.' This was what I did now, but, really fearing by this time to provoke a scene, I answered at once:

'Oh, I should imagine they're all right, wouldn't you? The little boy's father is enjoying him, I expect.'

It was more than fear of provoking a mere scene: I knew, now, that there were apparently no limits to what Lionel would say.

'That's just it, you see.' He began to talk quickly, keeping his eyes fixed on the flying road ahead. 'He didn't want it. That's why she walked out. She'd spent nine months telling him he'd like it when he got it, and at the last minute he made one of those awful scenes they do make—you know, sitting in the kitchen looking like a half-open can of beans and uttering every fifteen minutes— and she, poor sweet, just couldn't take another instant of it and walked out.'

I decided to let him go on. More trouble might result from an attempt to deflect him, and I also felt a slight interest in what he was saying.

'The trouble is, she's the strong one. (Too strong for me, you know how I detest strong women.) All he's got is a kind of sweet-ness . . . he's a sweet boy. No vice in him. Mad on gardening. But she needs a grown-up man.'

It occurred to me that this is what all women need. Because there are few of them about, and because none of the ones who had proposed to me had been as strong as my brothers were, I had remained unmarried. But this was not a remark I would have made to anyone, and especially not to Lionel, whose own defi-ciencies in the manly line must surely come home to him now and then. If I do belong to the world of the *Chanson de Roland*, it means that I understand the nature of chivalry.

However, I thought it safe, now, to ask him if we should be at Belair by lunch-time?

'You see, having known . . . what?' He broke off, looking as if he had been made to turn abruptly aside from something he had made up his mind to say, and turning to stare at me. 'What . . . ? no, no, of course not, we shan't be there until late afternoon—unless you want to skip lunch.'

'I don't mind, Lionel—if we can stop somewhere and buy some tonic water and a ham roll—'

'Naturally we shall stop somewhere and buy some tonic water and a ham roll!' he mimicked. 'What a maddening old Snow-Woman you are!'

It was his sister Frances's name for me. But I laughed, and so did he. 'Look at the map, will you,' he said next. 'I know up to here moderately well, but from now on I'm a trifle hazy—Laurette usually meets me at Alois, you see, and takes over the driving.'

'Don't you fly?'

'Oh God no—don't you know I detest flying? Three times a year I do this milk round, with a few minor variations. Now where are we? I've got an idea where the next place is but . . .'

While he studied the map I realized that not once during our journey had I asked him if he were tired with the driving? That was ungracious of me, and ungrateful. But if he *would* pretend that he was thirty-seven, he must expect such omissions to occur.

I had never met Laurette Handel, Charles's daughter-in-law. She was an American, and this was all I knew about her, beyond the fact that her father was an artist and that her family lived in Boston; but I had always had a vague notion, gathered from remarks dropped by Lionel and others, that she had begun by entertaining a *schwarmerei* for Charles, as the great art histor-ian and critic, and had gone on a visit—a pilgrimage, one of my acquaintances had called it—to France to see her hero, and had ended by settling at Belair as the wife of his son.

'Right, then.' Lionel slapped down the map. 'Now we make for a place called Azay and we skip lunch. And I suggest we go as fast as we can and finish this blasted run. I'm all in.'

I was not surprised to hear this. His skin had a greenish tinge. I felt some sympathy and some remorse, and resolved to say as little as possible during what was left of our journey. And how very glad I should be to arrive at Belair, and to shift the burden of 'coping' with Lionel on to other shoulders!

CHAPTER 9

WE WERE driving along one of the straight roads, which ran across a wide valley, and the distant foothills now showed dark and strong against the sky.

'Did Arthur die?' Lionel asked suddenly.

'Not unless it was within the last three months. I had a card from them at Christmas, as usual; from Toronto, this year; he and Florence were over there on a visit to their eldest daughter, to see the grand-children. He retired about eighteen months ago. I haven't seen him for years, of course.'

'Why "of course"? Aha—that slipped out, didn't it? You never could stand Florence.'

'You put things too strongly, Lionel. I simply felt that she was not the right wife for Arthur.'

'Well, you wouldn't have him, would you?—though God knows if ever anyone ought to have been made an honest man of, after the way you carried on—'

'I did not—'

But here the absurd expression, with its aura of flirtation and area steps, as applying to the dignified old woman I had seen briefly in the looking-glass that morning, struck me in all its incongruity. I broke into irrepressible laughter. Lionel turned to look at me, laughing too, and for a moment we were completely at ease.

I watched the wooded foothills gradually drawing nearer as we climbed the road winding up into their heart, and noticed that the fringe of beech shading the verges on the northern roads were seen no more; there was only the narrow-leaved acacia, as green, but more graceful, more feminine—or perhaps 'fairy-like' is better. How vast France is! How large her skies, how seemingly endless her Roman-spear-straight roads! This was the chief difference between her and my little England; her vastness. And I had so far seen only a quarter of her huge realm.

At a speed varying between seventy and eighty miles an hour we devoured the roads curving about the hills that cradle and overlook Lac Bourget. Across its shining water, on the opposite shores, were the little villages and towns given over to tourists and pleasure.

We tore through tunnels bored in the mountain where the stones were damp with the exudations of banked and hidden streams; past gorges with waterfalls like veils (again, as with *emerald*, no better word has ever been found for them), and ravines fledged with saplings that sprang, spangled with new leaves, from rifts in the crags.

In forests fifty feet above our flight I saw occasional dells, areas of solitude and peace, where I would have liked to linger. But we flew on. If Lionel had been fifteen and I twenty-three, we would have climbed those crags, and tasted the air of those miniature paradises.

We stopped for twenty minutes at a village called Les Échelles, beyond the tunnel of Col de Couz, and bought the promised ham rolls and some tonic water and fruit juice.

Then on we flew, past Saint Laurent du Pont and Voiron, Tullins and St. Marcellin, and now the country was opening out; there were no more gorges filled with trees and echoing with the sound of falling water; enormous hills cushioned with forests and patched with tiny fields of green grain were folding themselves around us, and always the road went upwards; up, up, towards the summits ridged with green young forests against the crystal blue of the sky. On our left we could look down into the vast valley that holds Grenoble, the distant view of which was dismissed by Lionel with a disparaging mutter.

Suddenly I saw him begin to brake. 'Let's have a swig of the wind-producer,' he said, and stopped the car.

Why was he suddenly nervous? I wondered. He is only coarse when he feels nervous. In silence, I filled a paper cup with Evian water and passed it to him.

He sipped it, looking absently out of the window into a coppice of acacia, through whose sparse clusters, scarcely in full leaf, we had a hint of the light and space shimmering upwards from the valley. The excited singing of birds at their nesting came to us in the silence, and the scent of the woods. Lionel jerked his head towards the coppice.

'The Chartreuse is over there, across the valley. But you'll get a better view from the top.'

I fell into a reverie. In Cornwall, especially along its north coast, the sea is in command; nothing else is important; it dominates the activities of man, making his presence a puny incident, and in these foothills there was the same feeling. I like that; the heart can rest upon it.

I became aware of movements at my side.

It was Lionel, fussing with a pocket comb and studying himself in the looking glass that serves as a reflection for over-taking traffic! I found it difficult to believe my eyes.

After a minute or two he put away the comb and started the car again, with no air of being refreshed by this glimpse of his own face. I had thought that he could no longer surprise me, but he had. I had thought that his vanity was well in hand. This little demonstration showed that it was not. I understand vanity in a handsome young man—I have seen my bonny Harry studying the set of his Sam Browne in the long glass—but poor Lionel has always been so exceptionally plain.

In five minutes he began to slow down again; we were approaching the grey, dusty-looking houses of a village. 'Here we are,' he muttered.

It was a long, straggling place, whose single street was broken halfway down by a small square *place* where a few lime trees flourished and tables were set out on the pavement outside one or two modest cafés. Beyond this *place* the road curved upwards again, half-obscured by the woods, and at the turn, strikingly noticeable because she wore a white dress, a woman was standing.

There was something that suggested uncertainty, even at that distance, in her pose; she was as if lingering on the grass at the edge of the forest, whose shadows fell on her; her dress gleamed in the shade.

'Hullo, there's Laurette,' exclaimed Lionel. 'Wonder what she wants? Something wrong, probably; there usually is.'

I couldn't refrain from observing, 'I hope not; I have always understood that Charles's household ran so smoothly.' I had not put up with four hundred miles of Lionel's company to be faced with domestic crises at the end.

'When someone's ninety you can never tell . . .' he gabbled, accelerating. 'If you're sure you won't mind I'll just park you here for a minute and go ahead and see what's up.'

He did not wait to be assured that I did not mind. I had never before been bundled out of a car and on to a hard French chair, and into the shade of a dusty lime tree. It was all accomplished before I could protest. There I sat, with my mouth open to say something, amidst a group of five old Frenchmen in berets, who were enjoying an apéritif.

They surveyed me with one hard, dry stare, and I, my annoyance with Lionel suddenly expressing itself in mockery, favoured them with an inclination of my head and a clearly enunciated, 'Bonjour, messieurs.' Immediately I was rebuked by a polite 'Bonjour, madame,' from four of the party; the fifth continued to stare inimically.

Lionel shot away across the *place* and towards the waiting figure, who had already waved and was coming leisurely down the road.

CHAPTER 10

I SAT there. One of the old men had begun to question me hoarsely, leaning forward and fixing me with an eye: where did I come from: England was not a rich country now; had I been to America, and so on. I answered without thought, using the manner I reserve for inquisitive strangers on park seats.

Lionel really could be *extraordinary*. I longed for a cup of tea. '"Detestable girl! But I require tea,"' I quoted to myself.

Now the pair, the slight elderly man in summer clothes and the young woman—I could see, now, that she was young—were slowly approaching across the *place*; not hurrying themselves, not even paying me the compliment of turning their faces in my direction; still absorbed in talk.

I dislike small breaches made in the wall of conventional manners. In this era, especially, the rampart has a value that we of the middle-classes never anticipated. Let the small breaches widen—widen—and in will pour the waters of chaos and down we shall finally go.

Young Mrs. Handel was not pretty; she conveyed an impression of fragility and earnestness; spectacles of the kind known as 'Billy Burners' gave an owlish look to a pale face crowned by short curly fair hair.

'Sorry to have kept you, love, but *what* has been going on in my absence you *would* not believe,' called Lionel airily as they drew near. 'It's high time I came back and took over . . . here's Laurette, Laurette, love, curtsey to Miss Barrington. If you're a good child perhaps she'll let you call her Maude.'

The young woman was smiling as if she knew all about Lionel as she held out her hand. I did not think that she would want to call me Maude, and the suggestion that she should do so would not come from me.

'I'm so very pleased to welcome you here,' she was saying earnestly. I liked the formal manner, and the slight cool pressure of her fingers. 'I hope the journey hasn't been too exhausting.'

'Not *too* exhausting,' I said, smiling, and she smiled in return. I felt that some sympathy had been established; it was based on a full and mutual comprehension of what a four hundred mile journey in the company of Lionel could be!

'In with you, dears,' he was saying briskly, holding open the door of the car. I had expected, I do not know why, that she would sit with him. But she settled herself beside me.

I was aware of a fragrance and coolness, rather than the usual disagreeable sensation of heat and compression when somebody sits down next to one in a car. I confess that it increased my first pleasant impression of Laurette. I do so prefer a thin body to a stout one.

'So far, so good,' as Jock would have said. But, as we drove across the *place*, I saw that Lionel's nervousness had increased;

it showed itself in a loud monologue about nothing in particular which continued while we drove along the last two miles separating the village and Belair, making it actually difficult for me to hear Laurette's quiet questions about our travels and quite impossible for me to study the rising spectacle of the Chartreuse.

At last I exclaimed roundly. 'Do please be quiet, Lionel, and let me enjoy the view,' and he gave his short laugh and was silent.

The road was growing narrower and steeper. It looked out over wooded slopes directly below; above, it was shut in by bluff upon bluff of thousand-foot hills, their forests and fields almost sage colour in the westering light. The car swept round a find curve and we confronted a wide stone plateau, scooped out from the hill, with a row of garages built of some white substance, and a smiling man in overalls to welcome us; the modern equivalent of the lodge-keeper's wife in white apron of my childhood.

Lionel hailed him with a flow of joking chatter and he assisted with the disposal of the car in one of the twelve garages. I think that this was my first hint of the scale on which my old acquaintance Charles was living; here were stabled the cars belonging to those guests who came on pilgrimage 'from all over the world'.

We began the slow ascent of a path winding upwards; wide, and paved with slabs of the same white substance. I commented, as we walked, on the garages. They were what I could only call 'strikingly individual' in design. Lionel laughed.

'I should hope so. Kessler did them.'

'The American architect?'

'Even so. Charles has this thing about mod. architecture. He said that garages needn't be dull or reactionary. Have you seen the new Elephant House at the London Zoo?'

'No. I don't go to the Zoo nowadays.'

'Well, it makes you think of elephants.'

'But isn't that natural, in the circumstances?'

'Yes, yes, of course. But Kessler designed these things so that you think of cars before you know they're garages.'

'I see,' I said, though I did not quite see; I only knew that the twelve linked buildings harmonized with the landscape in which they stood. Pondering, I continued the ascent.

The path, winding in a steep cutting, was bordered on either side by bushes of American currant, now in flower and alternating with dwarf white hawthorns trimmed almost into ball shape. The effect was charming—yet I did not altogether like it; I felt a slight, unreasonable repugnance. Wild nature had not exactly been compelled into artificiality, but it had been remorselessly made to do what Charles wanted it to do. It was as if he had gentled it along, so to speak, letting it go its own way up to the point where he took command and exploited it. I looked down with some relief into the immune woods below.

Lionel and Laurette regulated their pace to mine, but kept slightly in the rear. Occasionally one of them murmured something; once I thought I heard him ask, 'On the upper terrace—sure?' but I was fully occupied with making my slow ascent: conscious that I had been told I 'had a heart' and blood pressure, and the dear knew what else.

The track turned a sharp curve. Suddenly we were facing a very wide and long platform, which, made of the prevailing white stone-like substance, glared up at the setting sun. It overlooked the whole immense valley; the view took my breath; the strong air and triumphant light smote my eyes and my senses. It was like being suddenly swept into another world, and for an instant my whole being seemed to falter.

Then I was conscious of a wall on my right; it was a second terrace rising some ten feet above me and running the length of the great paved space. It was of white and yellow marble, shaped into blocks, and down it a bright flowering creeper fell.

The light beat upon my eyes; my heart struggled painfully. I stood for a moment to get my breath, feeling the discomfort in my old body, conscious of the overwhelming light and the crying of many birds in the silence, high up in the yellow sky. It was not hot. I felt the evening coolness touch my face.

Then—then something—a head—came up over the terrace wall, full in the glare and glow, and stayed there, silently, looking down. Horror seized me. I gaped upwards. Behind me, I could feel how still the other two were standing. A voice called down to me.

'Hullo there,' it said, 'Snow-Woman,' and I knew who she was.

CHAPTER 11

I THINK I moved my hand in a kind of wave. I know that I called out, as clearly as I could manage, 'Hullo, Frances, how are you?'

At that, she hoisted herself on to the balustrade and sat there looking down at us; a slight figure in a brilliant dress that showed her naked arms. Her white hair was tied back with a schoolgirl's chiffon bow. She did not say anything.

'For God's sake don't sit like that, I've told you,' Lionel called irritably, 'you'll fall. Does Charles want us up before dinner?'

'Don't think so; no-one's said anything.' Her chuckling voice had changed hardly at all.

'All right; we'll be along about six. This way, Maudie, darling. You must be worn out.'

I think he would have given his arm. But I moved on by myself, following Laurette. My bitter anger gave me the strength; if I had touched Lionel in that moment it could only have been to strike him.

The next instant an actual inward voice warned me. *Gently, it said, quietly, sober down. You'll hurt yourself,* and slowly I began to regain the control that has been my constant companion since the death of Edward. I would not *allow* myself to feel.

I remember the pungence of the air as we slowly made our way across the terrace, but I could not give a name to the scent; I steadied my feelings as we descended a flight of steps and made our way across a bright garden, by trying to decide what it was. A long, low house, built of that white material, faced us at the end of the garden, backed by trees and facing the valley. Now we were some way below Belair; I had seen no sign of Charles's house so far, but then I had not been in a condition to notice anything.

Frances!

Laurette left us at the entrance to Les Gentianes, saying that she hoped I would get a good rest, and adding that we would all meet later for a drink.

Lionel's house was quiet and cool. He led me down a passage with doors on either side and showed me into an elegant bedroom.

I remember his saying that there was a sitting-room, too, and a bathroom; it was a miniature flat, I afterwards found, just suitable for one.

He left me. He put me into a chair by an open window and muttered something about some tea, and I nodded, and he left me. I was so glad to see the back of him that that was my only thought; afterwards, I recalled his white face and expression of alarm.

Do you good, Master Lionel, I muttered viciously; repeating the words as if they were a charm to keep strong feeling at bay; *do you good*. I leaned back, breathing painfully and staring about me.

The window looked out on the slope of a hill near at hand, and wooded. The crowding pines and their shade presented a relief to the eye after all those vast distances, and I looked into the greenness and dusk, until my breathing grew quieter and the pace of my heart slower. Far into the depths, high up, last shafts of sunlight lingered, gold and still, and with the gradual quietening of my anger, and as I became soothed by the silence, tears began to rise. I had dreaded this; I have not cried for years. I turned restlessly in my chair.

The door opened and a young woman came in, carrying a tray. She set it down on a small table which she drew up to my chair, just lifting her eyes once, to give me the impersonal look of the properly-trained servant.

'Bien, madame.'

'Merci.' She went out, after a last glance round.

The tiny incident helped largely towards my recovery; at least, I thought, ruefully surveying the shattered picture of my holiday, I shan't be asked to be on friendly terms with some exuberant creature every time my bed is made; if the details of my life for the next three weeks are orderly, I shall be more able to stand up to the larger strains.

The tea was excellent; the bread spread with good butter. There were no cakes or jam; just first-class tea and first-class bread, and the butter.

Delicious.

Presently I felt able to explore my surroundings. It was all excessively up-to-date and attractive, in a hard style. I studied everything; walls, floor-coverings, ornaments (few of these, but even I could see that they were works of art; probably valuable; certainly ugly), curtains, lighting and all the unobtrusive small devices for comfort. The colours were clear and strong; everything seemed to be new. The place was as impersonal as a window-display at 'Habitat's,' but undeniably comfortable, and while I studied it I could keep thought and feeling away.

I did not dare, literally, to think or feel as yet. But I was aware of feeling, crouched on the edge of that region governed by my will; black, and raging, and raw with pain.

The door opened, and there was the plump maid once more.

'Pardon, madame, I forgot to ask if madame would like me to unpack for her?' She spoke her French with strong inflections of Italian.

'Please, yes.' I did not smile at her, but sat slowly down once more in that comfortable wickerwork chair facing the open window, and looked out at the pine wood. The sunlight had died off it, but the rusty trunks and rich dark branches looked softened yet distinct in the afterglow. I glanced at my watch; it was nearly five o'clock. The girl moved about the room almost noiselessly; she was light on her feet, for one so plump; and the small rustles and shakings she made as she unfolded my clothes and put them away in the built-in cupboards were rather soothing than otherwise. I shut my eyes.

At once, emotion began to shake me, and my heart started to beat faster. It was no use; I was not going to be able even to doze, and I sat there, keyed-up and wretched, until I became aware that the small sounds had ceased. I opened my eyes, to see the girl at the door, with some dresses over her arm; taking them away, to press I imagined.

'Is the amber one there?' I asked. It was my most becoming dress, and if there was one thing of which I was certain, it was that I meant to look my best when I next encountered Frances. Petty, even shameful—but I did.

She held it up. 'This one, madame?'

'Yes . . . that's right. I will wear it this evening.'

'*Bien, madame.*' She seemed to hesitate, and then, in the pause, I saw the mask which training had imposed upon her face break up into a smile. 'Such a beautiful dress, madame. Madame will look elegant!'

I was certainly not myself, and even more shaken than I had supposed, for, at the words, all my former satisfaction in the thought of being waited upon by a properly trained maid vanished, and I felt a small glow of pleasure . . . and comfort. Yes, it was comfort. I felt less alone, and not so far away from my home and my memories, because of this child's words. 'Thank you,' I said, smiling.

'Would madame like me to dress her hair? I have had lessons—I know how to make the hair look nice.'

'No, no, thank you. I—I will do it myself, I always do,' I said, and she said, '*Bien, madame*' again, and went out of the room, holding my dress carefully so that it should not catch on anything as she went.

I'm getting childish, I told myself as I got up, with humiliating slowness and difficulty, from my chair; I'll have my bath nearly cold, and see if that will knock the nonsense out of me.

I had had to give up really cold baths under the orders of my doctor when I was sixty. But that evening I snapped my fingers at James MacRae, M.D., and had it nearly cold . . . and it did do me good.

You cannot nurse even a righteous anger in a near-cold bath, and I was in, and soaped all over with some highly-scented French tablet, and plunged under, and out again and drying myself, in less than seven minutes: I timed it, by my watch lying on the edge of the basin. When I went back into the bedroom I was gasping, but I felt braced, and calmer. I soon ceased to shiver, and began that delightful glowing.

I was in my dressing-gown and putting the last comb in, at the back of my head, when the knock at the door came, a light, impatient sound. It was followed by the voice I remembered so well, with its chuckling undertone that always suggested she was relishing some malicious joke.

'Maude? Can I come in?'

'Of course,' I called, instantly. I was perfectly prepared, now, to face her. But I did wish that I had been dressed, and this slight irritation prevented me from noticing precisely what *she* was wearing; there was only a general impression of a dark purple, and straightness, and still that silly way of doing her hair. Absurd shoes, too, nothing but glittering straps. But elegance was the over-riding impression: Frances always did dress very well, and she never looked like anyone else.

I could not realize, though, that this thin, graceful person *was* Frances, whose letters I had been ignoring for years.

'Well, feeling better?' She sank into the chair by the window that I was already thinking of as 'mine', 'I've come to take you up to Charles when you're ready. It's easy to get lost, and there are bloody steps and things.'

'Thank you. I'm almost ready, the maid took away my dress—I suppose to press it.' I hurried on, feeling that I must say something, anything. 'Have you been here long?'

'Since last week. I've been staying in Cannes.'

Fortunately, at that moment, the maid came in with my dress.

'Nice, isn't it, Bianca?' Frances observed, fixing her eyes, still large and still of a light pretty grey, though less sparkling now, on the embroidered folds as Bianca hung it carefully up. 'What unusual stuff—good design—did you get it off the peg? Surely not.'

'No, I got it in a sale at Harrods, and my dressmaker made it up.'

'Put it on for madame,' Frances commanded, 'and mind her hair, now.'

Had I been myself, I should have calmly avoided being dressed under the orders of Frances.

But I felt as if I were carrying out some delicate task requiring the last ounce of concentration; I dared not relax into feelings; I had to think out every word, every intonation, every shade of meaning that might be read into what I was saying, if my imperious desire that Frances and I should continue to behave as gentlewomen was to be fulfilled.

I felt no need for scenes; I wanted—at least at the moment—no heaping of vengeance on that ridiculously dressed head; my one wish was to get through the next few hours in a civilized manner.

Bianca lifted the dress and slipped it over my head, so filled with angry thoughts.

'Pull the sash a little to the left—have you any foundation cream, Maude? You're so pale,' Frances added critically.

'No doubt. I'm tired.' That slipped out in spite of my caution, and the tone I used was not controlled. 'No. I have some rouge. I expect she's put it away.'

'That'll have to do,' and Frances added something to Bianca, who flew, so far as a plump girl could, to the dressing-table and began rummaging.

'I bought this years ago . . . thank you,' I said, as she held it out to me. I opened the box and stared unseeingly into it for a moment. Intruding on me, taking over my dressing, prescribing for my pallor—I could have stormed aloud, in my resentment.

'Let her do it, Maude, she's trained, I taught her last year,' Frances was saying, 'and a hare's foot!' she ended, in one of her mutters.

It was a return to her earlier manner, one belonging to nearer fifty than forty years ago, and, while Bianca was having the nature and use of the hare's foot explained to her, with laughter, I realized that it was partly the absence of this manner that had made Frances seem a stranger.

She was much less animated than formerly. It was of course to be expected, but I had not expected it. And I myself had contributed to her air of being a stranger, because, for all these years, I had seen her in memory and imagination as unchanged and as some kind of monster.

Bianca began, delicately, to manipulate the hare's foot; I felt the warmth from her young hand against my chilly, ancient skin. Her unsmiling concentration and the careful slight pressure she bestowed were beguiling; she seemed to be subduing the natural vehemence of her youth, in homage to my years. I looked steadily at the reflection in the glass. Yes, it offered some of the support I sorely needed this evening.

'You've worn a bloody sight better than I have,' was Frances's abrupt comment. 'Look at this—and here.' She pulled savagely at the cords visible in her throat and the loose skin beneath her eyes. 'And it's going to get worse.'

I glanced at her. 'Yes—but you're one of the people—one doesn't notice it, Frances, really one doesn't.'

She could always say things that would bring some kind of tribute from me—always, but what I had said was true. She was irrevocably old, she had worn really badly, yet the eyes in the fallen face carried off all the ruin with their signal of an indestructible greed for life.

'All the same, I wish I had your neck,' she retorted crossly, and suddenly we both laughed. I didn't want to; I suppose that by this time, thanks to shock and strain, I was slightly hysterical, and our laughter did not ease the tension between us because I instantly resumed guard.

'Ready? Come on then; Bianca, see that madame has everything for the night—did you bring a hot water bottle?' to me.

'I never use one,' I said, 'unless I'm ill.'

'I might have guessed it,' muttered Frances, making her way slowly ahead of me down the passage. 'Well, I've taken to one— had to. Central heating, those blankets, nothing's any good except a hot water bottle . . .'

I followed her out of the house and across Lionel's garden, through the dying afterglow. The small confession had relaxed me, I confess. *I* had not taken to a hot water bottle.

We climbed to the terrace, slowly, just not painfully, because we were two old women 'putting on a good show', and paused to look at the darkening valley and its lights under the sky while we got our breath. We didn't look at one another. I think that all the energies we still possessed were bent on arriving at wherever we had to arrive with no outward signs of distress.

We began the slow ascent of some steps made of yellow marble, at the side of the terrace, Frances leading the way.

A third person, knowing us both to be old friends, would have seen something most strange in our resumption of relationship without the smallest exchange of mutual news. It implied the existence between us either of a strong affection or a strong dislike. But the party at Belair, fortunately, was too old in years and too civilized in habits to comment, and Laurette Handel, though young, appeared to be civilized too. If she did ask an impertinent question or so, Frances and I were more than capable of dealing with her.

CHAPTER 12

WE CAME out at last on to another terrace, so high, and so as if it were lifted up into the solemn stillness of the air above the valley, that the presence there of a long, low, white house, and the light in a room visible through windows, seemed an intrusion. But at once my attention was caught, and held, by a figure seated outside the windows.

It was bulky, and its size and quietness were emphasized by the peculiarity of white hair falling almost to the shoulders, and a white robe that I at first assumed to be a kind of fancy dress but, as we slowly approached, saw was only a man's dressing-gown of unusual fullness, with a monkish kind of cord for girdle. This figure sat full in the sunless clarity of the light, gazing out across the vast valley at the heights of the Chartreuse still touched with an orange glow. Charles? It could only be Charles Handel.

Someone came out through the windows. 'Maude,' said a guttural voice that I remembered, and then I was having both my hands pressed in Mimi Handel's. She glanced at the motionless figure, then returned her eager gaze to me; she was small, withered, richly dressed in a dark material sparkling with jet and diamanté, and above the glitter there was a lively, ugly old face.

'My dear, I am so glad to see you after all this long, long time—how many years—? and so glad that you could come, and that dreadful journey! I said to Laurette, if only she could fly! But Lionel wanted to bring you himself, and you haf not changed at all—oh, your hair is becoming! So becoming,' as I made a foolish deprecatory gesture, confused as I was by my tiredness and recent shock. 'You have had a good rest, I hope? Come, then, come undt see Charles. Charles, my darlink,' and she turned towards him, 'here is Maude.'

She held my hand linked in hers as she led me up to him; and then, presenting me, as it were, she seemed to sink into the background. It was an extraordinary performance; I felt as if we were on the stage, in some drama of Ruritania in which the suppliant is brought to the old king.

He turned his head slowly towards me. 'Maude,' he said, in a faint, toneless voice, 'so delighted to see you here.'

And no more. His eyes had once been of a lively lightish hazel; they met mine, and instantly they were lowered. He turned his head away, fixing his stare again on the mountains.

'Always tired in the eveninks,' said Mimi in a half-whisper, and a jovial voice behind us said 'Mr. Handel? Ready to come in?'

Miss Bunsen, his secretary for thirty years, came out from the room on to the terrace, acknowledging my presence as she did so by a flapping gesture of the hand, intended, I supposed, to express recognition and delight. I had always found her a trying creature, but I was shocked by the greatness of the change in her; nothing was left of the slim, too-vital, gold-haired girl I remembered but a sandy woman with little in the way of bust and a ruined complexion. She was dressed in what I can only call a violent style, and there was a fixed brightness on her long face.

'Ready to come in, Mr. Handel?' she repeated.

'Not until the light has gone,' he answered, almost inaudibly, but with majesty. Yes, it was majesty. He did not turn his head, and Miss Bunsen instantly bowed her own as if recognizing the presence of some superior spiritual claim.

Mimi did not move or say anything, and it was only good manners for me to keep quiet and say nothing either, and there we stood, for what seemed like five minutes (and that is a longer time than most of us think, as you will realize if you recall how long those sacred two minutes seem on Armistice Day) while Charles waited for the afterglow to vanish.

Of course, it didn't. I was irresistibly reminded of King Canute and the waves. But, while musing over the incident afterwards, I did recall that I had twice thought of kingship in the first moments of meeting Charles Handel again.

From the corner of my eye I could see Lionel and Laurette in the room behind us, laughing together, but subduedly. Frances had paused while Mimi greeted me, and was now keeping up a kind of fidget in the background, picking leaves off a bush, and occasionally muttering, but when she began a stealthy movement towards the open window and the drinks-trolley, Miss Bunsen darted her such a glance that she stopped.

Knowing Frances, I thought that it was fury and amazement, rather than any assertion of authority on the part of Miss Bunsen that had stopped her. But she did stop.

Charles began to get up from his chair, slowly and with difficulty. Miss Bunsen did not move until he was on his feet, and had taken a step forward, then she went up and offered him an arm sleeved in a lurid African print. He made a repudiating movement.

'No . . . no . . . Lionel,' he said, more loudly than I had yet heard him speak, 'it's his turn.'

She darted back into the room and summoned Lionel, who came out unhurriedly. As he passed me, he winked.

I was relieved to see that someone could, yet I felt saddened, too. After Charles had walked slowly along the terrace leaning on Lionel's arm and disappeared through another window which Lionel slid aside, the atmosphere generated by this sorry bit of hocus-pocus vanished, as if on a breath of relief.

'Gaspard will put him to bed, he is like a baby with Gaspard, he has been with us for forty years, you remember him?' said Mimi. 'Now let us go in and have our drinks—Bunny, Frances my dear, come along, come in, we will have our drinks undt you shall tell me all your news, Maude.'

I have not had much news to tell anyone, for the last fifty years. But it was pleasant to be invited to tell what I had, and I followed her into the long, Roman room.

I call it Roman, because it reminded me of those reconstructions of Roman houses which I have seen in museums; there was the same impression of strong, grave colour, and richness, and bareness; there were even some busts of Late Roman emperors and the chairs were of reddish wood inlaid with ivory. I remembered that passage in *Marius the Epicurean* where Pater speaks of the hay-scent that floated along the passages in the old house of yellow marble in the country where Marius grew up, and at that moment, coming in from the evening fields, I caught the very smell.

Lionel appeared in the open windows and vigorously slid them together and pulled the ginger-brown curtains, bordered with a key-pattern in white.

'How many times have I got to tell everybody that I dislike being stared at by mountains?' he exclaimed, shivering, as he crossed to the splendid fire that leapt in a broad grate of brick and marble; '*and* hay. I particularly dislike hay. It means histamine, to me . . . thank you, Bunny,' as Miss Bunsen, who was dispensing drinks, held out a glass to him.

'Sherry, Miss Barrington? Is it still sherry?'

'Thank you. How clever of you to remember,' I said, and she turned away to pour it out, smiling. I caught Frances's eye, and she made one of her remembered grimaces, which I took to mean that she continued to share my distaste for poor Bunny. I was disconcerted to find us thus still linked.

Mimi made me sit close to the fire. The room was soothingly warm and quiet. Now the perpetual movement and ever-changing scenes of the last two days were over. Now I could be still, and recollect myself, and realize that my body was aching from the car's racing along the roads and my mind buzzing with the countless impressions it had received, culminating in the appearance of Frances on the terrace. I had not absorbed that yet, and while I was looking forward to being alone in my room that night, I knew that it would then come upon me in all its force.

So—one more effort, Maude. Only two or three more hours, and you can take off your mask. And at least you have not to deal with Lionel alone, now. You are supported by people who have known him, and you, for nearly half a century. The silence in the room was almost comfortable.

'Charles looks serene,' I said, turning at last to Mimi. 'More so, I think, than I had expected.'

It was not easy to find the right thing to say about a man of over ninety who had obviously become senile in a sad and embarrassing way.

'And well, too, I thought,' I added. Following on the shock of Frances's appearance, Charles's pathetic posing had been the lesser, but a still painful, one.

'Oh he *is* well,' Miss Bunsen said earnestly, clashing her bracelets about as she turned her starting eyes on me, with her horse's smile. Mimi murmured something, staring into the flames. And then Laurette said, her cool voice stealing out,

'I suppose we can look forward to having him—taking it all into consideration, his heart and his blood-pressure and everything, and his being taken good care of, that's so important, his being taken good care of—we can count on another two years, would you say?'

She addressed us all, leaning slightly forward, with her untasted drink cradled in both hands above her crossed knees. She wore her completely contemporary dress so badly! little Laurette was a frump: rather sweet, and a frump.

And no-one answered her. Frances took a gulp at her glass, looking at the fireplace; Miss Bunsen fixed her permanently startled eyes on the floor; I don't know what Lionel did, I wasn't looking at him. Mimi's head drooped lower, for an instant, above the jet and diamanté bosom of her dress. Then she looked up and across at me.

'Now, Maude, tell us. What have you been doink?'

'What have I been doing? Since the war, do you mean, or for the last year or so?'

'Everythink—since the war. Tell us all about it.'

'Oh . . .' I hesitated. My experiences, such as they were, had been typical, and of the slightest. I should have thought them small beer indeed to entertain the household of Charles Handel, and especially Mrs. Robert Gelfors 3rd (that was Frances). But I supposed that some allowance must be made for old acquaintance; even, perhaps, for some real interest and even for affection. I went on:

'I was looking after my parents for nearly ten years, after the war you know, and . . . that was a whole-time job.' Mimi murmured sympathetically, and I decided not to add that its difficulties had been increased by our lack of money, on my father's retirement from ill health, until the death of Great-Aunt Dorothea. 'Then . . . I'd had to let the house get into rather a bad state of repair' (that would sufficiently indicate our financial position) 'so . . . when I was left without duties or ties . . . I had it put thoroughly in order. Then Millie had come back to us, she was widowed—some time in the 'forties.'

'That lofely girl like a Greuze?' said Mimi, all genuinely sparkling interest. 'Oh, I remember her well, at your house. Such hair—the true ash-blonde.'

' . . . and she had no other home, so she stayed on with me . . . and I took up my music again, and . . . occasionally I play accompaniments for professionals at the Music Club in Hampstead . . . that's really all, I think.'

'Lionel said—didn't you have an interesting war job, with one of your women's services?' Laurette asked.

'The W.V.S.—Women's Voluntary Services. Yes . . . everybody did it, you know, it wasn't particularly interesting. But very necessary . . . I don't think I should call it one of the women's services, though of course it was. We usually use the word "services" for the women's auxiliaries to the Army and Navy and the Raf.'

'It must have been a satisfaction to work out your war-time tensions in social work,' said Laurette, with a kindly smile.

'It was. We called it doing our duty,' I said, smiling back, and out of the corner of my eye I saw Frances grin.

Laurette's gentle expression did not change. 'And did you continue to feel this need for self-expression by serving the community after the war?'

'I never did feel it, particularly. It was my duty.' I repeated. 'After my parents died I began to get—oh, all kinds of tiresome things, and I was told by my doctor to live more quietly. I cannot say that I was sorry.'

Laurette nodded, looking as if this remark had conveyed more to her than I knew, and I wondered if I were 'in for' three weeks of her being rather a tiresome girl? Bless me if she did not go worrying back to me and my war-work.

'You *never* felt a wish to take up any kind of public work again?' she persisted.

'I did once or twice wonder if it were my duty,' I answered, not as coherently as I could have wished; I was tired and bored by the discussion.

'This concept "duty",' murmured Laurette, as if preparing to examine it aloud, and then Lionel cut in, 'Maude's a genuine Victorian, you know, she was never "trained" for anything, were you, love?'

I shook my head, and was surprised by a sudden snap from Mrs. R. Gelfors 3rd. 'You don't know what a bore you are with your "training", Laurette. I feel sorry for all you girls—you've no idea what a good time is, have they, Maude?'

'Perhaps our generation is serious. But it has cause to be,' Laurette said quietly.

'At any moment you are going to be accused of personally starting both world wars,' Lionel said, getting up. 'Thank you, Rafael,' as a stout manservant put his head round the door and, rather casually I thought, announced that dinner was served. 'Come along, let us go and eat.'

He fell behind, to allow Mimi to lead our ill-balanced procession into the adjoining room.

CHAPTER 13

I WAS glad that the summons had come at that moment; not because Laurette's tiresomeness had really irritated me but because I had recollected that the peaceful country lying about us in the twilight had seen the martyrdom of many Frenchmen in the great Resistance movement in the Vercors; that mountain redoubt stretching away to the east. I did not wish to insult their memory by any talk of my own war-time experiences.

'Zo you still play, Maudie,' Mimi was saying as we took our places, 'ach, how beautifully you played to us that last night, when we dined with you! I haf always remembered.'

'Thank you . . .'

'I adore the piano, I wish you'd play to us after dinner,' Miss Bunsen exclaimed, drawing up her chair to the table with a painful screep: what a clumsy creature she still was.

'I shall be happy to, some other night. Tonight,' I turned to Mimi, 'I don't think I could play well enough to please you all.'

'No, no. Of course not. You must still be zo tired. Ach, that journey! Und Lionel, I am sure, was zo trying.' Unbelievably, she wagged a finger at him.

'Thank you, she was trying, too,' he retorted.

'But not zo trying as you, I am sure. Ach, I know—I know. I know what he can be, shut up with one in a car . . . haf I not been sight-seeing with him, years ago? Und now I do not go any more. But in a few days, Maude, when you are rested, he shall take you to see the Chartreuse.'

'What I would really like to see,' I said, as I unfolded my napkin, 'is the Vercors. I'm reading about it—I brought the book with me.'

But Mimi shuddered. 'Dreadful things . . .' I heard her murmur.

She went on at once, however, 'Another night we will eat in the other room, cosy by the fire. We will haf trays. This table'—she tapped the shining surface disapprovingly with her soup spoon—'is for the big parties. Charles had it made from our own walnut trees; the carpenter in the village made it. It vas too big.' Having handed our soup, the manservant had gone out of the room, yet her tone was lowered as she continued, 'But I did not want to ask them to gif us trays, this efening. There has been a little trouble while Lionel has been away. They will do thinks only for him.'

'My charm,' put in Lionel, swallowing soup.

I was dismayed to hear of servant-trouble in this impressive setting; but supposed that no setting is luxurious and splendid enough to prevent its creeping in somehow. Confining myself to a silent hope that it would not make my 'holiday' even worse than it threatened to be, I said nothing.

'Ten years ago we had good servants, Charles and I,' Mimi went on, 'but . . . but . . . there was trouble. Trouble always. Und,' she glanced at Laurette, 'Laurette's gompatriots—ach! it iss the same all over the world; they offer a "way of life" irresistible to all. Und that is why we have bad servants. Charles sacks all our French ones. Now we haf Italian and Greek. Not good.' She spooned up her soup with relish. 'I am zorry,' she ended.

We were quiet for a while. I addressed myself to my dinner, avoiding, with an effortlessness which was the result of years of practice, the peevish or lunatic demands made on my attention by the ultra-contemporary pictures crowding the walls of the room, which in its style was also what I thought of as 'Roman'.

I came to terms with modern art some years ago, after a sharp battle in which, in my opinion, I was victor.

While I was enjoying the delicate blend of sorrel and cream and other flavours which I could not identify, I suddenly remembered that there was a fifth member of Charles's house-hold, and that I had not yet seen him.

It tells something, I think, about the not-quite-tranquil atmosphere which I could feel in Belair, that I deliberately thought in silence, for a minute or two, whether I should enquire after Emil Handel.

No fifth place was set at the table; no-one had mentioned him in the four hours or so that I had been there, yet he had not died, so far as I knew; I had not heard of a divorce from Laurette. Was it just the casual behaviour of old acquaintances, who, in accepting me as 'one of the family', had simply not bothered to mention that he happened, that evening, to have another engagement?

That was the most likely explanation. Yet instinct did warn me, quite strongly, not to enquire.

I followed it. I joined in the conversation which was soon flowing round the table, its agreeably general current interrupted only by Frances's attempts to give it a more personal and malicious flavour whenever some name came up which she knew.

Again and again, my gaze returned to her face, where the leaden tints of age in her flesh seemed actually to glow with the fire of life that leapt and crackled within. Her eyes glittered, her brow gleamed moist, her voice made the harsh yet charming sounds I remembered with fascination from my childhood and with bitterness and pain from my youth.

She had not changed. A dinner-party, any kind of party, still brought out all the actress in her. She was a different being from the noticeably quieter one of our earlier meeting, when she had presumed to dictate my toilet.

I have often read, in older novels, 'The years rolled away.' Well, they rolled away as I marvelled, watching Frances. It seemed . . . so natural . . . to be sitting there, seeing her display herself. The detestation I had felt for her, for such a long time, seemed to shimmer and fade and change as I watched. I didn't know how or what I felt about her. I knew only that I should be very glad to get to bed.

Fortunately, we did not sit long after we had drunk our coffee by the fire. Gaspard, Charles's manservant, whom I remembered, came in to report that his master had enjoyed his dinner and was sleeping calmly; I remembered Gaspard, a thin little creature with froggy eyes, and we exchanged a few sentences which, I must say, can have deceived no-one by their pretence of a mutual interest.

After this, all sight or sound of the servants vanished. It was only half-past nine, but they might all have walked out of the house. Laurette had to go to fetch more cream for Lionel's coffee. The used cups were still about in their unsightliness when we rose to go to bed at a quarter to eleven, and when Frances, who had started on a tiresome defence of contemporary painting, marched into the dining-room to illustrate some point or other from one of the pictures there, I saw that the table was as we had left it. Mimi glanced at the disorder and made a little clucking sound.

'Yes, well, no-one's arguing,' said Lionel, who had lounged in after his sister.

'Maude was.'

'Indeed I was not,' I said.

'You were—you were. If you could have seen your expression!'

'She's tired.' He dropped a hand on my arm for an instant. 'We're all tired. Come along—bed.'

I received a particularly affectionate good-night kiss from Mimi—how much more likeable she was than I had remembered. Then I went off with Frances and Lionel.

Alone with the Croziers—at their mercy! I thought, as we began the careful descent of the terrace steps, and I actually laughed to myself, in a foolish way. I was so tired I could barely think.

'What's the joke?' demanded Frances, who was behind me.

'Nothing . . . I was being silly . . .'

Down we went through a darkness which gradually grew less, lit by a few very bright stars. Slowly, the blacker mountains loomed up against the black sky; it began to feel natural to be out on a hillside at night.

'Phew . . . phew . . . God in heaven . . .' Frances was muttering behind me, and then I caught a whiff of the scent she had used all her life, *Mitsouko*, and something brushed my face; she was waving her handkerchief about.

'That better?'

'It's delicious, but what's the matter?' I asked, and nearly missed the last step into Lionel's garden. I fell heavily against his arm.

I stood still and sniffed. 'Oh, yes, I can now—garlic, and very strong tobacco . . . what a horrid mixture.'

'Here . . .' and she thrust the handkerchief at me.

'Do come on,' Lionel said impatiently, and we set out, more quickly now, across the garden.

'Would you like Bianca?' Frances went on. 'That's better—how you all put up with it,' to Lionel, 'I do not know. She's not bad at taking one to bits—only I don't suppose you've anything to take, have you?'

'Not so far.' I laughed foolishly again.

'Well, you know what it is,' Frances said, sounding mollified, 'teeth, and one's face, and all the rest of it . . . it's the deadly grind that I mind. After sixty, you might as well be dead for all the use your body is to you.'

Lionel pushed open the front door, and we went down the corridor and paused outside my rooms.

'If you're sure, then,' said Frances. She bent forward, and the next instant her flushed, wrinkled cheek, bringing a breath of *Mitsouko*, had just touched mine.

'Good-night,' she said, 'You dreary old Snow-Woman, you.'

CHAPTER 14

I BREAKFASTED in bed. My night had been disturbed by dreams of ice floes and retreating figures far off in a frozen landscape, and as I awoke I did not want to face the day.

But there is no support like habit. It was a fine morning, and when I had breakfasted, and read some letters which Bianca brought in, I felt more or less my usual self. No-one came near me after Bianca had offered her aid in my toilet, which I declined, and it was nearly eleven as, dressed and calmer, I stood by the open window glancing again at my postcard from Tessa and a letter from Millie.

The latter had thought I would just like to know that everything was going on all right, and hoped I was having nice weather and a good rest. I thought these sentiments hardly worth the effort Millie must have expended in putting her ill-controlled pencil to paper, and, having reread Tessa's exclamatory remarks about nothing at all, I was going to put both communications into the waste-paper basket when a line on the back of Millie's sheet caught my eye.

'It is a lovely baby. I wish you could see him.'

Those Parkers! I had forgotten them. But evidently Millie intended that I should not continue to do so. She could be trusted, in her inevitable sentimentality, to follow up any situation which promised drama. She always ran, as the racing men say, true to form. The Parker baby, of course, was her reason for writing. I tore the letter into fragments.

Then I set out to explore. I crossed the garden, delicately scented more with young grasses and leaves than with flowers as yet, and brimming with sunlight, and slowly climbed the steps to the first terrace. I was pleased to find no-one about—and then, as

I came to the top of the steps, I saw a tall, drooping sort of man sitting at a table there, breakfasting.

He was staring into nothing, and I came into his line of vision. He raised a hand.

'Oh—hullo there . . . Miss Barrington . . . hullo . . .' He did not get up from his bamboo chair and a more awkward manner I had yet to meet.

'Good-morning,' I said, crossing towards him. 'It is Emil, isn't it?'

'Emil it is . . . sorry I wasn't . . . but here, do sit down.' He did get up then, and fussed with the chairs. 'Last night, I mean . . . do sit down . . . I'm flattered you remember me—I didn't expect you would . . . I came to tea with you when I was five. You let me play with the shells in the cabinet.'

'So I did.' I settled myself in my chair, and pulled my sun-hat more effectually over my eyes, noticing that last night's disagreeable blend of garlic and strong tobacco had reappeared. 'I remember, too. You were a careful little boy. And once, when you were at your first prep. school, I took you across London to Paddington.'

'Yes . . . you bought me an ice-cream.'

Then silence fell on these reminiscences.

'Could you manage another cup of coffee? There is some here. Or . . . you have had breakfast, haven't you?'

'Oh, yes, some time ago, no more for me now, thank you . . . How is your father this morning?'

'All right, I suppose. I'd have heard if he wasn't.'

I checked a startled glance, and he went on:

'Were you here in time for the evening performance?'

'The—?' I did turn, now, to look at him.

'That phoney business on the terrace—retiring with the sinking sun and all the rest of it—everyone rolling up for their turn to take him off to bye-bye . . .'

I think that my distaste was almost stronger than my embarrassment. I felt real distress, too. The 'evening performance' had been pretentious and absurd but Charles was ninety. He was *ninety*—cannot we just love someone of ninety as if they were again the child they once were? Seeing their little games, their beloved small rituals and their self-deceptions in the light of patience and love? I suddenly felt a protective affection for Charles.

'He is ninety and he is your father,' I said, as forthrightly as I knew how.

'That's the last thing I'm likely to forget . . . There's *The Times* here,' he turned to some newspapers lying on a chair, 'if you want to see it.'

'No thank you.' I thought the best thing was to change the subject. Emil Handel was not going to be shaken out of a disgraceful frame of mind by five minutes' conversation with me. 'Do you know if any plans have been made for today? I haven't seen anyone yet.'

'No idea, I'm afraid . . . I expect they'll want to drive you around. Bunny usually works out that kind of thing . . . oh, here she is . . . well, I'll be pushing. Got some work to do.'

'How is your painting going?' I asked as he got up from his chair: what a bean-pole he was! He must be all of seven feet. Bunny, clattering and jangling and grinning, was approaching down the steps from the upper terrace.

'Oh, so-so. Up and down, you know; I've usually got something on the stocks and I sell them, too. Make quite a bit. Chicken-feed compared with the old man's intake but it keeps me in cigarettes.'

I did not know quite how to answer, so I said, 'Well done.'

'Yes, isn't it? I really must be pushing, see you later.'

He shambled away; it is the only word that describes his movements.

'Good-morning,' I said, as Bunny came up.

'Good-morning . . . I *do* hope Emil hasn't been upsetting you?' was her disconcerting opening.

'We have been reminiscing about old times,' I said, smiling. I was not going to enquire why he might have been upsetting me; the last thing I wanted, on top of the shock given me yesterday, was to hear about the undercurrents at Belair (though I was beginning to fear that they existed). 'I was asking him—do you know if any plans have been made for today?'

'I've just come from Mrs. Handel. She sends you her love and says she thought you might like to take things quietly today . . . but of course, if you would like a drive this afternoon, you have only to say so.'

She paused, with her large, emotional eyes fixed on my face, and I received the impression that she wanted to pour out a flood of gossip. I had always heard her described as a highly efficient secretary; was she beginning to 'go to pieces'? after thirty years of service to the Handels, or did she feel herself as one of the family?

'No, I will take things quietly, I think. I shall stroll round the garden presently.'

'Mrs. Gelfors will be down soon, she's the gardening expert. But usually no-one except me shows up until lunch time. I *do* hope you won't feel yourself deserted.'

'Thank you, I am sure I shall not.' She went grinning away, and I picked up *The Times*, feeling a faint sensation of comfort at the sight of the well-known type—though, alas, the familiar dignified front page has gone for ever.

But soon I let it fall on my lap, while I stared unseeing across the hazy valley.

I had not yet fully faced the fact of finding Frances at Belair. I had been too shocked, and too exhausted by the journey, to think what it was going to mean. Now, sitting in the warm light, surrounded by flowering shrubs and sweet scents, I tried to confront it. But I was still too tired, I discovered; the fact and its implications seemed to slip away even as I grasped them. Last night's cold and alarming dreams had been caused by her presence there; that was as far as I could go, and the next moment my efforts were interrupted by the slow approach of Frances herself.

'Hullo,' she croaked, 'how disgustingly peaceful you look. What's all that mess? . . . oh, Emil's breakfast . . . things get worse and worse around here . . . don't think I shall come next year . . . did you see him?'

While she chattered she was dragging up a wicker lounging-chair, and packing it with many white cushions. She then arranged herself on it, sprawling at full length. She wore another exiguous sun-dress.

'Did you?' she said, lifting her dark glasses from one eye to look at me.

'Yes, I saw him.'

'Well,' Frances said impatiently, 'what did you think of him?'

'I thought he didn't look at all well,' I said at last.

'Who does?' muttered Frances, banging and shuffling the cushions about. 'You do, of course, but you're peculiar.'

I could feel myself rapidly falling back into my old habits with her. The years were melting away. I merely refused to be drawn, and I found that my silence, mild but decided, had the effect of discouraging her in what I may call her *bone-disinterring*, and presently she seemed to go to sleep.

The morning actually passed pleasantly. Had anyone told me, a week before, that I should pass some hours in the society of Frances Crozier and find them pleasant, I would have protested in pain and outrage. Yet there . . . we were. Two old women, resting in the sun.

'What are you smiling at?' suddenly asked her harsh voice, seeming to come from behind the black lenses masking her face.

'Oh . . .' I was beginning, then checked myself. I did not want to lead on to more bone-disinterring, on behalf, this time, of myself and her. 'Oh, nothing.' I said.

Mimi apologized because we could not lunch on the upper terrace.

'They will not bring the things out . . . it is so tiresome . . . und such a lovely day! Zo we lunch in the dining-room. You will not mind, Maude?'

I said the customary graceful things.

Lionel came out of the house at this moment, looking harassed.

'Some blasted New York paper on the line,' he announced. 'Bunny's talking to them. They want a story on Charles, on the state of his health.'

'But there has been no change,' almost cried Mimi, staring, 'no change for weeks. They had a story on his birthday in February—why do they want another now?'

Lionel shrugged.

'They are cruel,' Mimi said, as if to herself. 'When people zay the press is like vultures, it is true.'

Bunny came out to us, and she looked perturbed.

'I thought as much,' she said, in a 'significant' tone. 'Their contact has been on to them again.'

No-one said anything. Mimi looked stricken, Lionel stared at the pavement. Laurette came strolling towards us, remarking that lunch was ready if we were.

'In a moment. In a moment, dear,' said Mimi, dismissing her. 'Though why do I say in a moment?' she went on, her voice raised, 'when there is nothing to be done? Und nothing to be said. Maude is the only one who does not know what this is all about—'

'Then don't let's worry her with it,' Lionel said, taking my arm, 'there's no point in it.' He began to lead the way to the house.

In the afternoon, as no suggestions for any other entertainment had been made, I rested again. But I had not been lying down for more than half an hour before someone tapped at the door.

'Come in.'

'I hope you weren't nearly asleep,' said Laurette's lifeless little voice as she put her head round, 'but Charles would so like to see you.'

'Of course—I am very pleased.'

Fortunately, I had not taken anything off, or loosened my hair. I got up and smoothed myself and followed her through the sunlit, silent house. (I was becoming accustomed to everyone at Belair vanishing between meals as if they had disintegrated.)

'The afternoon is always his best time,' Laurette confided. 'Sometimes he has tea with us—just a cup of tea—and then, if it's fine, he goes on to the terrace for an hour to see the sun set, and then to bed. This time last year people came in in the evening, sometimes; he has some friends living in Grenoble, and there were always stray visitors, of course, driving up on the chance of seeing him, and people on their way down to the south. He usually did see them. He used to love people! He did; he loved them. But . . .'

If there was one thing of which I was certain, it was that Charles Handel did not love people, and never had. But from an Amer-

ican the statement was, of course, the highest compliment. I said
nothing but—'Yes . . . and all that has stopped now?'

'Oh, yes—months ago.'

We were climbing the steps to the second terrace. I was
conscious of the vast landscape spread below in its smiling
impersonal beauty, offering so much, demanding nothing, and
wished that I had been alone to look at it.

'Miss Barrington—' Laurette slowed her pace to a saunter,
then stopped, as we came to the middle of the terrace.

I suppose that I should have said, 'Won't you call me Maude?'
at this point. It presented an opportunity. I did nothing of the
kind. I looked at her enquiringly.

'Don't mention Emil to him, will you, please?'

'Of course not, if you ask me not to.'

I could imagine that a son looking and talking as Emil Handel
had that morning might well be a distressing subject for a nine-
ty-year-old father.

Laurette slid back the windows and admitted us into a room
large and light and full of colour, yet unmistakably invalidish and
unmistakably sad. My eyes went at once to the sole picture, on
a wide wall the colour of an apricot. It was Charles's Botticelli; I
had been wondering where it was hung. Its pallor and grandeur
were too serene to 'dominate' the room; they only seemed to have
nothing to do with this world at all.

'Maude, my dear,' said Charles's weak voice, and he was holding out his hand to me. Wearing his white robe, he was seated in
a low comfortable chair of canework by the window where the
fullest light came through. I went up to him, and put mine into his.

'You looked at my Botticelli before you looked at me,' he said,
with the teasing, charming note in his voice that I remembered.
'Now was that kind? when we haven't been together for so long.'

'I am sorry,' I said, 'it's no use lying, Charles. I couldn't help
it.' We were smiling.

'It's all right . . . if I have to take second place to anything, let
it be to a Botticelli. I am content.'

His eyes, which had a dim sparkle this afternoon, moved to
the picture, and for a moment we looked at it in silence.

'Sit down, my dear, sit down,' he said next, and I took a chair near him. Laurette had gone out on to the terrace and was attending to some plants there with a patent spray; the faint hissing sound as she drenched the tiny flies with poison came to us in the quiet.

'We . . . must talk about the important things . . .' he began to say slowly, 'no time now for small talk. You know I have always detested it,' and I nodded—though his views on this matter were not mine. I have a respect for small talk; it is one of the last few bulwarks of civilization.

'So I shan't . . . ask you . . . all the usual things,' he went on. 'I can see that all has been going well with you.'

Well with me! Yes, I have had money, and a home, and four meals a day for seventy-odd years.

'You are a beautiful creature still. You always were.'

'Thank you, Charles dear.'

'It's your taste in paintings. I . . . yes, that's it . . . your taste in paintings.'

For a moment I thought that I must have misheard him. His eyes were fixed solemnly on mine and his tone was lugubrious, as if he were a priest about to reprove a sinner.

I recovered myself quickly, however. Paintings had been the passion of his long life; paintings, and what he had said of them, had drawn him up from the poverty of his youth into a world of luxury and beauty culminating in Belair; painting and paintings were to him what the memory of my dead was to me: the centre of life. Yes, I could understand.

I said nothing, but sat looking at him with a smile which I hoped was not artificial. I think that Laurette could hear what was being said; I noticed that she kept close to the opened windows, moving from bush to bush with her spray of poison but never far away.

'Frances tells me you don't care for contemporary painting . . . we mustn't be . . . of course, after seventy, it does become difficult for some people . . . but . . . I wish . . . it has been the strongest desire in my life to open the eyes of the masses . . .'

'I know that,' I said quietly, slipping into the pause in the faint, slow sentences.

I could have had plenty to say. But naturally I was not going to say it.

'You must . . . realize, Maude . . . you *must* realize . . . I know . . . what I am talking about . . . seventy years . . . I have been learning and looking . . . I do *know*, Maude . . . I do know.'

'Yes, Charles . . . yes.' I resisted an impulse to pat the small, ugly old hand lying on the arm of the chair.

'I speak with . . . with authority . . .' he faintly smiled, 'as the . . . the Figure in the Christian myth spoke.'

'I know, my dear, I know.' My tone must have sounded too soothing, for he struck in quite sharply, with an access of energy:

'Don't butter me up, Maude, I'm old but I'm not a fool. Frances . . . talks to me as she did . . . always has talked to me . . . a wonderfully lively mind . . . a young mind in an old body . . . doesn't hide . . . her real opinions from me . . . what I would like . . . I want to hear you say . . . before you go, we must talk again and I shall convince you . . . these paintings are *veritable*. Veritable. Maude . . .' he began to struggle to sit upright in the chair, 'and I say it with authority . . . I would like to hear you say you agree with me . . . before you go. Accept my authority. Yes, accept me . . . before you go. Accept my authority. Yes, accept my authority.' He was looking at me, with a pathetic, haughty glare.

Laurette came in through the window. 'I think that's enough for this afternoon. I've shown 'em. I must wash my hands,' she said, dusting them off. 'Bunny's just coming up, Charles—and here's tea,' as Gaspard came in through the other door wheeling a wicker trolley packed with china and silver. 'Miss Barrington, you'll stay and have it with us, won't you?'

'Where's Mimi?' Charles demanded, sinking back into the chair.

'Coming,' Laurette said lightly. 'I *must* wash this off.' She dusted her hands again.

But she did not go, I noticed, until Bunny had hurried across the terrace to join us, and Mimi Handel had come in through the other door. I was relieved, I confess, to see them.

Charles's agitation, which was beginning to alarm me, subsided gradually. Mimi bent over him, murmuring, as she gave him his cup, and we drank ours to the accompaniment of quiet talk. Neither Lionel nor Frances nor Emil put in an appearance, and by this time I had been so worked upon by those undercurrents in the atmosphere that I felt it more tactful not to enquire where they were.

Setting, company, the tea table, were all elegant and pleasing. There was not an unharmonious object—if I except poor Bunny—in sight. Yet I was not at peace. I found myself, to my surprise, wishing that Tessa Halliday were there: I had often, goodness knew, been bored by her gush, but how she would have relished the exotic sandwiches and raved over the view! No-one commented on the beauty of the latter, and only Bunny and I tasted the former. We were all subdued and cheerless. I didn't, in the circumstances, expect hilarity. But it did seem a waste.

CHAPTER 15

AFTER breakfast the next day I was informed that Lionel would take me sight-seeing in the Vercors. Well, provided that I was prepared for the young Parkers to crop up, that should be both interesting and moving. I like to honour places hallowed by the martyrdom of brave men.

But I did not like to see Frances, approaching across the terrace where I was awaiting Lionel, vaguely raffish in trousers and a headscarf, and looking prepared to set out for somewhere.

'I'm taking you,' she said briefly, 'come on.'

I wanted to say, 'I would rather go with Lionel,' but what I did say was, 'Oh . . . is Lionel not coming?'

'No . . . it's just you and me,' and she gave her malicious grin and began to rush down the steps. I followed.

'Do go slower, Frances, you'll fall.'

'Nonsense,' and she continued her imprudent descent.

'Very well, but I cannot keep up that pace.'

'Could if you tried.'

I am ashamed to confess that I did try, and we arrived at the second terrace together.

'I cannot *imagine*,' I said, as we made our way down the long white slope leading to the garages, 'why Charles didn't have this continued up to the house; those steps are really dangerous, and in winter—!'

'He thought they'd look better, and so they do.'

While she was chatting with the garage attendant and getting the car out, I studied the view, trying to make out where the Vercors lay. The valley and the city, and the river with its marsh-lands—looking so primitive compared with the ordered landscape all about them—were veiled in a haze of heat. The white summits of the Chartreuse looked unearthly against a sky of blue-black sapphire.

'Will you put the hood up, please, Frances. I cannot stand the sun on my head.'

She grumbled to herself, but got the hood up and over our seats in the car, which was an open one, scarlet, and giving the impression that it could go very fast. It was a young woman's car; potentially dangerous, ultra-modern, and, I must admit, rakishly attractive.

'That suit you?' she snapped.

'Yes, thank you.'

'Get in, then. What a bore you are.'

I knew better than to answer, and she settled herself beside me, on a seat already hot to our thin clothes, and off we flew. I was certain that our pace was excessive, and nothing on this earth would have made me tell her so.

I had expected dramatic scenery in the Vercors; gorges, and caves where the Resistance could hide, and craggy heights where last stands could be made. We saw nothing of the sort.

What we saw was a region of wideish valleys, gentle slopes leading up to secondary mountains, and scattered farmsteads. A country less dramatic could hardly be imagined, yet it was just this ordinary, domestic appearance that gave to it the quality that impressed me. It was so easy to imagine, in this setting, the commonplace men who had died here for France. (I don't think

Frenchmen die for peace or international goodwill or any of the breathy abstractions, only for France.)

We did not touch its great forest, one of the largest in western Europe, but, as we drove (much too fast) through the high, hot, sunny air, I looked at any patch of woodland along the distant slopes and remembered a sentence about the great forest from my book about the Vercors—'then said still to hold bear'. That would have been in 1944 or 1945.

I checked the childish feeling of excitement, and turned my thoughts to the martyrs. Behind the individual heroism and suffering there was a wretched history of ill-timed attack and lack of the heavy weapons that might have given a different end to the story. Yet the heroism remained.

I mused on it all, my thoughts interrupted occasionally by some remark thrown off ill-humouredly by Frances.

'That's Villard-de-Lans. It's the capital.'

'What happened there?'

'Oh, I don't know—some business with the mayor. It all ended in the most ghastly massacre.'

'In the town?' I turned my head to watch the houses rapidly receding in the wide sunlit landscape.

'No—no—the whole business here, in the Vercors. If you're interested you can look it up, surely, when you get home,' she snapped.

It seemed that I would have to, for obviously Frances either knew next to nothing about what had happened in the Vercors more than twenty years ago or was not going to tell me if she did. I resigned myself to the prospect of studying the subject on my return to England.

She braked to a standstill and looked at her watch.

'It's twelve. Do you want to eat?'

'If you do.'

'We may as well . . . they've given us a basket . . . Will this do, here?'

I glanced around. We were on the edge of a coppice of beech in full leaf, with a stack of wood for the winter piled at the entrance to a narrow ride winding away into the trees. The soft wind wandered through the shade, cooling our faces.

'Nicely,' I said. It might have been anywhere in France, but I did wonder what those youngish trees might have witnessed.

'For God's sake,' exclaimed Frances, whose exasperation seemed, for some reason, to be increasing, 'let's eat in the car. You surely don't want all that business of sitting on the grass?'

So we ate: or, rather, I ate, and she did her usual picking and turning over and rejecting of some excellent food. There was a bottle of brandy, however, which she produced from a pocket in the car and drank at intervals, frowning silently into the trees.

'Frances, ought you to drink when you've got to drive?'

'Oh, for God's sake . . .'

She put down her glass and turned to me, and it suddenly came to me, with surprise, that she was nervous. She pushed her scarf back from her forehead.

'Look here,' she broke out in a high voice, 'you don't suppose I'd have come out on this excursion if I hadn't got something to say to you. We've got to have it out.'

She paused, and angrily lit a cigarette. (I have sometimes wondered what women did while making a scene before they took to smoking.) She held out her case to me, and I shook my head. I did not ask her what she meant, because I knew, and within myself I brought up every ounce of pride and loyalty to my dead that I possessed.

'For God's sake,' she said, still staring away from me and into the trees, 'come off it.'

'Come . . . ?' I could not believe my ears.

'Yes—drop it, come off your high horse . . . all this has been going on for fifty years . . . *fifty years*, Maude, it's fantastic . . . me writing to you, and you putting my letters down the loo . . . it's all so bloody silly.'

'It doesn't seem silly to me,' I said, and I made my voice very cold.

'What's it all about, anyway?' she went on, beginning to work herself up in the way that was oh, so familiar to me, 'I played around a bit with Jock and Harry and Edward—'

'Don't use their names—don't speak of them,' I cut in, quickly and uncontrollably.

'Why not? They aren't sacred, are they? Why shouldn't I use their names? I was fond of them. They were nice boys, and I liked kissing them and having them kiss me, and that's absolutely all there was to it, and if anyone in their senses could see us two hags sitting here squabbling about it fifty years later, they wouldn't believe it could be true.' She hurled away the stub of her cigarette.

I was silent.

'I know what you think,' she turned on me, 'you think I went to bed with the lot of them. Well, I didn't. In those days I wasn't . . . well, anyway, I didn't. Such a fuss about a few kisses.'

I swallowed the painful lump that ached in my throat and answered unsteadily.

'I won't discuss—certain aspects with you, Frances. That isn't . . . the point. I have avoided having anything to do with you, I have tried to cut you out of my life, because you . . . played them off against each other. You came between them. You know—you know, as well as I do, that there was . . . it wasn't exactly bad feeling . . . but . . . things were . . . And it was your fault.' I ended.

'Oh—' Frances said. I shall not write the words with which she sprinkled her retorts; they were ugly and dirty.

We were both quiet for a little while. I could not finish my lunch; I put the food back in its container and busied myself with getting out some table-water and drinking it. Frances sipped brandy and smoked and frowned at the trees.

'So how about it?' she snapped at last, turning to me.

I do not know why I answered as I did. But perhaps the quietness of the woods, and the cool wind, and the memory of the men who had died and suffered here, lingering at the back of my mind, acted upon me. I had been trying to keep up my bitterness but, as my eyes met those of Frances, I felt it go. It simply went out of me, or rather, it rolled off me like some sullen heavy cloud that had for years been obscuring what sunlight there was left in my life.

'Do you mean—forget about it?' I asked.

'Yes—and I should bloody well hope so.'

'Very well . . . all right then, Frances. I must tell you that I'm not quite sure I believe you—'

'Why should I bother to lie? It's all a hundred years ago, and in a few more we'll both be dead. If the boys are anywhere at all—I suppose you believe they are . . .'

'I won't let myself think about that,' I said, very quickly.

'—very well, then, all right, only if they *are* anywhere, can you *imagine* how crazy we must seem to them? "Fifty Years A-Feudin" or "The Fighting Grandmas". I'm having a drop more. How about you?' She held up the bottle invitingly.

'No, thank you.'

'Oh, come on.' She wagged the bottle about. 'Let's drink to making-up.'

'I don't *want* it, Frances. We can "make up" as you call it, without the help of brandy.'

'No—you're going to drink it,' she insisted. 'Come on, now, no more nonsense. Give me that glass.'

I shook my head and she snatched up my glass and half filled it. 'Drink up,' and she held it out to me, with her chin lifted and her eyes narrowed, in a way that I remembered. In a moment, if I did not comply, there would be an outburst. She shook the glass, thrusting it at me so that the liquor spilled. 'Go *on*, Maude.'

I took the glass and put it to my lips. It did not matter: it was only Frances being Frances. There seemed no point in arousing her fiery temper.

'Now stand up,' she commanded, getting unsteadily to her feet: there was barely room in the car for her absurdities, but I too stood up, suddenly feeling a lightness of heart that I had not known for years.

'Now what do I do?' I demanded.

'Drink a toast, of course. Come on—glass up! To our renewed . . . can't exactly call it a friendship, can we . . . to our renewed . . . re-re-*relationship*,' she ended solemnly.

'To our renewed relationship,' I echoed, and sipped. Frances drained her glass and flung it into the trees. She snatched mine, and that went after it.

'There. Ought to have smashed them, really, like officers in mess . . . oh, hell, you're quite right, I oughtn't to have . . . now I can't drive us home. Simply wouldn't be safe. I can see that. Even I can see it.' She sat down abruptly, and looked up at me muzzily.

'You'd better let me,' I said. 'I used to drive a lot at one time.'

'Charmed . . . I say, do we want to see any more of this old Vercors? No we don't, do we? That's settled. So we'll go home, and you'll drive and I'll tell you what's been happening to me for the last fifty years. Budge up.'

She moved, so that I could get into the driver's seat, then settled herself.

'I say, what happens if we're stopped and I'm asked for my licence?' I asked, as I backed the car on to the road.

'I was taken ill and you took over. And all the charm you can turn on.'

'Very well, we'll risk it. I don't suppose we will be.'

I found that I had forgotten nothing about the management of a car, and Frances's was a pleasure to handle. The small discovery increased my gaiety. Yes, it was gaiety. Frances always has been the most amusing company I knew and, in less than half an hour, she seemed to have worked the magic of putting her old spell on me. All her rudeness and sulkiness had vanished, and it did occur to me that she might even be glad—as I was—that our 'relationship' had been resumed.

'Now where shall I start?' she said. 'I know—when I was engaged to Johnny Ross.'

'But I remember him,' I exclaimed. 'Red hair, and a turned-up nose.'

'Yes, he was going strong at the time of the Great Divide or Schism. When you dropped me.'

'Never mind that . . . go on. What happened to him?'

'Oh, Lord, I don't know,' drawled Frances, like Lydia in *Pride and Prejudice*.

CHAPTER 16

THAT engagement had been a stormy one, and although Johnny
Ross was painted in the blackest of dyes, I felt sorry for him and
also for Paul Williams, Jeremy Randall, a man I met in Wash-
ington, Winford Alexander, Bob Harvey and a man I ran into in
Cape Town who I hadn't seen for years who was rather a lamb,
but was he mean with money!

The placid yet noble countryside unfolded before our homeward road, and the malicious chuckling voice babbled on. It was
all exceedingly entertaining, as a play by Vanbrugh is, for one
evening. It was starred, at intervals, by portraits of Frances's
husbands, one of whom had died, and one been divorced. The
third was alive, but Frances said that they did not often meet. (I
could only hope that none of these men possessed deep feelings.)

All the time that I was driving, and listening, I was feeling
faintly disappointed that I had not been given the chance of seeing
the Vercors with a guide who was well-informed, and impressed,
as I was, by its recent history. (Frances had lost no opportunity of
saying how tedious she found all war reminiscences.) But perhaps
I could come again, with Lionel; or the little Laurette, good tedious child, would make a perfect companion . . . and then, while
hoping that none of Frances's men possessed deep feelings and
still with my eyes and concentration on my driving, I went on to
remember how none of my brothers had ever shown signs, of
caring *deeply* for Frances. I had been closing my mind to that;
remembering only certain coolnesses and sarcasms. I had been
fighting on their behalf when there had been no need—or, at least,
not so much need as I had persuaded myself there was. Unjust?
Perhaps, a little, to Frances? . . .

We were approaching the small town beyond which Belair
lay, and the valley that held Grenoble was beginning to define its
contours below us. Frances had timed her reminiscences neatly;
she had started on her third marriage, and I calculated that the
end would be reached as we drew up to the garages.

'Did I mention Martha?'

'No . . . ?'

'My dear daughter. Can't stick her. Jeremy's daughter too. The only thing she's ever done that was any good was to pup Bill, and sometimes I'm not sure *that* was much use.'

'Your grandson?'

She nodded. 'The only one. I'm not on his visiting list, he finds me "embarrassing". Damned little prig.'

She kept her head turned away as she spoke, but the one large eye I could see in profile glistened.

'He's just down from Harvard. Here . . .' she rapidly unstrapped her wristwatch, snapped open the back, and held it out to me. Such a beautiful young face looked up at me; the American Boy incarnate.

'How good-looking!' I exclaimed. 'Quite exceptionally so.'

'But smug, isn't he? Smug.' She took the watch back and looked at the photograph for a moment. 'We got on all right when he was little—I blame Martha. He hasn't spoken to me since he was seventeen.' She shut the watch with a click that contrived to sound vicious. 'Well—that's the way the cookie crumbles.'

I was feeling sorry for her, for the first time throughout that long recital of troubles caused by lovers and husbands.

'Doesn't he even send to you at Christmas?' I asked, then realized that it was a tactless question. Yet I had wanted to show my sympathy.

Frances shook her head crossly. 'I told you—I'm in the Outer Darkness or whatever it is . . . he told Martha he "finds me *acutely* embarrassing".'

'I've always envied women with grandchildren,' I said suddenly.

'You need not envy me. Now I'll tell you about Martha.'

Frances's life at seventy seemed to be made up, so far as I could see, of three or four situations that could not change. All were painful, and all involved resentment or jealousy. I began to wonder if she were not lonely and unhappy, behind the hard façade?

It was odd to think of Frances in need of consolation, though what else had I needed, for fifty years? Perhaps we could console one another . . . and then—I remember it so dearly—I marvelled at the nonsense I was thinking.

We were entering the woods just outside the little town when we caught sight of two figures wandering along the strip of grass bordering the trees: Lionel and Laurette.

'Ha! the lovebirds,' said Frances, and as she spoke, at that precise instant, the facts glared into my eyes: a dozen tiny incidents that I had noticed without noticing ranged themselves into a pattern, and I knew that the two were lovers. I said automatically—

'Don't, please, Frances.'

'Oh, for God's sake. Why should you live in a plastic tower and everyone else grub about on the ground? They're only waiting for Charles to die. Emil's been no use to anyone since the war ended. He—'

'I thought he seemed unhappy.'

'Unhappy! He does exactly as he likes—which is to sit in the Bergère café half the day with his French buddies and chew over the good times they used to have blowing up bridges. The fact is, he died when the war ended. What's left is rotting.'

'He has his painting.' I wanted to soften the ugliness of what was going on at Belair, I felt that I *must* find something in the house and among its inhabitants that could be counted for comfort. I was going to be there for nearly another three weeks! How was I going to bear it?

'Don't kid yourself he cares about that; he turns it out by the yard.'

We were nearly up to the pair, who were strolling away from us. Frances leaned across and touched off a blaring note on the hooter, and they turned and waved. Such a calmly domestic expression was on both faces that the words *immoral* and *adulterous* in my mind seemed to die a natural death.

'Hullo! Had a good day?' Lionel said as I stopped the car beside them. 'You're back early.'

'All is forgotten and forgiven,' said Frances. 'I'm still a bit drunk.'

Laurette looked indulgently at us: 'The girls have made up', I presumed that she was thinking.

'I see. Well . . .'

'Let's get on, Maude. They don't want us,' said his sister, and I smiled at them, in a way that included both, but as if I did not see them, and we drove on.

'Now I suppose you'll be in a stew about *that*,' said Frances, after a longish silence.

'It isn't any use my being in what you call a stew. But even you must admit that the situation—isn't satisfactory.'

I knew that there was no point in saying to Frances that it was wrong.

'It's satisfactory for him,' she retorted instantly, 'he had this thing for years about an awful woman called Rosemary Jones who made awful jewellery. She would and she wouldn't—you know—had about seven children. If he's got sick of waiting for the youngest to grow up and leave home, you can't blame him.'

'I do blame him. Laurette is so much younger.'

'Well you've always been blaming him for something, haven't you? Young! She was born forty. She bores the pants off me, but she is one step better than R. Jones . . . We'd better cool off, or we shall be fighting,' and neither of us said any more.

I stopped in front of the garages, and the attendant, Jacques, came out and Frances handed the car over. Slowly, after she had fussed a little with him about its welfare and he had assured her that he would attend to it, we began the winding path. I did not know about Frances, but I felt so tired that mere movement was an effort. We trudged; we did not walk, we trudged up that impressive, hateful, death-white ascent. I glanced at her, and thought that she looked so frail she might at any moment falter and fall down.

'Tired?' I asked, mustering up a cheerful note.

'I'm never tired,' Frances snapped, 'and if you're comforting yourself thinking Mimi and Bunny are all right, you needn't. Mimi's only waiting for the old man to die to shoot off to her family in Hamburg, and Bunny's waiting to hear who's been left what. No-one's all right at Belair—'

To my own astonishment, I burst out laughing. I stood still in the middle of that wretched path, and laughed and laughed, while Frances stared.

'Oh, Frances! "No-one's all right at Belair"! it's like there always having been Starkadders at Cold Comfort. Come on, you're tired. We'll get Bianca to bring us some tea.'

I took her arm and she leant on me, and, both giggling, I got us up the hill.

CHAPTER 17

BIANCA got us tea with every appearance of willingness, and we took nearly an hour over it. I enjoyed that hour. Wonderful to say!

But I was not to have the other hour, the one I sorely needed for reflection and the rearrangement of some ideas. We had finished our second cigarette (we were in my sitting-room, overlooking the garden) when there came an agitated rapping at the door and Bunny blundered in.

'Mr. Handel is very bad,' she began breathlessly, 'I'm sorry to disturb you.' She stood there, with her gaudy dress and her beads looking incongruous below her alarmed face. 'But we don't know . . . Mrs. Handel told me to find you.'

'I am very sorry. Can we—I be of any use?' I asked. I think I heard Frances say, 'Speak for yourself, I don't go for deathbeds,' and could only hope that this had not been overheard.

'I don't think so, thank you, I have phoned for Doctor Nigrinus. But Mrs. Handel said . . . if you would all just keep near at hand, in case . . . he might want to see someone . . .'

'Shall we come up to the house?' I asked.

'If you would just sit on the terrace, as usual . . . thank you . . . You haven't seen Mr. Crozier and Laurette, I suppose? Anywhere about . . .'

'Should be here by now, we passed them on the road hours ago,' said Frances. 'I'll go and—no, I'm damned if I will. Can't one of those bloody servants go?' She leant back in her chair.

Bunny made a hand-wringing gesture. 'Oh dear . . . they're all resting or out . . . I don't want to leave Mrs. Handel for too long or I'd . . .'

'I'll go.' I got up from my chair, and it was disconcerting to realize how much effort was needed for the movement.

'Stern daughter of the Voice of God, three cheers,' said Frances.

'Oh, that *is* good of you!' exclaimed Bunny, 'of course we've been expecting this but it's the shock. I know I'm behaving unpardonably . . . I'll . . . be all right in a minute.' Her handkerchief came out.

'He is not dead yet, I think you said?' I asked mildly, as we went down the passage; I dislike people to go to pieces in a crisis.

'No, oh, no, and he may rally, of course, he's done this before.'

'Then we must hope,' I said. 'You go on and I will find the others and tell them to come to the terrace. I cannot hurry up these steps. Go along, now; it's all right.'

'Oh, Maude—you don't mind if I call you Maude, do you? you are kind—Yes, we must hope, of course . . . I'll be thinking of that, all the time . . .'

She hurried away, and I made a grimace at the steps and began to climb. We must hope, yes. But *I* was thinking that to live to ninety is to live too long.

I had pretended not to hear her request. Why the imminence of death should cause some people to lower the barriers of formality I have never been able to understand. Don't these vulgar fools realize that conventional behaviour helps us to bear the unbearable?

I was perhaps halfway up the ascent, and going very slowly, almost crawling, in fact—when there was a movement behind me and there was Frances.

'Sit down, you ass, we'll have you going west with a stroke, next,' and she pushed past me and went on.

I sat down, willingly enough, and watched her out of sight. She seemed to float up the steps like a girl. She always had been able to summon up these spurts of energy when necessary.

But what had knocked *my* small residue of energy out of me was the phrase *going west*. It struck straight at my heart. Words soaked in the blood of the young soldiers who died between 1914 and 1918. Into the fading light, into the sunset. Gone west; going west. *Harry, Jock, Edward.*

There were going to be disadvantages besides the obvious ones, in reviewing the 'relationship' with Frances. We belonged to the same generation, and we spoke its language.

'Maude! What's up? are you ill?' Lionel and Laurette were standing in the garden below, looking up at me, and Lionel actually sounded alarmed.

'No, only resting.' I stood up, dusting my skirt. 'Charles is not so well, I understand. Frances has gone to find you both.'

'Well here we are . . . I don't expect this is the end, you know. He's done it before, bless him, I really think he enjoys the extra attention,' Lionel said.

We mounted slowly, keeping our breath for the climb. Laurette's expression was stricken; but I supposed it too much to hope that an ordinary conscience was troubling her; she surely kept hers firmly trained on world problems rather than nearer home on the subject of adultery.

When we were seated in the cane chairs on the terrace, Lionel felt in his pocket.

'There's some mail for you, Maude, we met the postman and saved him a climb.' He handed me some letters, among which I recognized the large hand of Tessa.

'Will you excuse me?'

'Of course.'

The opportunity to occupy myself with something was welcome, for I felt as if my recent discovery must show on my face.

Tessa's letter was about nothing, as usual, and as usual consisted largely of exclamation marks, but on the second sheet she did announce something of interest, though of a tiresome kind:

'I'm seeing something of the Parker kid these days, your Millie seems to have taken them under her wing, they go past almost every day with the pram. Teddie is a real dish but a handful, I should think, no wonder there have been ructions with hubby!!!!'

So Millie had been confiding in Tessa. I could not suppress a sigh. There would be gossip and comment and speculation over this uninteresting matter when I got home, and affairs at Belair were already making me wish to go home and stay there. Tessa's comment, of course, was no more than in character.

I put the letters away in my bag, leant back and was quiet. Laurette had shut her eyes; Lionel was skimming irritably through *Paris Soir*, and observing at intervals that, thank God, it was about time for a drink.

Soon we were interrupted by the appearance at the top of the steps of Doctor Nigrinus, a dark little Greek-Jew, followed at a slower pace by Frances. He hastened across the terrace, ignoring us, and she came over and sank into a chair, grunting with relief.

'Where in hell did you get to? I've been halfway to the village, it's nearly killed me,' she threw at her brother. '*He* gave me a lift back,' jerking her head in the direction of the doctor.

'We came back through the woods. Laurette wanted some flowers.'

'Well her flowers nearly did me in . . .' Frances repeated. 'Do we get a drink this evening or is everything turned off at the main?'

'I'll see . . .' Laurette got up and hurried away, as if anxious for something to do, and Frances went on, 'Just how bad is he?'

'I don't know, we've only just got in . . . this happened before, you know, in the spring. Didn't you see the papers?'

'Never read them. I'm a MacLuhanite—reading's on its way out.'

I remembered that in the old days her conversation had always been full of the names of the newest fashionable crank of whom no ordinary person had heard. Who MacLuhan was *I* didn't know.

'It would happen again while I'm here, of course,' she added.

Lionel made no reply, and silence fell once more.

But I disliked the prospect of sitting there, drinking, while Charles Handel might be dying. He was not a man of whom it could be said, 'He would want us to go on as usual.' He would not want anything of the kind; he was a Jew, with all the Jew's feeling for the drama of the great human experiences, and he would want us to show, even to display, anxiety and grief.

It was doubtful to me, however, whether anyone was feeling these emotions, and my discovery and Frances's revelations, earlier that afternoon, made it impossible for me to believe in their sincerity had they been displayed. So, when one of the servants appeared, wheeling the trolley with drinks and followed by Laurette, I got up from my chair.

'I shall rest a little before dinner, I think.'

'Have a drink first—don't show us up—we can't all have the right feelings to order, you know. You're one of God's pets.'

I ignored Frances, but Lionel said, 'He may want to see one of us, Maude, he's quite up to staging something with his last breath. You'd better stay,' and what could I do but stay?

We must have sat there, in silence, for nearly an hour. I declined a drink; I did not want one, and if I had, I should still have refused it. I watched the light dying off the summits of the Chartreuse.

They are the most unearthly-looking mountains I have ever seen. I suppose it is the fact that their whiteness is not snow, and that one doesn't, on one's first sight of them, know *what* it is which gives this impression. The big snow mountains are a familiar, if an awesome and poetic, sight, but the heights of the Chartreuse have a beauty that is unfamiliar, because it seems spiritual.

There I sat, in company with two worldlings and an adulteress, between sacred and profane love as typified by the Chartreuse and the Vercors; and my feelings were with the men who had been martyred for France, but my spirit was drawn, unwillingly, to those heights above the hidden valley where the monks live.

Frances seemed to be dozing, Lionel seemed to be absorbed in an article in *Paris Soir*, Laurette was staring sadly at the dying light—thinking about Vietnam, I supposed. Then voices at the far end of the terrace broke the hush.

But we were not being summoned to Charles's death-bed. Dr. Nigrinus had come through the french windows, followed by Bunny, who was inviting him to stop for a drink.

'All Clear, for the time being,' announced Frances, who had apparently not been dozing at all, 'now perhaps we can be let off the chain.'

The doctor, having paused to give Bunny some instructions, passed us with an inclination of the head, and went on down the steps.

'He's rallied!' cried Bunny, approaching. 'Isn't it marvellous? Has anyone seen Emil? He was asking for him.'

'Enquire at the Bergère.' Frances swung her legs off the lounging chair, 'Where else?'

'But I *told* him his father might be dying!' Bunny cried. 'I told him just after Mr. Handel became unconscious. He was out here, on the terrace, picking flowers—to paint, I suppose—and I told him. It's too bad . . .' she broke off, looking tragic.

Lionel shrugged, and Laurette, saying, 'I'll call them up,' slipped away.

'Mrs. Handel's with him,' Bunny confided, 'he's still dreadfully weak and not out of danger of course. Dr. Nigrinus says . . . it . . . might come any time now.'

'Shall we stay here?' I asked her. (We usually changed for dinner; it was one of the minor pleasures, for me, at Belair; I could wear some of the pretty clothes I don't often wear at home; and it was nearly seven o'clock.)

'I don't know *what* to say, Maude, really I don't. He *is* better, but—' Bunny made one of her clumsy, inept gestures. 'I should think . . . so long as nobody goes far from the house . . .'

'Do we get any dinner?' asked Frances tartly. 'That's all I want to know.'

For the first time since I had known her I saw Bunny behave with something like dignity. Looking full at Frances, she answered,

'I know that Mr. Handel would want everything to be as comfortable as usual, Mrs. Gelfors.'

'I don't,' said Frances, in one of her mutters, as she began to descend the steps. 'Coming?' to me. 'What he'd like is to have us all hanging on gasping until he . . .' I could only hope, for the second time that afternoon, that no-one had heard her concluding *pops off*. I don't think anyone did: I am used, of course, to catching Frances's mutters.

Crossing the garden she slipped her arm into mine.

'How long has that ass been calling you "Maude"?' she demanded. 'I bet it *riles* you.'

'I don't like it. But just now, of course, in the circumstances, one can't say anything.'

'Blast the circumstances. I'll say something, if you'd like me to. It's sauce, that's what it is.'

'Really, Frances, it doesn't matter. But I do wish . . .' I broke off.

'What?'

'I do wish some of you would show a little affection for Charles. We are enjoying his hospitality—and—one has to admire him. He has climbed up from complete obscurity to world fame. I was reading an article somewhere, a week or two ago, in which the writer said that Charles had practically invented the standards for modern art, and also the vocabulary for appraising it.'

'Well, you hate modern art, so—'

'I don't hate it, it just irritates me, and the fact that it irritates me doesn't prevent me from admiring Charles.'

'Of course I *admire* him, he's as clever as a waggon-load of monkeys, but look at the people nearest to him. He's sucked everyone dry; a man I know once said he was "surrounded by maimed personalities". No-one can have any life of their own when he's around. Emil, *he's* Charles's fault. He was so determined that *his* son should be a great painter that he never let up for ten solid years. Drove him like a horse. Emil has about five ounces of ordinary talent, he can just about turn out those houses and trees in blobs of bright paint, the sort of thing people who get away for a fortnight once a year like to buy "to remind them" of a place, and that's all he can do. He'll never be any better, and he knows it. Laurette only married him because he was Charles's son, and she hoped he'd be a first-class painter.'

I had seldom heard such a long and shrewd assessment of anyone from Frances, who usually flings off generalizations that are brilliantly half-true. What she had just said, however, did seem to me true; painful, and all true. But I asked her how she could possibly know why Laurette had married Emil?

'She told Lion, and he told me.'

What answer was there to that?

'Well, please don't tell me anything more,' I said, turning away, 'it's all very squalid.' We were outside the door of my rooms.

Frances leant against the wall with folded arms, studying me. It has never ceased to surprise me that she will not try to turn a conversation threatening to be awkward or lead to a bitter argument, but always presses on. If this is a form of moral courage, it is a form I do not admire.

'Hell, Maude, what else do you expect life to be? You talk like a teenager.'

'No doubt. But I am too old to change. I really am tired, Frances. We'll meet at dinner.'

I shut the door gently, leaving her there.

There was a piano in my sitting-room. I judged that the sound of it would not reach so far as the sick-room, and I spent what was left of the daylight playing Debussy until I was more or less at peace again. No-one came near me until Bianca looked in, about eight o'clock, to see if I wanted anything.

'No, thank you . . . how is Mr. Handel, do you know?'

'He becomes weaker all the time, madame. Again, they phone for the doctor, and he will bring another doctor with him.'

A change for the worse. Well—it had been expected, and if I were needed I should be sent for. Bianca, who had assumed her correct face, presumably in deference to the occasion, went away, and I played on. But thoughts began to arise behind my pleasure in the cool sounds, and they were painful.

Was I jealous? Had I been taking it for granted that Lionel had no life outside the points at which his life had touched mine? Frances's revelation about the prolonged affair with the woman she called 'R. Jones' had come—I saw now—with almost as great a shock as the discovery of his affair with Laurette. Had I seen him as no more than someone known from childhood, who had been in my brothers' 'set', and with whom, for that reason, I had had for fifty years what contemporary slang calls 'a love-hate relationship'? And was I jealous? Jealous? I?

I played on, and presently found myself at the conclusion that I had been jealous, self-centred and quite remarkably obtuse. The decision was disturbing; I dashed at the notes, tumbling them out on the quiet air in glittering showers—and then the door opened to admit Lionel himself.

'Hullo . . . am I making too much noise?' I turned on the piano stool to face him.

'No, it's all right—I didn't hear anything until I got to the garden. He's going. Unconscious, and going.'

He sat down abruptly in a chair near the piano. 'I can't find Laurette anywhere. She had a fit of . . . what you'd call conscience, I suppose, an hour or so ago and she can't face it . . . she's gone off somewhere.'

It is a very, very long time since I have said just what came into my head. But I did now. And by the mercy of Providence, what came was nothing condemnatory. I heard my own voice say gently,

'It must have been a painful, worrying time. I am sorry things couldn't have been . . . happier for you both.'

He looked up, at that.

'Frances told me you knew. Oh, it hasn't been all misery, by a long chalk. Occasionally, of course . . . mostly on her part. I'm made of tougher leather, and the fact that Emil doesn't give a damn means something to me. It makes her feel worse, of course. Well . . . it can't be long now.'

'I am very sorry about it *all*,' I repeated. The one I was sorriest for was Emil. But that was one of the first things to come into my head that I did not say.

'Let's go up to the house,' said Lionel, rising. 'Sorry if I disturbed you, I . . . wanted your company.'

Next to Laurette's, I thought. Yes, I was certainly jealous; but what a surprising remark! He had wanted my company.

Well, not many people have wanted it since my parents died. I welcomed his want. I got up from the piano stool and I put out the lights.

The twilight was serene and beautiful. The faintest of afterglows was still on the heights of the Chartreuse, and I think we both saw it with a kind of pang; Frances would have said that anyone only has to be dying to induce tender pangs in the stiffest of upper lips, and there is no doubt, if the matter is regarded with detachment, that they do have an advantage.

'Where is Frances?' I asked, as we reached the second terrace.

'Gone out.' He offered me his cigarette-case.

'Again? She really is a miracle of nervous energy . . .' I shook my head. 'No, thank you.'

'In the car. She hopes it'll be over by the time she gets back; she's gone to the cinema, in Grenoble.'

We settled ourselves to wait, in the warm twilight deepening into dusk. I could smell the scent of the first jasmine flowers; this was the hottest day we had had, so far. I saw that the windows of Charles's room were shut.

We sat in silence for some time. Quiet sounds came up now and then from the distant town; a dog barking, the muted running roar of a train, a solitary bell-chime. Moths fluttered above the flowers. The only light was the faint one shining from Charles's room. Presently there was a soft footfall behind us and the slight shape of Laurette stole up, and, taking a cushion from one of the chairs, dropped it on the ground and settled herself beside Lionel; I think that she took his hand. No-one spoke. His pale summer clothes and her white dress blended into one blur. I could not see their faces, for the dusk had turned to darkness; I felt drawn to them both, with pity and understanding.

Later, much later, the windows of Charles's room were gently opened and Bunny came out and stood there for a long moment, looking across at the almost invisible heights. Then she turned back into the room as a sobbing and wailing broke out in there.

CHAPTER 18

MIMI 'collapsed', as the papers say—and we had our full share of the reporters and the television cameras that April, at Belair. She stayed in bed, and the management of affairs following Charles's death fell to Lionel.

But Emil was the one who talked to the press and television people, and who got us (reluctantly enough, with the notable exception of Frances) to provide material for their cameras; Bunny told me that Emil had been keeping the newspapers in America supplied with details about his father for years past; they paid him well; and this was a regular addition to the income he made from his painting.

I must confess that, during the two days preceding the departure of the coffin on its journey to America, I came to rely more and more upon the company of Frances. She was so plainly pushing what was past behind her, and already straining towards the future, that my spirits soared healthily when I was with her.

Laurette had fallen into a state I can only call lugubrious; she went about in almost complete silence, looking stricken. Had my opinion of this display been asked, I should have said that she had no grounds for such gloom; that had happened for which she had been waiting, and she should have been all reasonableness and happy anticipation.

But it was plain that she was laden with guilt: reason had no part in what she was feeling. She had done what was wrong, and it weighed upon her. The human creature, I thought, sometimes behaves better than its reason tells it to.

Of course, it had occurred to me that I should offer to leave at once. There was nothing I could do to help in this household about to make off in all directions. I suggested it, on the evening after Charles's death, to Lionel.

'Go if you want to, of course, my dear; I know the place is like a morgue. But can't you wait until Thursday? The Will is being read then. Frances is going to drive down to Antibes on Friday, and she can drop you at Grenoble; Bunny'll work out a route for you.'

He had apparently given the matter some thought.

'I had thought of going tomorrow,' I said; the day was a Tuesday.

'Oh, do wait . . . the fact is . . .'

'Really, Lionel, I see no point in my doing so. If you think it would show some disrespect and unkindness to Mimi, of course, that's different. But I am not interested, really, in the Will.'

'He's left you something,' said Lionel.

'Well, that was nice of him . . . but I . . . the lawyers can write to me or someone can.' Even as I spoke, I felt how eager I was to leave this beautiful, unhappy place, full of people whom Charles Handel had cracked, if not broken.

'The fact is . . . I'm not sure if you'll like it . . . and I'd rather you were here when you hear what it is. Then I can explain.'

'Oh, mercy, Lionel, no more mysteries, please! Very well then, I will stay until Friday.'

As I went out of the room I heard him say, 'I've always wanted to see someone flounce,' and I was weak enough to put my head round the door and say, 'I did *not* flounce,' on which the interview ended in mutual amusement.

So I stayed. The servants were in process of being dismissed; only my friend Bianca would remain until we had all gone, tempted, as Frances told me, by a large bribe. I was sorry to hear that; I had been so ingenuous as to suppose that she might have some affection for her employers. Frances said, of course she wanted more money, she had a little girl who was delicate and a husband out of work. She was the best of that bunch, Frances added; and she had agreed to cook for us. *I* planned to give her a handsome tip.

The last newspaper telephoned; the last of the television cameras rolled away on its unmistakable van. The coffin had already started, by car and rail, on its long journey to America, where Charles would lie in one of the cemeteries in his birthplace: a village in the 1870s, and now a huge, prosperous city.

'He was always zo loyal to America,' Mimi said fondly, 'he used to zay—it gave him all; all but beauty. For that, he had to come to France.'

As no-one said anything to me about remaining in the house on Thursday morning, I made sandwiches for myself, in the long kitchen at the back of the house which was white as an Arctic landscape and full of square appliances with dials which looked as if they might at any moment erupt into computing something.

Bianca's little girl was there, cherishing a doll at the kitchen table. It was a highly contemporary doll, wearing a mini-skirt and a brassière, but her manner towards it was satisfactorily old-fashioned. She and I exchanged only smiles and small gestures of mutual courtesy. Then I filled my Thermos with wine and water, and went off to explore the heights rising behind Belair.

What a delightful day I spent! The most serene, the most full of happy interest, since I had left home. I found a farm that did not seem to have changed in the last hundred years; I got into talk with a boy herding sheep under a great oak tree; I watched a *troupeau*, or mixed procession of sheep, goats and cows, come down from the pastures through the late afternoon light in charge of a girl who looked like a gipsy, in full cotton skirt and corsair's head-scarf; I found a rare orchid; and sauntered down through the woods into Relair as the dock in the village was striking seven. I felt bathed in sunlight and dear air, and my eyes were soothed by the old and beautiful things I had seen, and I was at peace.

And ready to face those two dragons, Progress and People.

The party was sitting on the lower terrace, avoiding as if by mutual agreement the upper one haunted by the memory of Charles awaiting the end of the after-glow; and Bunny, Lionel and Frances looked old, and Laurette looked sad—or was it only the contrast with those eternally youthful forests and fields where I had been wandering?

'Where the hell have you been? We were just thinking about informing the police,' said Frances, as, having taken fifteen minutes to wash and change, I came slowly up the steps leading from Lionel's garden. 'Sherry?'

'Please.' I sat down between Laurette and Bunny. 'How is Mimi?'

'She got up for an hour or two to hear the Will. Talked about it a bit. She's gone back to bed. You have to congratulate Bunny, Maude,' Lionel added, 'she's set up for life.'

'I do congratulate you,' I said, turning to her, and she ducked and mumbled, 'very heartily,' I added. She had been crying.

Indeed, when I thought of the atmosphere at Belair and realized that she had been living in it for more than thirty years, I was able to give my congratulations the ring of sincerity. Poor Bunny had earned her fortune.

'The pictures,' Lionel said, 'are divided between the Metropolitan Museum of Art in New York and a new gallery for modern art to be built in Paris and called after him, the Handel Gallery. All the money goes to Mimi except a thousand for Frances, and

Bunny's legacy. This place is to be a museum and I'm to be in charge of it and may God have mercy upon my soul.' He drank off his glass at a gulp. 'He gave me my house and the land in advance, you see, so I only get the Botticelli.'

'Only!' I said, and Laurette laughed miserably.

'And only *He* knows what it would fetch if I auctioned it,' Lionel went on, 'so, I'm all right—we're all right, aren't we, love?'

He laid his hand on Laurette's arm. 'And Emil?' I asked—moved to some disgust by that gesture. 'What about Emil?'

Lionel shrugged. 'Nothing.'

'Literally nothing, Lionel?'

'Not one solitary cent, dollar or sou. Charles was bitterly disappointed in Emil, you know . . . don't you want to hear what you've got?'

'I can wait,' I said; I had a strong premonition that my inheritance had been inspired by some malice, some desire to punish, on the part of poor Charles; and to strengthen this feeling, I remembered Lionel's remark about my not liking what I should get. . . . 'what kind of a museum, Lionel?'

'Oh, for regional flora and fauna; also geological, antiquarian and sociological, and the proceeds—I'm to decide what's to be charged for admission—are to go to the "embellishment and amenities of St. Benoit". Nice for them, if we can ever get tourists to crawl up those ruddy steps. I shall have to put in a lift, I think.'

'Cost you the earth.' Unasked, Frances leant across and re-filled my glass. 'Maude, you are, without exception, the most unnatural human being I've ever met up with in the entire length of my life. Haven't you any normal curiosity at all? Here's to your awful uniqueness.' She drank, then poured herself another. I turned to Lionel, questioningly.

'It's two Picasso drawings. Late ones. I'm sorry, dear.'

'I'm not surprised. The last time I saw him he gave me a little lecture about my opinion of contemporary painting. I don't *quite* see the motive, but . . .'

'Mischief. Pure mischief. He could be like a small boy,' said Lionel. 'Christ . . . I'm going to miss him. What a character! You talk about Maude being unique,' turning to his sister, 'but Charles was the kind only thrown up once in a hundred years. And courage! with his entire reputation based on a "lie in the soul" as big as this house . . . whew!' He shook his head as if dazed, 'the risk!'

'Mr. Crozier,' Bunny said shakily, 'I don't think you ought to say things like that, now he's dead.'

'I wouldn't if Mimi were here, bless her. She believed in every judgement he ever made as if it were something in the Talmud. But you know—I know—don't we all know—he thought modern art the greatest swindle ever brought off at the expense of the public. He was a marvellous conjuror, and he built up that terrific edifice of criticism, with that wonderful and ludicrous nonsense of a vocabulary, with genius. That's the word for it. It was genius. He was a genius. What he really adored, what he really believed to be great, were Botticelli and Titian. And now what we've all got to do is to take damned good care no-one ever finds out.'

Lionel was rather drunk, I thought. He stared straight at me, as if daring me to speak. When I did, it was to say, 'I suppose there would be no objection to my giving the things to the Tate?' I was actually feeling a little sick.

'Why not to the Handel Gallery, Miss Barrington?' Bunny put in eagerly.

'I would prefer to offer them to an English gallery.'

'No objection at all, I should think, why should there be? But why not sell them?' asked Frances.

'I couldn't do that . . . I should feel dishonest.' I heard my voice sounding hard as glacier ice.

But I was feeling dreadfully sad. This revelation, coming at the end of a day spent amidst scenes which had refreshed and rebuilt my spirit, struck me with doubled, trebled, pain. And shame, shame for poor Charles's weakness and greed. I felt that I could hardly bear it. I got up from my chair.

'I'll give Bianca a hand,' I said (we had all, even the most domestically inexperienced of us, become more familiar with that kitchen and with dusters, saucepans and vacuum cleaners too, during the past few days, and very uncomfortable it had been). 'Is dinner going to be elaborate, tonight, do you know?' I turned to Frances.

'Eggy,' was all Mrs. Gelfors said, but her face expressed distaste.

'That sounds simple enough. Give us half an hour,' I said, and made my way across the terrace and through the pseudo-Roman luxury of that wretched house to the back premises. I wanted to do something ordinary and useful.

I left them sitting in silence. The afterglow on the Chartreuse was particularly beautiful that evening.

I don't want to remember anything more, at this moment, about the time I spent at Belair.

CHAPTER 19

LIONEL had to conquer his detestation of flying in order to be present at the cremation of his friend, and he left on the following morning, accompanied by Mimi and Laurette.

Our words of farewell were brief, though Mimi did give me a hearty kiss and told me I had been 'a gomfort'. Frances and I stood watching as they all got into the big white car, with the garage attendant at the wheel; he was to drive them to the airport.

'Mimi looks as old as God,' Frances said suddenly, 'Jews always do, of course, after about fifteen.'

'Do you remember how pretty she used to be, in those big black sombreros, and her cloak?'

'She isn't pretty now,' Frances said with smugness.

'. . . it must have been a terrible grief to her, Emil and Charles not getting on,' I concluded.

'Not getting on! For God's sake, Maude . . . they hated each other's guts.'

The car was moving swiftly away, now, down the long white incline. 'Good-bye—good-bye!' I called, while Frances waved fiercely, without a smile and in silence. Her next remark, I felt sure, would be a demand for a drink.

She glanced at her watch. 'Let's get that old so-and-so Rafael to bring us a drink.'

'I'd rather go down to the village—if you *must* have one.'

'In that dust, and the locals gawping? Thank you . . .' She turned away and began to climb the long ascent to the first terrace, with me unprotestingly following.

We had seen nothing of Emil since the departure of the last television cameras; he had simply disappeared; and it was not until our final evening there that Bunny came on to the lower terrace, where we were sitting, with a copy of an American paper, in which there was, she said, a 'very bitter' interview with him; they had hunted him down to a remote village in the Vercors, twenty miles from St. Benoit; there was even a photograph, in which he looked taller than ever, and the smell of rank tobacco and garlic seemed to rise from the page as I looked. I declined to read the very bitter interview, and silently passed the paper to Lionel.

I had been musing all that day, and had come to a decision. I would break my journey on the way home and go to my brothers' graves, in the north.

I had been there once, forty years ago, with my parents. I had not had the courage, and I am not a cowardly woman, to go there again. I could not, I could not.

But now I had found both the courage and the desire. I didn't know how, or why: but now both were there, and as the time wore on, and Frances's car spun, endlessly as it seemed, down the straight white roads beyond the foothills, and through the Rhône Valley (which we had made a détour to see) and as we began to drive past sign-posts saying 'Paris', I found myself even eager to stand on the sacred ground.

I had not told Frances about my plan, merely saying, one day during lunch at Belair, that I wanted to break my journey at Paris; and shortly afterwards she had announced that she would postpone her trip to Antibes and drive me there.

'That's nice of you, but . . .'

'You know I never do things I don't want to . . . go on about that suit . . .'

For, on our last day, alone in the empty house but for Bianca, we had fallen into a random discussion about clothes, in which we had both always been interested, and we carried it on for most of our journey northwards. I realize that this must sound rather heartless, but I was more than weary of the situations at Belair and felt no desire to talk them over, and I suspected that she felt the same.

The smiling summer country ran by as we reminded one another of clothes we had worn in the past, and compared fashion and prices in America and England, and our respective ways of spending money (I planned, she squandered).

It was a thoroughly enjoyable gossip, dropped sometimes in favour of an hour-long silence and then resumed. I have never talked clothes with anyone since I parted from Frances, and now I knew that I had been missing the small indulgence.

Beneath the light to-and-fro of our talk, the true purpose of my broken journey lay quiet and sad; not for a moment did I forget it.

She would leave me, I knew, at the airport before my plane took off; I remembered her dislike of valedictions.

Early in the afternoon the car drew up at Orly, more than two days after leaving Belair. We certainly had not hurried.

'See you late October,' said Frances, almost before I was out of the car; her hands had not even left the steering wheel.

'Do you intend to take my cases to Antibes?' I enquired.

'Oh, you know how I hate hanging about at these places.'

'Yes, but I would like my cases. Thank you,' as she scrambled out, and attacked—it is the only word for her actions—the fastenings of the boot. We were both smiling.

'There are your flaming cases. Can't think what you're going to do here . . . what *are* you going to do, anyway?' she ended, eyes glittering with curiosity.

'I'm . . .' I hesitated—'I'm going north, to see the boys' graves.' How the words hurt. It was like scraping a jagged stone past my throat and lips.

'Oh . . . all right then.' She started the engine, then turned to look at me, keeping her foot on the brake. 'Your brooch is undone,' she added.

'Will you stay with me when you come over?' I asked.

'No, thanks all the same. I have a hunch your house is like a museum.'

'Thank you.' I was still trying to fasten the little diamond bar on my lapel.

'Have all your brooches got pins as long as that?' she demanded.

'What an extraordinary question . . . I don't know.'

'You'll have to get short ones soon . . . I'll stay at the International.'

'Why shall I have to have short ones? (Just as you please, of course.)'

'And I'm not so fond of your Millie—she's wet.'

'I'm used to that,' I said. 'She always has been . . . why shall I have to . . .'

She shot away, to the roar of the engine's acceleration, and I just caught her answer—'You'll see!' as she disappeared into the traffic. My last glimpse of her was an arm in white jersey, briefly waving. She did not look round.

The village I was bound for was some thirty miles to the north of Paris.

I was fortunate enough to find a room for the night at a small hotel. I went through my preparations calmly and slowly, speaking my correct French, checking the smallest detail, eating luncheon, then resting for two hours in the pretty, impersonal bedroom, and all the time my heart thudded relentlessly. All my eagerness had gone; I only ached with old pain and sorrow.

In the late afternoon I got up and tidied myself and set out through the shabby narrow streets for the cemetery. It was a small place, I remembered, on the side of a small, bare hill.

Villages in the north of France lack what I can only call the comely Frenchness of those lying further into the country; exposed as they have always been to the invasions of war, and ignored by tourists hastening to the beauty spots and historic towns, they have a dirty sameness and poverty, reminding one of back streets in the older coast towns on the other side of the Channel. St. Vaast-aux-Puits was no exception, though a hurrying grey sky and whirling miniature dust storms helped the depressing effect; it was grey and black and dun; shabby washing hung in the untidy gardens and faint bad smells floated out from passages opening on dark and crowded little rooms.

But the cemetery had such a cherished air that, by contrast, it appeared almost beautiful. Only the lower part of the ground was given over to the graves of the English; at the summit of the hill the elaborate Celtic crosses of the French, weather-worn and grey, tilted against the grey sky, looking forbiddingly foreign.

The English graves were tended with great care. As I walked between the rows of small crosses, each bearing a name, his age, and also the regiment he belonged to and the name of the battle in which he fell, I felt grass soft and short as turf beneath my feet, and saw each cross, and each stone guarding its piteously small piece of ground, gleaming white as sea-washed bone in the lowering light.

My own two graves were side by side, in the last row given over to the English. My father had seen to it that the crosses were of marble, and below Jock's name and his age (His age. Twenty-two.)—had caused to be engraved the refrain of *Lightheart*—

But Lightheart, O, Lightheart, when will you come again?

I suppose it could be said that Jock had had the lightest heart of the three, but I had never wanted the line to be added to the stone. The poem had at one time been known throughout the Western world, and had brought tourists to gaze at Jock's grave: I could never think of that vulgar curiosity without a frightening anger.

The dust-laden wind tore at my skirt and flapped the scarf I had tied over my head. The grass had evidently been cut only that afternoon, for the fresh, raw scent lingered. I stood staring down at the graves, lost in a pain-filled dream.

'Madame?' I turned impatiently. Was there no privacy for grief anywhere?

It was a bent, dirty little Frenchman in clothes matching the black and grey of the village; who had crept up on me unobserved. He at once began to retreat.

'Pardon, madame, I thought it was the other lady.' His surly tone sounded anything but apologetic. The smell of grass was all but obliterated by that familiar reek of tobacco and garlic. But I put out a detaining hand.

'It is nothing, monsieur . . . what other lady do you mean?'

He shrugged, but kept his sly little eyes fixed on mine.

'I don't know, madame . . . I am the guardian here; I cut the grass and keep the stones clean of moss—ah, it's a devil of a job, that—the other lady who comes here.'

'Here? To these two graves, you mean?' I pointed.

'Yes, madame.' His stare wandered over me, taking in my clothes, my shoes, handbag, everything. I think he was trying to work out my income.

'Do you mean that she comes here regularly?'

'Once a year in the summer, madame. Every year, she comes.'

'But . . .' I paused. I was wondering if this regular visitor might be Ida Kingsley, to whom Jock became engaged during the last months of his short life. I had kept up a regular correspondence with her until her death a few years ago. She had married late in life and apparently happily, but she might have made one or two visits to Jock's grave, for old love's sake.

'Did she come last year?' I asked.

'But certainly, madame. A lady not quite so tall as madame, not young, you understand, but *chic*, very *chic*.'

Last year. Then it could not be Ida.

'She always speaks to me, madame. And she brings flowers—such flowers! Once, I remember, there were orchids, with many roses, in a gilt basket.'

His eyes wandered away from mine for the first time, and I remember thinking that he had certainly taken that basket and kept it for his own purposes; sold it for a franc or so, perhaps.

'Has the lady large grey eyes and white hair?' I asked suddenly; the notion was absurd, but it had come to me; it was there; irrevocably lodged in my mind; and I had to know.

The guardian nodded.

'But yes, madame. White hair, lately; these last few years. As for her eyes—me, I do not look at the colour of a woman's eyes—unless she is young,' and he leered unpleasantly. 'She is always *bien coiffée*. Not young, you understand, but *bien coiffée*. Very *chic*.'

I don't know how I felt. Just astounded, I think.

'For how many years has the lady been coming?' I asked.

He shrugged again.

'Many years, madame. I have been the guardian here for thirty years, and every year she has come. Not during the war, Madame will understand, but the first year afterwards. Madame knows her, perhaps?'

'Yes, I know her.'

I could not bear his company for another minute, and I began to open my bag. His bloodshot eyes at once became fixed on it and he muttered something about 'madame always remembers the guardian' as I took out some notes and handed them to him.

'Thank you, madame, thank you.' He turned away at once, and made off slowly down the smooth grass path between the graves. No doubt Frances's *pourboires* had been on a scale to match her standard of living. She was not going to out-tip me *here* . . .

With horror at my thoughts, I tried to pull myself together. I stood, staring down at the twin, peaceful shapes of the graves; shaken, tortured helplessly by what I realized was jealousy.

Yes, I knew Frances; had known her for more than fifty years; and it appeared that I had never known her at all.

CHAPTER 20

ANOTHER kind of surprise waited for me at London Airport; Tessa, accompanied by a man who proved so attentive and thoughtful for our comfort on that awkward journey back to town that it was some time before I realized that my brothers would have dismissed him as a bounder.

'You won't mind if Alec does ninety, will you?' coaxed Tessa, as we settled ourselves in his large and fast-looking car. 'He does so love letting her out, bless him, and it is legal on this road.'

'Certainly not, if he can square his conscience . . . this is nice of you, Tessa, how did you know which flight I was coming by?'

'I worked it out with Millie . . . well, you *have* been in the lime-light, love, haven't you? We saw you on television, at least, not you, but the house, and that Mrs. Gelfors, what's *she* like? and your friend, that was him, wasn't it, the one who talked about the art gallery, the one you had lunch with and you were so ratty with, have you made it up?'

'We did that before I left, if it can be called a making-up.'

Alec was in process of letting her out; as an ex-driver myself, I could understand the temptation of that motorway running broad and wide and high above the little houses and the derelict meadows, but I did have to grasp my hat; it was a hot day and all the windows were open.

'Oh . . . well, go on, tell me all about it . . .' Tessa said impatiently.

I was realizing that it was because I had grown accustomed to Frances's face, her delicate features and sallow but exquisitely tended skin, that poor Tessa's now seemed so unnecessarily large and florid, and I was ashamed of myself; Tessa was by far the nicer woman.

'Well, there isn't much to tell; the weather was good, and I had one drive with Mrs. Gelfors and one delightful day by myself, exploring, but Charles became ill almost at once, you see. I was to have stayed for nearly a month but as it was . . .'

I paused. Belair, and the days I had spent there, already seemed as remote as last night's dreams. I had been in a place where everything surrounding me—the landscape, the house, the gardens—were beautiful, and only the moral climate ugly and false. Now England had taken possession of me again; familiar, ugly, noisy, cosy England. 'He left me two drawings by Picasso,' I ended.

'Lucky you!' squealed Tessa. 'Alec, did you hear that? The old boy left her two Picassos . . . worth thousands, I expect?' Alec, who was prudently reducing his speed nearer to the accepted seventy, made an attentive movement of his head.

'You'll sell them, of course?' Tessa went on.

'No. I shall offer them to the Tate.'

'I can't understand you,' she sighed, 'you are funny . . . most people . . .'

'I don't like Picasso's work. Surely you must have heard me say so? And it would seem . . . ungracious to Charles, I feel, to sell them, whereas he would like the Tate to have them. He would like to think of them hanging there, "Presented by Miss Maude Barrington."'

Something, I knew now, had happened to me at Belair. Before my visit, I would not have made this gently-spoken explanation which, in parts, was not quite true.

'Yes, I do see,' Tessa said, after a moment's reflection, 'him being dead, of course, you don't like to think of hurting his feelings.'

This was a little too much: I had a sudden picture of Frances's grin, and exerting myself to change the subject, I painted for Tessa a detailed, yet rosy, picture of the household at Belair, which was a better work of art than those Picassos.

They declined my invitation to come in for tea, and after Alec—I never learned his other name—had helped Millie to carry up my cases, and I had thanked him, they drove off.

There was yet another small surprise in the hall; Millie had made me one of her beautiful bowls of flowers. The arrangement of flowers is an art which I have never possessed or been able to master, and she has it. Jasmine and the large white convolvulus which gardeners detest, with white sweet peas and honeysuckle, were in the silver bowl won by Harry as a prize for shooting, the scent filling the hall as the flowers filled the bowl.

'Oh, Millie—how *very* pretty. Thank you.'

But it was more than pretty—the graceful sprays resting in the clear water, all the whites and creams reflected in the glittering silver. It was poetic; fairy-like. I just touched the jasmine with one gloved finger.

'Lovely,' I said.

'I'm glad you like it, miss.'

Millie was looking well. The woodwork gleamed, and the windows; the house was at its best, and I told her so.

'Thank you, miss; I gave everything a good going over. I'm ever so sorry you had such a sad end to your holiday.' She paused. 'But it's nice to have you back, miss.'

'Has it been lonely?' I asked over my shoulder, on my way up to my room.

'Not really, miss.' She paused, and I wondered whether she would confess to the walks with Mrs. Parker and the pram; she must realize that Tessa would tell me about them.

'It was a bit, at first. Then the young girl, Mrs. Parker, she rang up and asked to speak to you and . . .'

'To speak to me?' I turned at the head of the stairs and stood looking down at her as she stood by her bowl of flowers.

'Yes, miss. I told her you was away. She—she wanted to show you baby, I think, miss, and—you not being here, I thought you wouldn't mind—the sofa has been done, miss, there isn't a mark on it now, you'd never know—so she brought the baby up two or three times and we went out over the heath with the pram. Ever such a lovely boy he is, miss. Gaining every week.'

She was standing easily, relaxed and smiling up at me, as she spoke, and something in her expression, a shade, a hint of the unusual, struck me, but I could not define what it was.

'I'm glad you had company,' I smiled back as I went into my room and shut the door.

I saw that she had put an even more beautiful bowl of flowers on the table beside my bed. As I bent to smell the jasmine and the salmon-pink sweet peas and feathery wild grass, I suddenly knew what it was in her expression that had been puzzling me; she had looked at me as if we were equals.

I was glad to be home, yet restless too, unaccountably restless. The secretary of the Music Club in Hampstead to which I belong had written during my absence, asking if I could accompany a professional singer who was engaged to come to them in October, and enclosing a list of the songs he was to give. I wrote an acceptance and settled down to learn two songs by Hugo Wolf which I did not already know, Warlock's 'The Droll Lover', and a whole group by Duparc, who is one of my favourite composers of songs for the piano. I practised for two hours each day.

A week or so passed quietly. I was irritated at having to accept an invitation from Tessa to go to tea one afternoon and tell her 'all about my holiday', yet, when the event took place, to my surprise I mildly enjoyed it.

I came back into the house at the precise moment that Millie was turning away from replacing the receiver of the telephone, and was informed that she was 'just having a word with Teddie' and her manner was not apologetic.

But my irritation on such occasions—for this was not the last—was not strong. She had always been one of those women who make friends within their family, seldom or never looking beyond it for companionship, and I knew that her circle was very small; there was a much older sister, I gathered, now bedridden and living in Dorset, and a brother and his family in Canada who sent cards on Millie's birthday and at Christmas, and that was all.

We had ceased to hear from her since 1918, when she had left us hurriedly to be married, and at that time—it was during the appalling week when the news had come of Edward's death—we were all so distracted with grief that her departure had passed almost unnoticed.

Then there had been silence, from Millie and about her, for more than thirty years. She had reappeared, in the early fifties, widowed, and asked my mother to employ her as housekeeper, for old time's sake, and my mother, already in failing health, had been thankful to do so. When my parents died, within a few years of one another, we, she and I, had both taken it for granted that Millie would remain with me. She was a link, though an oddly uncommunicative one when her garrulous nature was remembered, with the past.

It had never occurred to me that a woman of her childish nature, who lacked intellectual resources, must often be very lonely, but it did now, and if she had made a young friend and enjoyed fussing over the girl's baby, I was pleased for her.

She might entertain them as often as she liked in her sitting-room, so long as I was not pestered to gush over the child or disturbed at the piano by crying or chatter.

But during those first weeks of my being at home again she did no more than have long conversations with Mrs. Parker over the telephone, and report the progress of the baby to me at intervals.

I have already said that I dislike ambivalence. But, once more, in those weeks, I found myself in two moods, which contradicted each other, and which I felt simultaneously; I was relieved to have leisure and solitude to think over all that had happened at Belair, yet at the same time I missed the interest of a house full of people. I could not help wondering what all the members of our late party were doing?

Search as I would for excuses for Charles's 'Lie in the soul' I could find none that would satisfy me. I managed to *explain* to myself why he had behaved so for sixty years, but the unforgiveable lie remained.

I believed what Lionel had said: so many details, now that I came to recollect them and add them up—and Charles's taste for luxurious living was among them—bore the story out. I was left with the large, unattractive fact, which could neither be climbed over nor worked round. There it stood, in the middle of the path leading me into serene memories of Charles, and there it stayed.

I have always tried to face facts. Sometimes there is a kind of harsh comfort in them. I suppose this habit of mind has helped me through life, hardening me, perhaps, in the process.

With what ugly care Charles had built up his reputation! He must have seen, at the time of his first encounter with the more 'advanced' painters before the First World War, the road down which art was to go, and had made his decision and his plan accordingly.

Quickly, with whole-hearted and cynical concentration, he had constructed the house of his fame, and each false expression of opinion, each ruthless verdict in favour of the newest *avant garde* painter (*ruthless* in the sense of his having ignored the promptings of tradition and of his natural tastes) had made him into a worse man. I recalled, without an indulgent smile, the prolonged fierce arguments about 'advanced' paintings that he and I used to have in my youth.

Well, so far as I was concerned his reputation and his authoritative opinions had not altered my views one jot: I disliked the irritating nonsense of which he had made himself the prophet and interpreter more, if anything, than I had when I was nineteen.

How well I remember the Charles of those years! A man in his late thirties, sporting a great black wide-awake hat and a floating cloak of the same dramatic cut; a copious talker, a frequenter of the 'artistic' cafés and the clubs that put on advanced plays.

As age began to sap his energies, he had left the more tedious activities of his career, the exhausting journeys, the weary bargaining and the spellbinding, to Lionel, who, I was certain, must have revelled in the task. I did Lionel the credit to believe that, after he had grown to love Laurette, he may have felt some remorse at having wooed so many dollars out of so many ingenuous American pockets: she may have shown him another kind of satisfaction, into which lying and manipulating didn't enter. But at the same time I was sure that the part he had played for forty years was so suited to his nature, so 'up his street', that I could imagine his revelling in it.

Well, it was all over now. And—do you know?—I just found myself fond of Lionel, and fond of the Charles of my memories. And that was all. Reason and justice continued to give me their verdicts, and old acquaintance tossed them aside as if they no longer mattered.

This indifference was part of the peculiar lightening and stirring which had begun to take place within me after the first sight of Frances looking down at me from the upper terrace at Belair. It was like that delicate sense of night having ended and dawn drawing near; there is no light, thickest darkness shrouds the world, yet there is a nameless scent and the almost inaudible rustling of a soft fitful wind.

It was like that with me.

Doctor MacRae has forbidden me to dig, or mow, or reach up to tie ramblers, and therefore my activities in the garden are restricted to strolling, sniffing, gazing and feeling frustrated; I used to enjoy working in a garden. So I am fortunate in having Mr. Crofts, twice a week in the summer, and once a month in the winter. He is older than I am, and feels, I am sure, that his seniority gives him the right to be even more self-willed than most jobbing gardeners; inevitably advising me to pull up my favourites and replace them with something more 'showy', digging the weeds in and thereby assuring their resurrection, and pruning when the fancy takes him, and so forth. There is no end to it.

One morning, a month or so after my return from Belair, I came in from the garden feeling exhausted after a longish tussle with Mr. Crofts. I had read somewhere an article by a gardening expert, in which he said that Ipomoea Rubra (Morning Glory) should be planted when the evenings are light and long, and I proposed, this being the smallest of tasks and the time of year suitable, to plant the seeds myself. I am more than fond of the heavenly blue flowers; if they possessed scent, they would seem not to belong to this world at all.

Mr. Crofts had not been content to continue forking over the stiff clay soil between my rose bushes (which he was doing exactly as I continue to play the piano, with a surprising ease due entirely to years of practise).

After darting a keen but furtive glance down the garden at me, he stuck his spade upright in the earth, leisurely wiped both hands on his trousers and proceeded to plod down from his end, over the grass and between the purple phlox and glowing Sweet Williams, to mine, where I stood before an old ironwork table, with some three-inch pots, a bag of John Innes seedling compost, and a packet of seeds.

'You're busy, then,' began Mr. Crofts. His tone was accusing.

'Yes, Mr. Crofts.'

'You leave that; I'll do that for you; might find time before I pack up.'

'Thank you, Mr. Crofts. But I will do it.'

He lingered, temporarily baffled but not defeated.

'Ought to have had them in weeks ago; they won't do nothing, not planting them this late, they won't. Ought to have been in end of April, middle of May.'

'I read an article in a newspaper, Mr. Crofts. It said that they should be planted when the evenings are long,' I retorted, annoyance betraying me into explanation.

'Newspapers don't know everything, not by a long chalk they don't. You mark my words.'

'The writer was an experienced gardener . . .'

'They do a lot of 'arm, them chaps do,' cried Mr. Crofts, suddenly aroused, 'all my ladies round 'ere they read them chaps and there's no doing nothing with them arterwards. I don't wish never to hear nothing about experienced gardeners in the newspapers never again. Stop you getting forward with your work, they do.'

We continued to exchange remarks of this kind for some minutes, and it developed into a struggle of wills; I insisting that I would plant the seeds and Mr. Crofts obstinately vowing that he would. Finally, as eleven struck from the spire of St. Michael's, I dusted my hands, and went off towards the house.

'You will like your tea now, I am sure, Mr. Crofts.' I spoke over my shoulder.

'I'll just put these in, won't take a minute,' said Mr. Crofts, standing over the table and looking at me from under his old cap. 'Let's 'ope they comes up, that's all I say.'

Oh, the lower classes! I swept into the kitchen, where Millie sat shelling peas.

'Can you spare me a cup of tea, Millie, when you make that tiresome old man's?' I asked, and she looked up smiling.

'Been having an argument, have you, miss?' She got up to attend to the kettle fussing on the cooker. 'It's not like you to want tea in the morning.'

'No . . . but I do today, please. I'll have it here, if I may,' and I sat down at the table.

Millie keeps her kitchen beautifully; and I like the old-fashioned air which its shape, and she herself, have contrived to give to it. There is her loudly-ticking ancient alarm clock, and a built-in wooden dresser, well stocked with pretty china, and one of those high pseudo-stone mantelshelves, painted black, which are more usually seen in houses in the country than in a house in London. She has a white plush cat sitting on it at one corner, with a red ribbon bow round its neck, and a pottery pig to hold savings, and other small childish possessions. It is a quiet room; it lies at the back of the house. Her bedroom and sitting-room, both rather dark, I fear, are in the front.

When she had put the cup and some biscuits on the window-sill and called to Mr. Crofts that it was there, she returned to the table and poured out for ourselves. She passed me my cup and helped herself to sugar, which I do not take, and we sat in silence sipping, and looking absently out at the garden, where Mr. Crofts was applying to the consumption of his elevenses the energy which he had recently employed in defeating me . . . because it was defeat; from where I sat, I could see the three-inch pots on the table, and two of them were already filled.

I was regretting having referred to him as a tiresome old man, because Millie was quite capable of repeating the remark to him one day when she lost her temper with him, when, turning towards me, she said in a low, hurried tone,

'Miss, I was thinking . . . the weather's so nice just now, and she does want you to see baby . . . could I . . . would it be convenient, miss, if I was to ask Mrs. Parker over for tea one afternoon?'

'Yes, Millie, that would be all right . . .' I was beginning, when she hurried on, her eyes fixed on my face, 'I expect you're busy with that concert coming on, miss, but we'd keep out of your way, except for . . .'

'The concert is not until October, you know . . . you need not do that, Millie. Does the little boy cry much?'

'Oh no, miss, he's ever so good.'

I put down my cup. 'Very well, then. You choose a day, and let me know.'

'I thought—next Wednesday, miss—if that's convenient?'

'Yes, that will do very well. I'll keep it free, if she wants me to see the baby. And you make all the arrangements, Millie. Perhaps you might like tea in the garden? And don't they live in Rothbury? That's a long way to come just to tea—wouldn't you like to ask them to lunch?'

'It's very kind of you, miss, but I don't think so. Teddie likes to have the mornings clear to do the house down and get things ready for Ron in the evening.' Millie's expression was what can only be called smug.

Indeed, I thought. Such excellent habits seemed incongruous with the swollen figure, flopping hair and the eccentric, unbecoming tunic which I remembered. 'Very well, if you think so . . . How will they come? It must be difficult, getting a perambulator on and off buses and in the train.'

'Thank you, miss, but Teddie'll manage. She's a wonderful little mother.'

Again I thought that there must have been a transformation at some time.

'Is she feeding him herself?' I asked, 'or is he having some patent stuff?'

Emotional Millie! Her eyes filled. 'Oh, yes, she *would* do it, miss. Why not get him on to something ready made up, I said, but no, she must have her way. Very determined, Teddie can be. You won't like it when you can't get out to the pictures, I said to her, but you might as well talk to the wall . . . very well, then, miss. I'll tell her next Wednesday.'

A pause. Millie put her head on one side, and appeared about to say something more.

'Yes, Millie? What is it?'

'It was only . . . miss . . . I was just wondering . . .'

'Well? Wondering what?' I tried to make my voice kind.

'Only . . . I *was* wondering if you'd have tea with us, miss? In the garden? With me and Teddie and baby Eric?' She had a melting, tears and smiles expression that was exceedingly irritating.

I managed somehow to make the pause between the question and my answer almost unnoticeable.

'Of course I will . . . it's nice of you to ask me. I am looking forward to seeing the little boy.'

This was a flat lie. I have had as little to do with infants as most unmarried women; and have only once held one in my arms; that was Lionel, of all unlikely things, when he was two weeks old and his mother called me in from their garden gate, where I was loitering with Frances, after our walk home from school, 'to see the baby'. From the visit on Wednesday week I anticipated nothing but boredom.

I got up and went back into the garden to see whether Mr. Crofts, 'in victory, magnanimous' had left me any Morning Glory seeds to plant.

*

That was a beautiful day, that Wednesday.

I remember that I put on a grey dress patterned with large, pale red roses, and a necklace; I wanted Millie to see that I could take a little trouble for her friends.

I was still dressing when they arrived; I remember it so well. A taxi drew up at the gate, and I was just wondering who had tiresomely chosen this one afternoon of all others to descend upon me—when I heard the front door open, and then a loud, decided young voice.

Millie seemed to be protesting.

'Of course I did. That's what they're there for, isn't it? Don't fuss, love.'

I saw the elegant reflection in my looking-glass raise its eyebrows. Somebody seemed to have found her tongue. It appeared improbable, now, that a conversation would have to be manufactured. I sat down, and was reading, to give them time to settle in—not that I supposed the owner of that voice would need much time to settle—when there came a tap at my door.

'Tea's all ready, miss.'

I went across and opened the door. Millie was in her best clothes and smiling, but strikingly pale. She always has felt the heat of course, that was what I thought: it is the heat.

'Thank you . . . Millie . . . in the garden?' I knew that it was in the garden, but she likes every small event to be surrounded by a frame of unnecessary little questions and sentences. I think it makes her feel less nervous.

'Yes, miss . . . you did say we could, and it's such a lovely day . . .'

I followed her down the stairs. The gentle ancient wood of baluster and tread gleamed softly, the worn old Indian and Persian rugs glowed in reflected sunlight. Millie had put bowls of every yellow flower in season wherever she could find a place. I wished, as we descended, that I were going to have the afternoon to myself, to enjoy my house in solitude.

CHAPTER 21

WE WENT through the kitchen, out into the blazing sunlight.

The old iron table was covered by a white cloth bordered with four inches of crochet lace, disinterred by Millie from some cupboard, and had been arranged, with the second-best china given over to her for her use, under the pear-tree, which throws a large cool shadow. Our three old wicker garden chairs (looking smarter than usual; she must have washed them) stood in a circle, and there was the perambulator, a light contemporary affair which folded up, I judged, when necessary, with a mound of gold and white lying motionless in it, and in one of the chairs sat the girl.

It must be she, because of the colour of her hair, the vivid sovereign gold. But for that, I don't think that I should have recognized her. She wore a brief, sleeveless tunic of light blue, and her head was turned sideways, giving to me a profile clear as one on a stamp.

She turned round slowly as we approached, and, still slowly, got up and stood awaiting me. It was certainly me; her eyes did not wander to Millie; she kept their grey-green light fixed, with an intentness just short of rudeness, upon my face.

Where had the shapelessness gone? She was unusually tall for a working-class girl, and slender; and the only fullness was in her bosom, which was that of a nursing mother. I was so surprised as actually to feel a slight confusion; I had expected to see one kind of creature, and was confronted by its exact opposite.

Millie was dithering in the background. (I suppose it is foolish of me to expect that she might have 'picked up' some kind of social training during the years she has lived with what she still calls gentry.)

'Here's—here's Teddie, miss,' she was saying breathlessly, 'and—and this is Miss Barrington, Teddie, who's so kindly—'

The girl and I put out our hands at the same instant; and I smiled, but she remained grave.

'I am pleased to meet you,' I said—which was *so* stupid of me that at one time I used to frown and colour when I remembered the blunder.

'How do you do,' said Mrs. Parker, in that rather loud, rather deep voice I had heard at the front door. 'I was just saying to Millie, before she went to tell you that tea was ready, that I hope the sofa is quite all right now?'

As she finished the slowly-spoken sentence, colour ran up under her neck and over her face. So she was less poised than she seemed! But she kept her eyes on mine.

Again, I was a little thrown off balance. I was so surprised by the brave plunge into the awkward, the now almost unbelievable, incident of three months ago that I found myself wanting—even anxious—to say something reassuring.

'Thank you, no real harm was done. I hear such good things of your boy from Millie that I am glad my sofa was there when it was needed.'

'It did come in handy, didn't it?' she said, and then there broke from her a sudden delightful sound, a laugh that seemed to escape through her carved, firm lips like some irreverent fairy, and, looking back at me—she had glanced away as she laughed—she caught my eye and laughed again, and I laughed too.

Millie had taken the opportunity to go across to the perambulator, set carefully at the edge of the shade so that the babe's almost naked body received the strength of the sun while his head and face were protected.

'Just look at his hair, miss,' she breathed, 'exactly the colour of his mum's.' Indeed, it was the same improbable strong gold, though there was the merest fuzz of it. He was asleep.

Having looked down at him for a minute, I sank into one of the wicker chairs, finding all at once that I was glad of its support, and Mrs. Parker sat down a fraction later.

'Will you pour out, miss?'

'No, it's your party, Millie, will you, please?'

I knew that she would be glad to have something to do. She gradually became less nervous as she asked us our preferences in the way of milk and sugar, commenting on them as we replied, and even murmuring 'Sweet enough,' with a glance that was not quite free from what I can only call, in her own language, sauce, when I said 'No sugar, thank you.' (She has known for fifty years that I don't take it.) Mrs. Parker said, 'Plenty, please; you know me,' and Millie put in three spoonfuls. The boy continued to sleep deeply.

'It's so fresh up here,' the girl said suddenly, in the midst of the silence while we sipped, 'Down where we are there's no hills or anything like that.' She looked slowly round the garden.

'But Teddie and Ron have got ever such a dear little home, miss,' Millie put in eagerly. 'Three bedrooms, and a frig. and all. It's a dream kitchen, isn't it, Teddie?'

'The house is all right; I like the house. It's having everything so low-down and sort—of flat,' the girl said with a kind of stern-ness which I was already recognizing as a part of her personality. 'I like hills, myself. When I was a kiddie, I lived in Wales with Mum's cousin; after Mum died. I liked the mountains. I've always remembered them.' She bit largely into a piece of bread and butter.

I was puzzled. The impression she made on me today was so different from that made by the silent, grotesque creature who had begun her labour in my drawing room that the girl who sat here, self-possessed and, in a hard style, both beautiful and cour-teous, might have been a different creature. Her very features seemed different—but I supposed that the general uncouth swell-ing of pregnancy might account for the shapelessness on that first occasion.

At every chance that presented itself during the pauses in our conversation I studied her, and I knew that she was doing the same to me. I supposed that we were in the same situation; this was the first time that I had met a girl of the working-classes socially, and the first time that she had had tea with a lady.

Millie showed a strong tendency to bring the talk back, again and again, to the baby, but Teddie—it was a most incongruous name for this rather alarming young creature; surely she must possess a more suitable one?—deftly steered it round to other subjects: the difficulty of reaching Highgate from Rothbury, perambulators large and small, the weather and holidays, and managed to say something characteristic and even interesting about each. It was the strength and decisiveness of her personality, I decided, which gave interest to these ordinary subjects.

An unusual young woman. By the time she was forty, that manner might have hardened into something less than attractive. Now, combined with her undeniable beauty, it gave her the aura of a severe young angel. And then the bubbling laugh—I could imagine that young men of any spirit would find her irresistible.

I was wondering a little, I must admit, about the husband, of whom Lionel had said he was 'about a third of her weight; that's the trouble'.

Then the boy woke up, thanks to the passing of what Millie calls, 'that four o'clock jet', and his mother got up at once and went over to him. She picked him up, and, cradling him upright in her arms, put her cheek against his, which had been pressed into a tiny mimicry of wrinkles where it had been resting on the cellular blanket. Then he tinily, copiously, yawned.

At this point in my memories, I must plead embarrassment. No-one can describe the appearance and behaviour of a three-month-old creature, whether baby or puppy, without the use of adjectives which induce distaste; even Swinburne, even Francis Thompson, failed in the task. The capacity to utter foolish words, to make silly fondling gestures, is reserved, I sometimes think, to the lower classes, and I could not see the two gold heads pressed side by side, I could not hear her murmurs of love while a wide smile softened her face and showed her large white teeth, without wanting, after a moment, to turn away my head—though the sight was pretty enough.

Millie, of course, was completely at home in the situation, at once assuming a special face and a voice which made her appear idiotic, and beginning to make sounds in which the word—if it can be described as a word—*wuzzer* frequently occurred.

She became arch when it was discovered that the boy was wet, and insisted that he should be taken away to have his napkin changed—I remember thinking, *so I should hope.*

'Mum'll bring him back when he's a nice clean boy again. Naughty aeroplane, waking Eric up, wasn't it?' and so forth.

The girl glanced at me 'I'll take him indoors,' she said. No apologies, no smile . . . I had to admit that she had poise. Was it natural, or had she somehow acquired it?

She walked over the lawn towards the house with a longish stride, Millie almost running beside them like a dog beside a car, and persistently pushing her face into that of the child.

I leant back, my tea cup between my hands, and stared up at the six poplar trees that grow at the end of my garden and do not quite conceal that of my neighbour, the inquisitive Mr. Grayshott. I *thought* that I had already discerned him once that afternoon, peering through the leaves of his hedge. He knew that I had no young relatives, and what he must be making of my entertaining a baby to tea I could not imagine, but I enjoyed the notion of his bewilderment and curiosity.

I had just finished my first cup when they returned, Eric now wide awake, and clad as to his lower limbs in a blue garment that matched the shade of his mother's tunic and reclining in her arms with . . .

I was going to say 'a kind of languid grandeur'—an absurd phrase. But he was an unusually fine child; large, solid, fair skinned, with an unmistakable air about him of deeply-based health, and he *did* look grand.

'Here he is. Not worth tuppence,' Mrs. Parker said cheerfully, and Millie began to busy herself at the table with more tea for everyone, and that plate of coconut kisses which only appears in our house on special occasions.

'He is a beautiful child. You must both be very proud of him,' I said.

I brought in the *both* deliberately, because it had occurred to me, having, so to speak, now seen young Mrs. Parker in action, and the size and beauty of Master Eric, that the 'poor bastard' of a young husband and father must occasionally feel himself rather in the background—or, as Millie would put it, 'his nose was properly out of joint'.

'Oh, Ronnie's mad about him. Doesn't know which he likes best, Eric or me,' said Mrs. Parker, laughing again with the same helpless effect, as if the mirth were bubbling out of her.

'He likes to do everything for him, bath him and change him and all,' she confided, sitting down again and accepting a cake with a casual 'Thanks, love,' from the plate held out by Millie. 'I tell him it's his job to bring the money home, not change the baby . . . he's a bit soft, Ronnie,' she ended on an indulgent note.

'But ever such a good husband, isn't he, Teddie?' Millie put in eagerly.

Mrs. Parker considered. 'He's all right,' she at last conceded. But there was an expression on her cameo-face that convinced me her feelings were more tender than her words, though her next remark was: 'He's got no *go*. Let anyone walk over him. I'm always telling him, "Stand up for yourself, no-one else is going to."'

She drank some tea, looking sternly into space.

'You do wear the trousers, don't you, Teddie?' Millie put in proudly, 'I couldn't do nothing with—with mine, but that suited me. Very set on his own way, Stanley Miller was,' turning to me, 'and I had to knuckle under . . . but we got on all right, me and him,' she ended softly.

Millie's face has still something of the Greuze look remembered and praised by Mimi Handel; if you can imagine one of his girls grown old, then you can imagine Millie at nearly seventy, and when—as now, speaking of her husband, tenderness lights it—the cockney inflections in her voice can be forgotten. Her looks are as different from my own as they could be, and as for tenderness, I don't know whether my face can express it. I do know that I have always had painful difficulty in expressing my feelings in words (my loving feelings, that is); though I have no difficulty in expressing them inwardly to myself.

I had been fearing that Mrs. Parker and Mrs. Miller might find themselves incapable of facing the fact that the visit must end.

But, on the stroke of five from St. Michael's Church, the former looked at a pretty watch on her wrist and observed that it was three minutes slow. She then adjusted it, frowning, and said that they must be going; it took over an hour to get home, and Ronnie got in at half-past six.

'But he don't create if his tea's not ready, he's not that sort, is he, Teddie?' said Millie.

'It always is ready. But—no, he doesn't create,' Mrs. Parker said in a considering tone. Then she caught my eye, and, unexpectedly, bubbled into that uncharacteristic laugh again and added, 'might do me a bit of good if he did.'

The remark was in bad taste as all her references to her husband had been, yet her expression and the laugh gave it a kind of charm.

I got up at once from my chair. We had said all there was to be said at a tea-party; I had admired the child; and now I had the excellent excuse of the long journey eastwards to refrain from pressing them to stay another fifteen minutes.

'I am sorry you can't stay longer,' I said to Teddie, 'but I can quite see . . . Millie, wouldn't you like to give your friend some flowers?' The garden was in the full richness of a hot June.

I was surprised to see colour run up and over the girl's face and neck again.

'Oh . . . that's kind of you. Ronnie does our garden, and I've got more flowers than I know what to do with,' she said coldly, 'but thanks—all the same.'

She looked full at me. Millie was rearranging the pensive Eric's coverings. I did not reply: I was again taken aback. What could be the matter?

'We'll be off, then.' She turned to Millie. 'For goodness' sake leave him alone, love, he's all right,' then back to me. 'Good-bye then, and thank you, Miss Barrington . . . I'm glad the sofa was all right.'

Suddenly I seemed to be in her place: owner of a proud young heart and a sensitive young conscience. I could understand both. I put out my hand to her.

'Now you must forget that,' I said, speaking with sincerity, 'to me, it's exactly as if it had never happened.' I paused, and what I said next was not completely sincere, 'it might have happened to anyone,' I ended.

Her expression became agitated, even . . . was it afraid? . . . for a second, then she said quickly, 'Oh, no, not to anyone, Miss Barrington, only to me,' and turned away once more to the boy, scarlet. Well, if she were embarrassed, that was to her credit.

A few moments more and our farewells were over, and they were going down the path towards the house, Millie wheeling Eric and chattering as she went, and Mrs. Parker carefully balancing the tray loaded with tea-things.

I leant back again and began to look up into the blue sky, where mountains of snowy cloud were becalmed. *It was the time when lilies blow*, I thought, *and clouds are highest up in air*. So they were; the bodiless ranges hung toppling directly above my head. I was unaccountably tired: my thoughts were not irritable, they only ran through my head too quickly for comfort. The visit must have taken more out of me than I had anticipated.

That's over, I was thinking, and it went off well enough. The girl is strikingly unlike what I had decided she would be like, and strikingly individual. Interesting, too, I should think. But I'm old and I'm tired, I don't want to get involved with interesting young people.

The boy is grand, of course. I smiled at the memory of his yawn.

It's a good thing, perhaps, that Millie has taken them up; she shows every sign of being exceedingly tiresome when she gets really old, and perhaps they will help to absorb her energies, I mused.

What was going to absorb my own energies?

Well, I had managed somehow for fifty years; I would go on managing, I supposed.

Of course! The girl had just left her husband when she came here that first time. That would account for her blushing, when the sofa incident was recalled.

I'm glad she went back to the poor . . . young man. That splendid boy will keep them together now.

And that's the end of the Parkers so far as I am concerned, I remember thinking, with a sense of relief.

Millie had tip-toed back unobserved (I think I had dozed for a minute or two) and when I tinned my head, I saw her looking at me with *the* most irritating of her many irritating expressions, over the top of the tablecloth she was folding.

'I do hope you enjoyed yourself, miss. I know I did—'

'Very pleasant' . . . or some such phrase, I muttered.

'. . . Teddie won't rest now, miss, until *you've* been over to tea with *her*. Very nice manners, Teddie has. Not one for taking all and giving nothing. She was at the Hilda Marshall Grammar School for Girls. A very good school, it is; everybody speaks well of it. You . . . you will go if she asks you, won't you, miss?'

I am sorry to say that I got up and stalked back to the house without answering. Whether Millie read any sense of my annoyance into the storm of Liszt that shortly floated out into the garden, I don't know.

CHAPTER 22

MILLIE may have felt that she had been hasty in her attempt to carry my relationship with the Parkers further, because for some time she did not mention them. And I was quite ready, of course, to let them and their affairs drop; I had more matter for active thought than I had had for years.

My picture of Frances had undergone a complete change since my visit to the cemetery at St. Vaast-aux-Puits.

At Belair, I had decided that I must accept her as she still was, faults and distasteful habits and all, because it had been such a relief to lose at least one of the situations rooted in the past which gave me so much pain.

But at St. Vaast I had learned that she was faithful, and that she possessed a heart; and now I could feel gratitude and affection, as well as the half-century old fascination. And a little jealousy too?—oh, yes, a little jealousy. She had found the courage to go to *their* graves when I lacked it.

At first, in those monotonous weeks of early summer, I used to make excuses for myself. I had loved my brothers so very much; they had been my all; my life had been empty since they died; I had only had my duty to my parents to sustain me, I had never wanted to marry anyone: and so on. But, gradually, I had had to face a fact. It was as if some gentle but remorseless force were compelling me.

My grief had been selfish.

Staring inwardly at the new idea, I began to understand how my agonized drawing back from life, during half a century, must have meant fresh suffering for my father and mother. They had lost three children, and the fourth was turning into a kind of frozen *thing*, a Snow-Woman, as Frances had called me, a creature crouching behind barriers of pain and pride; icy walls mile-high and so thick that the faint cries for help from her father and mother could not reach her.

I used to despise them for showing the world their grief. Yes, I used to do that. I was bitterly angry—always in silence—with my father for writing the poem *'Lightheart'*, only seeing how it laid open our loss to strangers' eyes all over the world—for it had been translated into many languages—and never realizing the reconciliation, small but real, which it must have brought to him, and to others; how it must have kept memories in hearts unknown to me fresh and green; full of pain, but alive.

But Lightheart, O, Lightheart, when will you come again?

All these thoughts, it will be understood, were exquisitely painful and a martyrdom to my silly pride. It drained my energies to track down my guilt and set it face to face with the judge of my conscience, and condemn it.

I spent hours of that June merely lying back in a chair in the garden or sitting in silence at the piano, my hands idle in my lap. The distant voices of those Beatles, with whom Millie had of course become besotted, sounded faintly from her transistor in the kitchen throughout the long, hushed, sunny afternoons and I would sometimes 'come to' out of my torturing thoughts, and frown at the cacophony. Yet it was a harmless enough noise; it was only that it hurt my ears, and pulled me back again into what we think of as 'the real world', and my thoughts were, to me, so desperately important.

Enough of this; I think people are bores when they are introspective, especially when they will tell you about it. Let it be sufficient to say that by the middle of July I was beginning to feel more at peace. My thoughts had cleared; I was able to see my guilt in perspective, and to be humble enough—yes, I used the word

to myself, the word I had never used before without contempt—
to make up my mind to do better in future. There might not be
many years left me in which to try! I began to be very, very tired.

It would have served me right, as the children say, if Frances
had stopped writing to me. But she did not; she wrote at least
once a month; in fact, we began a correspondence which became
a pleasure. Whether she wrote from old affection, I did not know,
but I liked to think that it was affection; the grumbling, reluc-
tant, deep-rooted affection of the oldest friend, and now I know
that it was.

More than I deserved. More than I deserved.

From her, I had the news of the household at Belair that I
had wanted. Laurette had started divorce proceedings against
that unfortunate Emil, who had 'taken up with a French woman,
ten years older than he is, and a right bitch on the make', as Mrs.
Gelfors plainly put it, and was meanwhile still living in his father's
house, and turning out his gaudy, pleasant pictures for tourists.

Lionel was in America, to arrange matters in connection with
Charles's bequest to the Metropolitan Museum of Art. The coarse
description of Emil's mistress fell short, I feared, of the reality,
and strengthened my conviction that, of all the unhappy people in
that house, he has had the harshest fate. But it is always possible
that he does not think so.

It was a relief to read of Bunny swooping down to rescue
her sister from a miserable little secretarial job in Norwich, and
carrying her off to Geneva, where the goodwill and premises of a
confectioner's shop, on an excellent site in a main thoroughfare,
had been secured. Bunny proposed to capitalize on the English
taste for afternoon tea when abroad, and open 'The English Tea
Shop' there, 'resisting, God knows how, the temptation to call it
"Bunny's",' Frances wrote. This, it appeared, had always been
Bunny's private dream.

Lionel was overworking, his sister pronounced. He sent me
his best love. And Mimi Handel was safely settled in the midst
of her 'enormous, madly chatty tribe of Jews in Hamburg'. That
was pleasant to think of, too. I was certain that she at least had
loved Charles, and that she grieved for him. Her family, living

with that absorbed intensity characteristic of their race, must yet be a consolation to her.

And then, one morning, late in August, there was a letter awaiting me on the breakfast table, addressed in a bold modern script and with the postmark 'Rothbury'. When she brought in my breakfast I saw that Millie could not keep her eyes from it. I was glancing over *The Times*, but I noticed her eager look.

Well, I supposed, I had better do what was kindest. Some months ago I would have done what I wanted.

'I think your friend has written to me,' I observed, holding it up.

'Oh, yes, miss, that'll be from Teddie, she did say as she was going to ask you over to tea.' Millie lingered. 'Aren't you going to open it, miss?'

I was smiling as I did so; the childishness which is Millie's most marked trait seemed to me, that morning, endearing.

> 14 Brotherton Close
> Rothbury
>
> 'Dear Miss Barrington,
>
> Ronald and I and Eric would be very pleased if you and Millie could come over to tea next Sunday. The front garden is looking smashing and we would like you to see it.
>
> Millie knows the way. Please come at three o'clock.
>
> Yours sincerely,
> E. Parker.'

It was strange—as I read this aloud, I saw Millie pale. It happened at the end of the letter. The colour actually left her lips, and her expression was so alarmed that I exclaimed, '—What's the matter?'

'Nothing, miss—it's only the heat, it's boiling today, there isn't a breath. You'll go, won't you, please, miss?'

I remember the extreme strength of my disinclination to go. I thought of that long, awkward journey in the heat, among the crowds of people whose tastes and background were so remote from my own that I could feel no point of communication with them anywhere; the weariness of churning out a conversation with the girl and her probably shy or aggressive husband, and the embarrassment Millie would feel, and show in her most irritating way, at going anywhere with me in public. But the idea of *refusal* never entered my head.

'That's nice of her,' I said, trying to choose words that would please Millie. 'We'll go, shall we? You would like to, wouldn't you?'

'Oh, yes, miss! Oh, thank you ever so, miss! It won't be too bad a journey, there's a train for about an hour, awfully slow, they are, and then a bit of a bus ride. Stops quite close to Teddie's, it's only a five minute walk after that.' She was smiling again and her colour had returned.

'Very well, then. What time do you think we ought to leave here?'

I was having thoughts about hiring a car. But I dismissed the idea at once; Millie would be even more embarrassed, and I didn't know what kind of a place I might be going into; it might cause tiresome interest among the inhabitants to arrive in my Mr. Jones's large and handsome Cortina.

I glanced again at the letter, as Millie placed my breakfast before me.

'What does the E stand for?' I asked, still trying to be pleasant. 'Edna, miss.'

Millie whipped out her handkerchief and deftly removed two little pools of tea which had fallen from my cup when she knocked her hand against it. I could feel her nervousness.

'But Teddie never did like it, she won't let anyone use it.' Bless the woman—what was the matter now? She had lost all her colour again.

'Well, I prefer it to Teddie. That's most unsuitable—it doesn't suit her at all.'

Millie said no more but went rather quickly out of the room, and I was left to my scrambled eggs and my *Times*. I resigned myself, unsoothed by their Women's Page to the prospect of Sunday.

CHAPTER 23

I HAD expected to find the streets less crowded than on weekdays, but soon saw, as Millie and I sat in the bus going down Highgate Hill, that my expectation had been ingenuous.

True, the weekday hardly-broken stream of roaring traffic was absent. But a brisk procession of cars, each laden with a family in place of the solitary driving father of the week, accompanied us down the hill, or darted out from side turnings; and our own bus was crowded with women and children, the babies smart and staring, and the mothers cheerful through the preoccupation of their natural cares. Sunday, I discovered, is the day of the weekly family visit.

I was pleased when Millie, muttering apologies for 'ever such dirty old trains, miss', led the way to the booking office of a steam-train station in the heart of Kentish Town which must have been there for a hundred years. I enjoy travelling on small old railways. Dirty yes, but quiet compared with the roads, and passing through almost deserted stations where high banks of sooty grass loomed over us, and the brown brick houses of the inner suburbs, shaken and frail, gazed down on us like the ghosts of a lost solidity and comfort. Our carriage, again, was full of young women and children, but their chattering, suggesting the chirruping of birds on a fine morning, was rather pleasant than otherwise.

But oh, that bus ride across the former marshy farmland to Rothbury! Mile after mile of low new houses, their stucco already darkened by the smoke from the squat, clumping factories, each set in its municipal-style garden of clipped sooty grass and staring flowers. Flashy shops, and occasionally an isolated group of cottages that must have been nearer two hundred than a hundred years old; roofs sagging, windows dark and glaring where louts had smashed the glass, and through it all cut the broad, featureless road made for motorists, arched over by those terrible lamps that throw out their shadowless glare at the hour which was once twilight.

Not a tree above three years old, not one single feature, either beautiful or hideous, to startle the monotony. A low cloudy sky hung over the low clean roofs and the road where sheets of news-paper whirled in the wind of passing cars. I saw one meadow, a fenced-in patch where what was left of a hawthorn hedge lived on; it was labelled as 'a site acquired for development' and surely the sooner it was developed, and that reminder of a lost, humble poetry was rooted up, the better.

It was only the sight of the cheerful young mothers and their sturdy children that stopped my spirits from sinking to zero.

'Nearly there, miss,' observed Millie, who had been watching the nearest baby with a smile and her head on one side.

I managed a nod, and a smile of sorts.

It was difficult to rest my eyes anywhere; the babies evidently found my hat and gloves of novel interest, and stared at them and me unsmilingly, and if I looked out of the window there was that depressing view going past. However, I happened to be doing so when something began to grow out of the horizon some miles away; tall leggy things, towering above the houses, dark and slender against the dull sky. Cranes! Nearer and nearer they came, exaggerated in their ominous length, tilted at beauti-ful dangerous angles. That I should live to thank heaven for the sight of some cranes!

'That's where they're building the new oil-factory, miss,' said Millie, 'right on an island in the river, it is.' Among many annoy-ing habits is her continual, stealthy study of my face. She so often says something that proves she knows what I am thinking . . .

The bus stopped. 'Here we are, miss.' We stood up, and I had to step over two pairs of robustly extended feet, male and (presum-ably) white, as we made our way out; a (presumably) coloured pair, in smart Italian shoes, were withdrawn with a polite murmur. On the way home, exactly the reverse happened, which somehow pleased my sense of justice . . . or something.

'And here's Ron,' cried Millie, 'brought Eric to meet us! Well, there's a lovely surprise.'

Ronald Parker was standing by the bus-stop. A big, gentle boy, was my thought, and his shirt, striped in pink and blue, looked fresh against his clear dark skin. Eric was lying in the perambulator, surveyed the scene. On my venturing to smile at him, he turned away with hauteur.

Millie and the young man were exchanging a kiss, I caught his eye as he looked over her shoulder. The glance was shy and sulky.

I had expected it to be. But oh, dear, what was the time? Five to three, and we certainly could not leave before five. Two hours of it.

'This is Ron, miss,' said Millie, beaming between us—from one to the other, 'Ron, here's Miss Barrington . . . come to see you.'

'Good-afternoon,' I said, putting out my hand. 'How kind of you to come to meet us.'

'That's all right . . . good-afternoon.' Well, at least he shook hands properly; neither too hard nor too weakly. 'I thought I'd better, seeing it's the first time.' I could imagine a girl's heart turning over at his smile, but somehow I could not imagine Mrs. Parker's doing so, or only against her considerable will.

'I'll push Eric . . . come along, lovely, come with . . . Millie.' She hurried on ahead and I was left with young Parker.

I could see the effort he made as he turned to me.

'Find the journey very long, did you?'

'No, not really. It was all new to me, you see. I—'

'No, I don't s'pose you'd be likely to know this part,' he muttered, 'it's a bit of a way from . . . up where you live.' Then he looked guilty. I knew exactly what had been going on; madam had been impressing on him that he must bring out his nicest manners for me, and he resented it.

'About fifteen miles,' I said mildly.

'How long did it take to do it, do you reckon?'

'An hour and a half exactly. I timed it,' I said, turning to look up at him. I could see those cranes out of the corner of my eye; they, and his face, were the only beautiful things in sight.

'Half an hour by car,' he said, on a note of longing, and then I knew what to talk to him about.

'Have you got one yet?' I asked. 'No, of course, Millie told me you hadn't . . . what kind will you get, when you do?'

'I fancy one of them open jobs; with—' and then he said something technical, which I did not understand and can't remember, about the engine. 'Fat chance. A family man, that's me. It'll have to be a mini, with plenty of room for the wife and kids. *When* I get it.'

It was difficult to reply. Married too young, I thought; what answer is there to that trouble? None; Nature herself has made it unanswerable.

'Teddie'd like a Jag. Not what you'd call modest in her requirements, Teddie isn't,' and he smiled. I wondered if she were always worrying him for new things; electric nonsenses, and so forth. Such nagging did not seem congruous with her personality, but one can never tell about people.

We had stopped in our walk down the neat, featureless road, in a little square of houses grouped round a central bed of grass. This was railed off, presumably from the local children, by ugly wire and concrete posts, but its neglected grass was scattered thickly with all kinds of rubbish.

He was holding open a small gate. My attention had been on the railed-off space, but now, as I turned, I saw two long narrow strips of radiant colour, low-set and glowing, running down either side of the path, up to the house door. 'Oh, how pretty!' I exclaimed. 'They're like carpets.'

'That's what it's called, Oriental Carpet. You get the packet at Woolworth, a shilling, it is, and I got twelve and spread them well out. It's funny how the coloureds vary,' he went on, following me up the path, 'there's one lives next door but one, stops every day to look at that and have a word about it, and another, lives across the green, I caught him chucking rubbish on it the other night when I was coming home late. Started a bit of a race riot for two, that did. *He* won't do it again.'

I realized that 'coloureds' had meant black people, not the flowers, and just managed to control a startled glance at him when the bright blue front door opened and there was Teddie—Edna—with Millie, holding Eric and doing what I can only describe as mopping and mowing. There was not quite room for two in that hall; she had to stand halfway in an open door on the right.

'Good-afternoon, Miss Barrington,' said our hostess, with perhaps less of welcome and more of severity in her tone than was quite conventional. And that was all.

'Good-afternoon,' I said. 'I have been admiring the Oriental Carpets.'

'They do look pretty,' Mrs. Parker conceded. 'Come inside. Ronnie, take Miss Barrington's coat and hang it on the pegs by the door.'

'I remember where the pegs are, now!' he exclaimed, as if in surprise, and, busy as I was with getting myself uncoated, I saw her beautiful young face suddenly *crack*—into what promised to start wild giggling. It was instantly controlled, and I was relieved that there should be laughter between them, yet annoyed that my visit should be the cause of it. Then, as she ushered me into the living-room, I put the incident down to a natural nervousness.

'It's a funny kind of room, isn't it, miss?' whispered Millie, as Mrs. Parker, announcing that she would make the tea, disappeared into the back of the house. 'Teddie won't have a nice suite.'

Uninvited, I had sat down; I was unnaturally exhausted; I suppose it was strain.

'It's quite strikingly pretty and unusual,' I snapped. 'Do be quiet, Millie.'

'I'm sorry, miss.' But her eyes—why?—were bright with triumph. She danced Eric up and down, crooning to him and I shut my eyes. Then I opened them and glanced round.

Everything was blue or a clear scarlet. The walls and ceiling were sky blue, the plain carpet the scarlet of a guardsman's coat. A small central table had been lacquered blue, and it was set with cups of scarlet plastic. The half curtains at the windows were blue; the thicker ones the same strident red.

I lay back, remembering Proust's description of the theme in music that is like a cock crowing in the scarlet dawn, and felt too old and too tired for the headlong youth blazoned out in that tiny room. Nothing was old; nothing was quiet; nothing was made of stone or metal or natural ancient wood. As irrevocably as Charles Handel's house in France, it belonged to the new world that was coming, just as I belonged to the old.

The girl—though I felt her to be more the young wife and mother this afternoon, here, in her home—came in with a teapot on a blue tray.

'Tea's ready,' she announced. 'Will you sit here, please, Miss Barrington, and Ronnie . . . Millie, you and Eric over there, please.'

Millie observed that she and Eric would keep each other company, wouldn't they, though indeed the exiguousness of the room made their places at a tiny table in one corner almost joined on to the one at which we sat. Millie perched upright on her chair, Eric half-reclined in the invaluable pram, raised on pillows.

'I can't make cakes yet,' observed Mrs. Parker, 'and as I expect you don't like shop cakes any better than I do, Miss Barrington, I decided we'd just have bread and butter. That's nice bread; it's rye; I hope you can eat it? I went to East Ham to get that. I did make some jam. Six pounds of it. Plum.'

'Quite the best, unless—perhaps—greengage,' I assured her. 'Bread and butter will do beautifully. When we were small, we sometimes had 'a bread and butter tea' just that, and no cake. Are you going to learn to make cakes? I can't.'

'In time,' she promised, passing me a cup which, I noticed, was full of tea the exact strength I like; she had remembered. 'There's a lot of things I want to do in time . . . *don't* give him his cake till he's drunk all his milk, Millie, *please!*' she interrupted herself to address poor Millie with sternness.

Eric, I noticed, had been provided with a small slab of pink and white cake upon which his eyes were fixed eagerly, and I was rather relieved to see, in this provision, some relaxation of the awful severity of the lines along which the Parker home appeared to be run. I wished that someone of my own generation—Frances, perhaps—had been there with me, to enjoy the afternoon afterwards in retrospect. I was finding Mrs. Parker at home both funny and endearing. Yet impressive, too, so much character! Quite alarming.

'Is gardening your great hobby?' I asked, turning to Ronald, who was masticating rye bread with no expression of enjoyment.

'Gardening and cars,' said his wife, and was going on to say something else when he said, 'Just let me get a word in, will you?' in a mild voice, more pleading than commanding, and she smiled suddenly at him and was silent. He turned to me.

CHAPTER 24

'THAT's it—only I can't do much here with the gardening. Most blokes round about just don't try. The gardens are dumps, mostly. Then when you do get something to come up, someone comes along and . . . vandals, that's what they are, vandals. It's the kids, mostly. There is a bit of ground at the back, but . . .'

'Perhaps you would show it to me, after tea,' I said.

'There isn't much to see. I got it dug over, and raked down. It's good soil, too. A bit sooty, now, but that don't hurt . . . there was farms round here right up to the war. Then they started buying them out to build the war factories—'

'Before they started building them further out because of the bombing,' Mrs. Parker put in. 'Not that I'm *interested* in the bombing, come to that,' she ended, as if excusing herself for mentioning it.

'Yes, well . . . and after the war the speculators started in, building these estates for us poor slaves at Glovers, and after that the Council bought them.' He drank some tea thirstily.

'Glover's is where Ron works, miss,' Millie put in; her eyes had been fixed upon us most of the time during the meal, and I observed that Eric had secured his cake, either legally or illegally, and eaten every crumb. 'A big firm, it is.'

'Never mind them now, it's Sunday . . .' said Ronald.

'Been a bit of trouble down there,' said Millie in a low tone, as if to herself. 'Communists, and that.'

'But about the garden . . . I want to grow vegetables, lettuces and potatoes. I reckon you could even save a bit on your lettuces, apart from the interest of it . . .'

'Ronnie should have been a farmer,' his wife said. 'He really does love it.'

'Oh, belt up . . . love it,' said the boy, 'that's a corny thing to say . . . no, it makes something to do, week-ends and evenings, the pub's a mile down the road and—we have got a telly, but Teddie doesn't go for it. Have to keep it upstairs.'

'I like the educational programmes,' said Teddie primly, where-upon, I passed my cup up for more tea, exclaiming vigorously, 'My dear child, you sound like a prig! Are you quite sure you mean what you say?'

For an instant she looked angry, and then she laughed. She considered.

'Well . . . p'raps I . . . like it a little better . . . than I . . . think I do,' and we all three laughed, Millie alone continuing to look scared.

'Well, *you* haven't got one, Miss Barrington, Millie told me so,' Teddie said.

'I haven't one for various reasons; I read, and I practise the piano, and one hasn't time for everything. Also, a great deal of the singing and the modern music, both popular and serious, literally hurts my ear drums. And I dislike the shallowness of the discussions between "personalities", and the general smoothing out and streamlining of topics and problems which are full of insoluble difficulties.'

I drank some tea, feeling that I had been 'pontificating', as Jock used to say, and the girl said abruptly, 'I like to hear you talk. Go on.'

'Now did you ever know anyone who could "go on" after hear-ing that?' I turned, smiling, to her husband. 'Suppose *you* go on, about the carrots? That's really interesting.'

'No, but I do,' insisted Teddie. She checked herself, colouring. 'I didn't—mean to be personal.'

I was more flattered than I cared to admit to myself, 'and Eric?' I said, turning towards the silent pair in the corner, 'does he say anything yet?'

'Miss Barrington! He's only five months!' Teddie's laugh rang out.

'Well, I know nothing about babies. You must forgive me.'

'He's forward,' said his father, giving the baby a cool look which in no way hid love and pride, 'but they all are nowadays. That one'll be married, time he's turned thirteen.'

'Not if I have anything to do with it,' said Teddie, 'he's going to be properly educated, aren't you, Hijjus?' She moved her fingers at him, and he responded with a sudden wriggle and a wild smile.

'Poor little beggar,' said Ronald Parker. 'Teddie, this here bread's enough to break your teeth.'

'That's what it's meant to do—exercise your jaws,' she retorted; with her eyes full of domestic lightning—then, suddenly, her giggle came out. 'All right, love, I know it's a bit tough. There are some biscuits in the tin . . . p'raps you'd like one too?' to me.

'I'm sure our baby could eat a biscuit,' from Millie, 'couldn't you, Millie's lovely?'

'He's had cake . . . and before he'd finished his milk, too . . . oh, I saw you, don't worry . . .' his mother said relentlessly. 'No more muck for him today.'

I enjoyed a plain biscuit, fetched from the kitchen by a sulking Millie; the plum jam, though of perfect consistency, had been over-sweet for me, just as the rye bread had been too hard for me to eat with enjoyment.

Tea was over. It was just after four o'clock. I was wondering how soon we could with decency begin murmuring about the long journey home.

'The worst of living here is that there isn't much to do or show you.' Teddie was starting to collect cups on to the blue tray. 'It's all alike, round here.' Her tone was not discontented; she was just stating a fact.

'But do I need to be shown anything?' I ventured to ask. 'It's pleasant, just sitting here talking.' She hesitated, plainly divided between courtesy and her own need to keep things moving.

'Sure?' she asked.

'Quite sure, my dear.'

'Oh, all right, then . . . we'll leave it . . . Ronnie always hates me rushing the things off the table.' She sat down again.

'I'll just rinse them through; it won't take a tick,' said Millie eagerly; the harder you snub Millie, the more she wags her tail, and it is a trait I have found hard to live with. Teddie shook her head fiercely at her.

'It's like living with an electric saw,' said Ronald Parker suddenly, 'you know, they start up at six in the morning and go on all day without letting up.'

'Thank you! I'd like to know where you'd have been once or twice, without your electric saw!' his wife cried, absolutely rearing herself at him and seeming to flash with pride and self-confidence; it was quite shocking, and, to me, most embarrassing.

'What a thing to say,' Millie murmured, 'we don't like to hear Daddy say things like that, do we, Eric?'

'I'd have managed. Not so well as you, of course, but some-how . . . come on, Miss Barrington, like to have a look at our back garden?'

I was glad to follow him. And, as we edged past his wife in the tiny room, I was astonished to see him unhurriedly, gently pull one of her ears and to see her answering smile. We went through the minute, speckless kitchen, where, so far as I could see, most of the contents were made of bright plastic, and I was reflecting that of course there are aspects of marriage which to the unmarried must remain mysterious: consolingly mysterious, sometimes.

The small oblong of freshly dug and raked earth appeared, to me, menaced by the little houses overlooking and crowding about it, whose untidy gardens were separated from it only by thin rail-ings on either side. Ronald exclaimed irritably, and went to pick up a crumpled carton. Some three or four children were in the left-hand neighbouring garden, squabbling rather than playing over an elaborate metal stand, brightly painted, which supported a swing: an expensive-looking toy. From a garden on the other side a black face looked across and smiled, and a hand waved, and Ronald called some remarks to his neighbour about the weather. There were some beautiful roses in the black man's garden, and Ronald confided to me that he spent a lot of money on his roses.

Yes, there were the black man and his roses, Mrs. Parker's blue and scarlet parlour and her embattled beautiful youth; and the little boy. But these things seemed to me to be blessings shin-ing against an atmosphere of strain so great that only Ronald's own youth must have enabled him to support it. There might be consoling mysteries in marriage, but about this particular marriage I was troubled, and, having so many old griefs and questions of my own past to muse over, that summer, I resented my concern.

'Can't make up my mind to go for vegetables or flowers,' the boy was saying, standing with shoulders slightly hunched and looking out (God knows, there was not far to look) across his rented sliver of England. 'I . . . I'm not one for making up my mind in a hurry. Never was. Teddie, she gets fed up with me sometimes. But I like to *go into* a thing, once I've started . . .'

I was aware—may God forgive me—of distaste. Was he asking for sympathy? Or having the extraordinary disloyalty to complain to me of his wife?

'I suppose it depends on what the soil is best suited for,' I suggested, and stooped quickly and sifted a little of it through my fingers. 'It's sandy . . . your idea about carrots was a good one . . . I expect your coloured friend has to spend a lot on fertilizers to get roses going on such a sandy soil. They like clay.'

His hand had been out to help me regain my balance, but, seeing that I did not need it, he smiled. That smile, and the ear-pulling—well, I supposed and hoped that, in spite of appearances, things might be 'all right'.

Perhaps it was just that I was unused to the manners of young married working-class people. I must remember that these were the first of their kind that I had known.

We lingered for a little while, under the colourless sky, with the tiny neat houses crowding in and staring at us. There was a muted stir of Sunday afternoon life over all the back view from Brotherton Place; old faces peeping secretively from curtained windows, young women gossiping across the sagging fences, children crying in perambulators or squabbling over their games, a few men toiling over the strips of garden. The sense of being overlooked was beginning to make me feel irritable, and I was relieved when Ronald, saying, 'Well, that's about all there is to see,' led the way indoors.

'I was just saying to Teddie, miss, p'raps we ought to be thinking about going,' Millie said instantly. Her eyes were reddened, and I assumed that her young tyrant had been scolding about Eric's illegal cake. 'It's a long way, and there's always a lot of traffic Sunday afternoons. People coming home early, like, to avoid the rush.'

'Yes, well, perhaps . . . but may I talk to Eric a little, before we go? I have hardly seen him,' and I sat down in a painfully modernist chair, of, I assumed, Swedish inspiration, reflecting that we still in some respects suffer under invasion from the Vikings. 'Will he come to me, do you think?' I added to Teddie, and, as she lifted him, I held out my arms. But first, I carefully took off my brooch, that it might not scratch his miraculous face.

'Is he—all right, Teddie?' his father put in, in a lowered tone.

'I've just changed him . . . of course he's all right, and another month or so and we shan't have to bother with *that* any more,' she said gaily. 'He'll be house-trained . . . here, catch!' and she almost tossed him into my lap.

He took it quietly. He was sleepy, and in a moment, after one stare, he leant back against my shoulder, settling himself, and blinking. I could hardly believe in the clarity of his eyes, and the texture of his skin and the shape of his little head under the red-gold down. But best of all, I liked the warm, heavy weight against my breast. I wanted to hold him closely, to clutch the breath out of him—I was shocked at the strength of my feelings. I was afraid, too, of something unspecified and vague going amiss while I held him, yet the joy was stronger than the fear.

And, all the time I felt that I must not let that donkey, Millie, see what I was feeling. Her eyes, I knew, would be fixed upon me.

'There . . . back to mother,' I said in a moment.

I looked up. How quiet the room had grown. They were all three staring at us, the little boy and me, with the solemnest, strangest expression, and I was quite startled. 'Take him, my dear,' I said to the girl, and she moved quickly forward, her face alive again, and received him, with a muttered word of thanks.

A disagreeable idea had insinuated itself, following the strange little silence, and I wanted to rid myself of it. The best way was simply to put it straightly to Millie on the way home; if my frankness broke up the acquaintanceship between myself and these young people, well, it might be as well. It would be better than their continuing in an illusion that I would 'do something for Eric', as a rich, soft-headed old woman.

Our farewells were friendly. There was even a plain invitation, on my part, that Teddie must bring Ronald to tea 'the next time you come', which, I said, must be in the autumn when my six apple trees were in fruit. But the unpleasant idea persisted; and I only waited until Millie and I were seated in the railway carriage on the ancient line that would carry us back to Kentish Town, which we fortunately had to ourselves, to begin.

In fact, she spoke first—which I had expected.

'Well, that went off ever so nice, didn't you think so, miss? and I'm glad you didn't mind the parlour, I can't get over it somehow, all that red and blue, a nice three piece suite and one of them contemporary wallpapers—'

'Millie,' I interrupted, 'I am sorry, but I have something that I must ask you—something rather unpleasant.'

She gaped piteously, then burst out—

'Oh, miss, is it about the cake? I couldn't help it, I swear I couldn't, I took my eyes off him for a second, it couldn't have been more than that, and he'd reached out and got it . . . they're like lightning, when they want anything . . . and Teddie took on about it ever so while you was out with Ron—carrying on, you'd think . . . *after all*,' her voice suddenly rang with a furious resentment and she actually writhed, as if in pain, '*I am* . . .' She broke off, looking terrifiedly at me, then turned her head away and stared out of the window.

'Of course it isn't the cake, don't be silly,' I said, 'I am sorry she upset you; we have to make allowances for young mothers, they take things so seriously. No. It's something else. I enjoyed my visit, Millie, and I liked Ronald. There's something very taking about him. And the little boy is beautiful, and I find Teddie interesting, though not an easy person to live with, I should think. Exceedingly strong-willed. But I *must* ask you something, and I wish you to answer me *truthfully*, please.'

I paused. Her head had come slowly round while I was speaking, and now she was facing me, in a silence brimming with what, I could see to my surprise, was plain terror. Her eyes were widening and widening, and her lips were parted, and through them little breaths came fast.

'Don't look at me like a rabbit at a snake,' I said crossly, 'it's only this. Are they hoping to get something out of me?'

She was silent. She continued to stare, and once she swallowed. But she answered not a word.

'It occurred to me,' I went on, already beginning to feel, as I gave voice to it, that my suspicion had been vulgar as well as unfounded, 'that they might hope I would take a fancy to the boy—help to pay for his education, or something of that sort. His mother said that she wants him to be "properly educated".'

I paused. Millie seemed to pull herself together, and when she spoke her tone was cold and resentful—and I remember being pleased at these signs of a proper pride in the defence of her friends.

'Teddie isn't a bit like that, miss,' she said quietly. 'I'm downright surprised you should think it of her. And neither is Ron. A bit too much the other way, if anything. Why, I can't get Teddie to take a thing from me, hardly, for my Eric. Get something out of you! Teddie's been brought up proper, and she went to a good school, too, and . . . and . . . young people, they aren't *like* that, nowadays, miss. They get ever so well paid, they don't want anything, nowadays, from us older ones, they'd sooner make their own way. I'm surprised, miss, *you* should think that of anyone. It's . . . it's not like you.' She looked straight at me, with her usually mild eyes full of a kind of disappointment.

'You always think the best of everyone—in a way,' she went on. 'Except me. Not me.' And then, of course, she began to cry. 'Never a good word for me, you haven't got,' she sobbed, 'and never have had.'

I sat in the grimy, ill-lit carriage as it swayed along below the brown old suburban houses where the dull evening was coming down, feeling ashamed.

But happier, too.

It was true, then; this young family liked me for myself. Even the boy had rested contentedly in my arms. I remember the warmth that crept up in me, as if my cold heart had unexpectedly encountered the glow of some beautiful wood fire. They liked me. I turned briskly to the blubbering Millie.

'Now you know that's not true . . . never a good word for you. What nonsense. Why, how should I get on without you?' I patted her hand, which she jerked away. 'We've known one another fifty years—'

I broke off, disturbed by the memory of a certain Victorian comic song, which I hoped had not also occurred to Millie, and she nodded, sobbing, 'Nearer fifty-five, miss,' which I took for an indication that she was beginning to feel better.

'You ought to know me by now,' I conceded, feeling about in my handbag. 'My bark is worse than my bite.'

'But you *can* bite, miss,' she said in her mildest voice, looking at me over the edge of her sodden handkerchief.

I had to laugh, and a smile crept over her face while she mopped at her eyes.

'Now have one of these,' I said, getting out my case full of the strong French cigarettes which Frances' bad example had lured me into becoming addicted to during our drive across France, and holding it out to her, 'it'll soothe your nerves.'

'Oh, I couldn't, miss,' she said automatically.

'Nonsense, you often enjoy a cigarette in the kitchen, don't you? Come along, then.' I shook the case slightly at her, modelling my bullying upon that of Mrs. Gelfors.

'All right, then, thank you, miss. I will if you will too,' and she mincingly helped herself.

So we sat and soaked ourselves in rank French tobacco while the heavy London evening went past, almost silently except for the old-fashioned rattling of the wheels. Once Millie sighed and I heard her mutter something about 'wishing I'd never got mixed up in it—' which I took to mean that she regretted encouraging my acquaintanceship with the young Parkers.

I did not regret it, now.

CHAPTER 25

THAT year, I had been more conscious than ever before of what I had thought of for years as 'the tempting note' in summer, the suggestion that each long day gives of moving onwards to some superb climax that never comes. Edward used sometimes to talk to me about 'the tempting note'; this year, the suggestion of promise was so persistent that I could hardly believe it when the calendar said October 1st, and the newspapers began bellowing about Christmas shopping, and summer had done nothing but— be summer.

One morning I answered the telephone because Millie was out, and heard the well-known, not unpleasant American intonations in the voice of Frances. She had arrived that morning, and was staying at that hotel whose colossal alien shape I could see down in the valley from the window of my back drawing-room.

'Oh, I'm not trekking up there,' she retorted, in answer to my invitation, 'you come down here and we'll lunch and do a movie— if there's anything worth doing?'

I suggested a new musical which had been highly praised by *The Times*. (I keep my respect for their critical opinions, and, having learned to read between their critical lines, so to speak, am often thus preserved from wasting money on a depressing piece of rubbish in a theatre, or starting to read some tedious and disgusting book.)

'Oh, God, not a *musical*,' exploded Frances. 'Aren't there any French films on?'

I should have remembered that, with her frivolity, Frances combined a most dismal taste in the arts.

'Plenty,' I said, trying not to even think of the name of that creature Bunuel, lest I should telepath it to her five miles away.

'Then come on down—how's things?—no, you can tell me later. This place is a hole. 'Bye.'

I spent much of the next fortnight at the hole, otherwise her comfortable and well-run hotel, and I spent a great deal of money, too, on lunches and theatres and cinemas, alcohol and new clothes—such nonsense, but I enjoyed the latter—while Frances encouraged me, saying that I 'might go old all of a sudden' and have to spend it all on geriatric specialists and tablets.

Off by eleven in the morning, never in bed before midnight, I did notice vaguely that Millie was not looking well, but I was so over-occupied, and so rather disagreeably, but also irresistibly, rushed, that I could not find the time to think about her, or to ask her what was the matter.

The truth was that Frances retained her witch's spell; she could take me out of myself and make of me, for a short time at least, another being. There was affection and gratitude on my side now, as well, but the witchery remained.

Behind her unflagging, bitterish gaiety she was, I knew, a tormented creature. Occasionally, too, she hinted at unbecoming attractions to men years younger than herself, which naturally came to nothing, and which scorched her vanity. She suffered agonies, I am sure, from growing old. And I could do nothing to help her.

The rattling, wasteful fortnight drew to a close. She had bought her clothes for the winter ('cheaper here than in Paris'), and had had some attention paid to her teeth by the dentist who had looked after them since she was fifteen, and now it was the last evening before she flew back, and we were dining at her hotel.

'You know that song of Cole Porter's; "I get a kick out of you",' she said abruptly, between two bolted mouthfuls of unfattening salad, 'it's like that with you and me. You're a prig, and we don't agree about a thing, do we? . . . well, you know we don't . . . and you're dreary. Snow-Woman. But *somehow*, we've managed to have fun.' Her tone was not questioning; it stated a fact.

'What I've enjoyed most is laughing. No-one says things quite like you, or ever has, or ever will,' I said, continuing to eat my creamy Italian pasta with perhaps a slight additional sedateness; I was going to miss her. 'I almost never laugh, usually, when Millie and I are alone.'

'Now that I *can* believe. Quite well,' said Frances. '. . . did you ever see any more of that girl who pupped the baby on Great-Aunt D.'s sofa?'

'Oh, yes. She's made great friends with Millie, and she's been to tea with us, and I've been to tea there. They've quite . . . er . . . taken me up. What amuses you?' I added, as her painted, deep-scored face broke up into laughter.

'Oh . . .' She stared round the large, softly-lit room for a moment. '. . . I don't know. It's just funny, that's all . . . mind you call me up if anything ever happens there. Reverse the charge . . . it'll be worth it.'

'Why should anything happen? The Parkers are all young and strong . . . and why on earth should *you* want to know, at considerable expense, if anything happens to them?'

'Haven't you been reading your old *Times*? There's trouble at t'mill, lass.'

'Which mill?' I asked patiently.

'Not a real one, dolt . . . the firm where Ron works. I suppose *The Times* has condescended to notice it.'

'I haven't read *The Times* for a fortnight—I'd sooner not read it at all than skim through it—and you know I haven't been in bed before midnight . . . what trouble?'

'Oh, God—I don't know, just trouble . . .'

She was looking at me, so oddly, out of ancient, sparkling eyes.

'How do you come to know anything about it?' I persisted, 'and how do you know his name is Ron? I thought you never read the papers.'

'Oh, I was glancing through some rag yesterday under the dryer . . . the other chaps have sent him to Coventry, for the last week.'

'I do wonder about the derivation of that,' I said thoughtfully, 'Why Coventry?'

'No-one but a frozen old Snow-Woman,' burst out Frances, dashing down her fork, 'would think about derivations when someone's being *crucified*. You're a psychopath, Maude, that's what you are,' she announced with more than usual drama.

'I don't think I really am, you know . . . but I'm sorry if they're in trouble; I'll ask Millie about it tonight,' I said. 'And I still think it's odd, your knowing.'

Frances was looking calmer now, and the next thing I heard was,

'*Look* at that *coat*. Gamages's must have had another sale,' and we began to discuss, not kindly, I fear, the garment which had just come into the room on the back of a lady who should neither have bought nor worn it.

Poor Frances. She had brandy sent up to her room, and there we sat until nearly midnight while she became steadily drunker and more bitter in her talk. I listened, unaffected by the brandy (I have always possessed an excellent head), and I tried to say what I could to comfort her, expecting at every second to have her turn on me.

We had become so much closer in the last two weeks that I would have been capable of venturing to try and comfort her with talk of God—but that I had no conviction with which to do it. For half a century, where there should have been the sense of God within me, there had been only bitterness and resentful pain.

At last, talking quietly and with dry eyes, she told me that I was her only friend now; she had quarrelled with everyone who hadn't died, and her daughter hated her and her grandson wouldn't come near her. I didn't know *what* to say. I could not get out any words.

She did, at last, look at her wrist-watch and say that I must go home, and I got up, with some guilty relief (poor, poor Frances) and began to get ready.

She leant back in her chair beside the coppery face of the heater, with the slight folds of a minimal red chiffon dress pulled up well beyond her knees and her white hair sweeping back in its lacquered, shaped, trained elegance, and backed by a flat bow of red velvet. She watched me, while she slowly turned the balloon glass round and round between her fingers.

'The Snow-Woman's beginning to melt,' she said suddenly, in a tone so different from that of earlier in the evening that I almost glanced at her. But I was concentrating upon fastening the clasp of a fur hood which always had been difficult.

'Isn't she?' Frances insisted, not jeeringly, not loudly. I had never, in all our years together and apart, heard affection in her voice, but I heard it then.

'I think so—a little,' I answered, and then I did look at her. 'I do feel—different. It's just these last few months.'

'Since Belair?'

I nodded.

'And have you got a new pin for that brooch yet?'

'It's odd you should ask me, because—Frances! The first time I nursed the Parker baby, I took that brooch off first, before I took him on my lap, in case it should scratch him . . . but how extraordinary! You said something about it months back, in the summer, before I'd even seen him . . .'

She nodded, still looking at me, still turning the brandy glass. The hot, bright room was silent.

'Did Lionel tell you about the Parkers? And did you imagine I might perhaps get fond of the little boy?' As I spoke, I felt again the warm, soft weight against my breast.

'Something like that, I guess.'

She got up with a little difficulty from her chair, and pulled down the dress suitable for an eighteen-year-old, and came across the room to me—and put both hands on my shoulders. 'Well . . . *ciao* for now . . . you won't believe it, but it would have been hell over here without my dreary old Snow-Woman,' she said.

'Until next May,' I said, 'we'll meet then. Good-night, dear Frances, take care of yourself.'

'So likely,' she said. And then we kissed lightly, and so we parted, and I never saw her again.

CHAPTER 26

ALLOWING myself an extra half-hour in bed on the following morning, after my dissipations, I was yet breakfasting by a quarter to nine. I noticed that Millie still looked worried and ill, and after I had finished I went through to the kitchen.

She was standing with her back to me, facing the sink and staring down into it, with her arms hanging at her sides, motionless.

'Millie,' I said gently.

She turned quickly. 'Oh, miss—I didn't hear you—I was just coming—'

'It's all right. I came to ask you if anything's the matter? You don't look well, to me.'

She darted to the table—in a movement of startling violence compared with her former stillness—and snatched up a newspaper, held it out, thrust it at me.

'It's Ron, miss. Missing. Never turned up for work yesterday—Oh, God, please, please let it be all right,' and she shook her head dazedly with both fists clenched against her cheeks.

The inch-tall headlines said, '"Coventry" Man Still Missing'. Then, in slightly smaller type beneath—'I'm Not Worrying. Ronnie Can Take Care of Himself', and as I read that I could hear the words being said aloud, in a young voice that rang with hard confidence.

'Ronald Parker, 21, the boy who stood out against his Union and three hundred of his mates and refused to pay a percentage of his overtime earnings to the shop fund, is still not at work in the big, light factory at Rothbury this morning.

At his neat little home with its gay front garden, near the Works, Mrs. Edna Parker, 19, said, 'I'm not worrying. Ronnie can take care of himself. I've stuck by him all through this and I'll go on sticking. I think sending him to Coventry was a dirty thing to do, un-British and cowardly.' Mrs. Parker said that she would wait until this evening for news before informing the police.'

There followed a short summary of the events leading up to his disappearance; apparently he had not been home for twenty-four hours.

I have always found the details of industrial life so tedious that I have never bothered to master their vocabulary, but I managed to gather, in spite of poor Millie now crying loudly and distractingly beside me, that a sum, based on overtime earnings, had been demanded from a number of the men at Glovers by their Union, as a contribution to a shop fund; that they had refused to pay it and been fined by the shop stewards; that a number had still at first refused to pay but had afterwards agreed to do so on being threatened with expulsion from the Union, and that Ronald Parker alone had held out.

This had all started some two weeks ago, just at the time that Frances had arrived in England and swept me up into a fortnight of ceaseless expensive activity.

The Union had expelled him, and the rest of the men had unanimously voted among themselves to send him to Coventry. He had continued to go to work.

I let the paper fall on to the table and put my arm round Millie and held her gently.

'Don't cry, my dear. This is all news to me—I haven't seen a paper for more than a week—you should have told me, Millie . . . Would you like to go over and see Teddie? I could get a car for you—'

'Oh, no—no, thank you all the same, miss—it's kind of you, but I've written and written—four letters and a card I've sent, and not a line . . . I'm nearly out of my mind with it . . . and my little Eric . . .'

She sank into a chair by the table and bowed her face down on her arms. It was a dull morning; the kitchen, always dim, was in a half-dusk. I went over and switched the lights on; there was no point in being more depressing than we need.

'You see . . . miss . . .' she was muttering, with her face still hidden so that I could hardly hear, 'there's something else . . . it's been on my mind *something fearful*, 'specially since all this happened . . . I don't know why some people have to suffer so . . . losing . . . losing . . . and then my Dusty . . . it isn't fair . . . it isn't *fair*.' She sobbed again.

I stood beside her, keeping my hand on her shoulder and occasionally moving it in a gentle stroking.

'I'm afraid there's nothing to do but wait, Millie. We'll hear the news at one, and there may be something then. Meanwhile, I really think the best thing is for us to get on with our work . . . I haven't touched the piano for a fortnight. It will be best for us both.' I paused, and steadied my voice.

'You know, lately, I've thought that if I'd had some kind of work that I *had* to do, when . . . when my brothers were killed, I should never have . . . got into the state I did . . .'

'Yes, miss.' She slowly lifted her face from her arms and began wiping her eyes. She looked up at me. 'You . . . I've often thought, miss, how dreadfully sad it was . . . none of them marrying.'

'Yes,' I said. 'Yes, it was sad. Well, now I'm going to practise . . . come in and have a word with me whenever you feel you can't bear it, Millie.'

'Thank you, miss,' she said subduedly. But it was plain that the outburst had relieved her. I went out of the kitchen, leaving her quietly settling to her work.

Thank God—or something—I was thinking as I salt down at the piano, I'm able to hear those sort of remarks now—about their not marrying, about the 'sadness'—without the former inward blaze of resentful agony. I suppose I'm beginning to get really old. Poor young creatures. (But this time I was thinking of the Parkers.)

I concentrated upon a peculiarly hideous sheet of 'music' that had been sent to me by an intellectual acquaintance who had decided that my taste needed widening. With it had come a note, explaining that the piece was not meant to be music in the, and my, former sense. It was 'music' in inverted commas; a temporary use of the old name until a new one evolved.

Presently I actually became interested in trying to link up the isolated chords and single notes with appropriate themes, and making some kind of a shape. It sounded, if anything, worse than in its original 'form', and I was just about to crumple up the sheet (and the black patterns made by the charmingly-shaped notes were still as pretty as ever!) when Millie came in to say that Mrs. Halliwell was on the phone and would like to speak to me.

It was easy to guess what about.

'*Well*, dear, for a retiring maiden lady you *do* manage to get yourself mixed up with what's going on, don't you? First all that hoo-ha at Belair, and now your Teddie's boy . . . I suppose you hadn't had any private tip-off where he is?'

'No, I haven't, unfortunately. Millie is very worried and unhappy—'

'And I s'pose *you* think it's all a shocking bore, as you usually do when anyone gets into a jam?'

'I'm worried too, Tessa, nearly as worried as Millie. I've grown fond of them in the last few months.'

'Wonders will never cease!'

'Yes, I think one might call it wonderful . . . I didn't expect it.'

'It's about time,' Tessa snapped; I think she felt irritated because she could not, after my confession, fly out at me for coldness, peculiarity, inhumanity and so on.

'Do you think he's walked out on her?' the coarse, warm voice went on.

'I should think nothing is less likely . . . Tessa, I am practising, and I think I'd better get back to it. Forgive me, but it takes my mind off the worry . . . I really *am* worried. I will try to telephone you later, if there's any news. Good-bye, for now,' and I rang off before she could protest.

I was becoming increasingly anxious. A weight of unease hung over me, brooding and dark. I could feel it like a load; the *heavy heart* of the Bible and the old novels, arising not so much from the fact of the boy's absence from home and work, as from those 'pressures', as the moderns call them, that I had suspected were hidden within the privacy of his marriage.

I remembered my earliest contacts with the young pair, and Lionel's voice saying, 'No harm in him and not much else either,' and 'About a third of her weight. That's the trouble.'

I judged Ronald to be gentle and slow-paced rather than weak. But that he was 'about a third of her weight' I *did* believe; it was plain to see; and from this brute fact my uneasiness was writhing up.

The one o'clock news had only a few sentences about there being still no news of him. Millie could eat nothing, and I sat with her, because she was unable to stop crying. In the midst of my apprehension and the kind of inward darkness that had slowly invaded my spirit, I tried—I did try with all my heart—to do my best. I remained with her in her little sitting-room, all that afternoon.

But it was to get worse, the time of waiting. The day had been singularly bright, with a soft autumnal air and long misty beams from the sun . . . Light lingered in rose and grey, the poplars in the garden gleamed rusty gold in the last glow. I wondered if Millie would go to bed or if I should have to sit up with her all night.

I must confess that once or twice I wondered at the extremity of her anxiety: what fathomless depths of affection, what torrents and leaping springs of love she must have been dowered with, to feel so much for a young pair and a baby she had known for less than a year? And how she must have been starved of an outlet for her riches during all these years with me. Well, I had been starved for longer . . . Yes, it was riches.

There was no news at six or at ten and none in our evening paper, but late that night, sitting side by side at the table in her stuffy little room, we heard on Millie's television that Mrs. Parker had called in the police and a search was going on—dogs, frog-men, groups of police with walkie-talkies and lights, the routine to which we of the twentieth century have grown accustomed.

They were covering the miles of still open marshy land left unbuilt on near Rothbury; where Ronald's father had once worked an allotment; Ronald used to play there as a little boy, and had always liked to walk with the family dog over the blackened mead-ows. His father had suggested that a search should be made there.

Through the mild, damp October night, now dark with thick cloud, they were moving; while the ghouls in their cars drove up the nearest road, to get as close as they could in the hope of seeing a dead body.

I sat there; imagining the slow advance of the searchers, the voices calling to one another through the darkness, the stealthy ripple and slide of the great river along its shores of mud that gleamed greasily where the turning lights struck, and the sigh-ing wind going through the rushes and past the ruined huts of abandoned allotments.

The corpse-viewers did not have long to wait for their treat. In the small hours he was found near the hut that had belonged to his father, lying in the midst of the largest expanse of reeds.

Twisting miniature paths ran through it, down which a dog and a boy would have liked to run; and there was so much litter scattered about that the man who found him had at first taken his white face, among the dark reeds, for yet another crumpled carton, and had not troubled to go nearer.

CHAPTER 27

IT WAS another bright day. I had been to bed for a few hours and had gently compelled Millie to do the same. She was quiet, now, dressed and sitting by the table sipping the tea she had made for us both. I felt dreadfully sad, and exhausted as well: it was more than forty years since I had tried, in my crippled way, to give out love and comfort to anyone as I had tried to give them to Millie last night and that morning; and in those years, of course, I had grown old, and more frozen into my snow-tower.

'Twenty-one,' she said at last, almost dreamily, staring out into the bright, soft morning through the kitchen window. 'It's young, isn't it, miss? My . . . my boy was the same age, and . . . and there was Mr. Edward . . . but not so young as Ronnie. It'll seem funny without him, miss. I felt . . . he was like another son, in some ways . . . . I always have got on with young lads, (since I got old, I mean, of course). It was having one of my own, I s'pose.' She sipped her tea again.

'I didn't know your child was grown up, Millie,' I said, surprised, 'I—we—always took it for granted, I don't know why, that—your boy—died as a baby.'

'Oh, no, my . . . my boy was twenty-one, miss. In the regular Army. The Middlesex Regiment. Killed at Dunkirk . . . George was.'

'I am so dreadfully—' I broke off. What *had* we, my parents and I, been made of, that we had never heard this before? But I knew well enough what *I* had been made of: myself. I had taken it for granted that, because *I* would not have wanted questions, however kind, Millie would not want them either.

'He was a fine boy,' she said, very softly, so softly that I could hardly hear the words. 'I was that proud of him. A lieutenant, he was. Commissioned in January 1940.'

'I wish I had known all this before, Millie dear.'

'Well, you never asked nothing, miss, and I thought you wasn't interested, like.'

She spoke in the same unusually soft, exhausted voice, sitting with one cheek supported in her hand, and leaning forward looking down at the table. A sunray was glittering in the bright silver and ashy gold of her hair.

'Married young, George did. Me and his Betty got on ever so well. And then she died too, miss, not long after having a little girl.'

'Then you're a grandmother, Millie! And I never knew! But—where is the little girl now? Surely—nothing happened—?'

'Oh, no, miss.' She lifted heavy eyes to my face. 'That's Teddie, the little girl. I never told you because I thought you . . . wouldn't like it, somehow.'

'Teddie! That explains everything—but, Millie dear, that really was rather silly, not telling me because you were afraid I "mightn't like it". I'm so glad, I'm delighted for you, even with this dreadful thing having happened—it's lovely for you to have a grand-daughter, and now that splendid little boy.'

I reached out to her across the table—kept white and well-scrubbed by the hand that I remembered, unwrinkled but already rough with work, at seventeen—and took it in my own, where Edward's signet gleamed.

'I always was silly, I s'pose,' she said with a faint smile, not looking up. There was a silence. The sun shone into the room with the effect of a third person being there, so brilliant and warm was it. I could hear a robin singing in the garden. Outside our house the world was streaming off to the day's work, brutally going ahead with living. All that makes the world real to you has gone, and people go ahead with getting the day started . . . how many millions of times has that thought gone out from someone's heart, I wonder?

'Millie, would you like to have Teddie and the little boy to stay here? She might be glad to get away from the fuss—there are bound to be reporters, at first, and the neighbours . . . would you like me to get Mr. Jones to take you down in the car, and you can bring her back with you?'

'Oh, I don't know, miss,' she answered dully, 'won't it upset you, the noise and that?'

'Of course not . . . and if I do find it a little strange at first I shall get used to it.' My heart was already sinking. I swore at it.

'It might be nice . . . I could put my Eric to bed . . . bath him.'

'Yes, well, that's settled. I'll go and telephone Mr. Jones,' I said briskly. 'If he's booked, we'll try for a minicab. You get your things on.'

I got up, feeling the effort that it was to move. The robin's crystal song seemed to blend with the sunlight, as if they were one presence, unearthly, yet sweet and warm, like a comforting spirit pouring itself into the room . . . I was over-tired I suppose.

Mr. Jones was free, and, I think, a little interested at being drawn into 'a case in the papers', though showing the mingled kindness and reserve to be expected from a sober family man and a veteran of the last war.

'That's all right,' I said, coming back into the kitchen. '. . . They can have the big front bedroom.'

'Mr. Jock's room!' came Millie's voice, half-scandalized, from her own little dark bedroom.

'It's sunny. I'll have it all ready when you come back. Can you just telephone to let me know if they're coming?'

'Yes, miss.' Millie emerged in her grey coat and with the grey and gold scarf I had given her for her last birthday arranged round her white face. She did, however, look a little brighter.

'You can't think, miss, how I'm longing and longing to see my Eric . . . I do keep it all done once a week, miss.'

'Yes, I know, Millie. And I can think how you're longing to see him. He's—the most comforting thing I can think of, at the moment.' (And he'll give you plenty to do and then you'll be all right, I thought.)

'I only hope Teddie won't be in one of her moods,' Millie murmured, standing at the door.

'Oh, well . . . we must make . . . you know her better than I do,' was all I thought it best to say. I was thinking that such natures as I judged Edna's to be could react quite incalculably to sudden shattering grief: she might even have run away. She had once before. 'Poor child. Give her my love, and say I do hope they'll come. There's Mr. Jones.'

I ushered Millie gently but decisively out into the hall at the sound of a long well-bred snore on the hooter (this unprecedented signal having been arranged between Mr. Jones and myself in order that not a second of time might be lost).

Mr. Jones was looking concernedly up at the house, as if our sorrow would be visibly stamped upon it. He got out and said good-morning, and helped Millie carefully into the big saloon and arranged the rug over her knees. I heard her murmur something about 'might be the Queen', and then she said,

'Thank you ever so, miss, I'll phone as soon as I can, but what phones there is *down there'*—she spoke as if Rothbury were Hell—'is all broken by them vandals.'

'That's all right . . . bless you, dear. Good-bye.'

They drove away, and I turned back to the house, but not before I had been seen by that Mr. Grayshott who lives at the bottom of my back garden, and who, no doubt, says that I live at the bottom of his. He was on his way to the shops with a small bag and had his tiresome little dog, Meggy, with him as usual.

'Hullo, hullo, what's this—your housekeeper not leaving, I hope?' he cried hopefully. He has long envied me Millie; no housekeeper can put up with him for long, bachelor and rich as he is.

'No. She has gone to fetch her grand-daughter and great-grandson to stay with us for a while. The girl's husband has just committed suicide,' I replied, thinking it as well to tell him enough to give him facts to gossip about; he would gossip anyway. 'Will you ask Meggy to come out of the garden, please, she is scratching up my dwarf dahlias.'

'Dam' good of you, I must say,' cried Mr. Grayshott, ignoring, for which I was thankful, the suicide, 'brats making a mess all over the place . . . noise . . . no, *I* could never stand it.'

'I expect there will be trying moments,' I said, 'but I am fond of the little boy and . . .'

'Dam' good of you, dam' good,' was all Mr. Grayshott repeated, as he made to hasten away in search of fillet steak, 'Meggy, come here, girl, leave Miss Barrington's flowers alone.'

Meggy, of course, took no more notice than of the prevailing wind, and had to be coaxed out of the clump ('never lay a hand on a dog') and offered steakies before she reluctantly emerged, with her black snout all over earth and bits of my dahlia petals.

'She's in splendid condition,' confided my neighbour over his shoulder as the pair made off. 'Seven, but you'd think she was two. It's feedin' that does it.'

Reflecting that Meggy's splendid condition was hardly good news for those of us in the village who enjoyed our gardens, I went back into the house. A year ago, even six months ago, I would not have thus confided in Mr. Grayshott and horrid Meggy. The Snow-Woman, as Frances had said, was indeed melting.

Of course, Jock's room had not remained absolutely as he left it after his last leave; the furniture had been re-arranged.

My mother had a theory that deliberate cultivation of the memory of the dead was sentimental and false, and she may have been right. (In my case, I had had no choice; their memory had become my life.) This had not meant that she had not sorrowed dreadfully for her sons; only that her sorrow had taken a shape different from mine.

So I felt the familiar hopeless pang as I entered, and began pulling off dust-sheets and wiping a duster over polished wood, but it had little to do with what I saw around me. The sunlight poured in, the October wind blew out the curtains. I was busy for an hour, perhaps, with clean sheets and the vacuum-cleaner, and cosmea and tobacco flowers from the garden, and then I lit the gas heater (a modern one, installed there only a year ago) and went downstairs. The room, I thought, looked comfortable and welcoming. Later on, the baby boy might like Jock's series of prints of comic dogs that ran round the walls, which Lionel had always called 'profoundly un-funny'.

Later on? I had not yet thought of any time-limit to their stay.

The telephone bell rang, startling in the sunlit quiet.

'Oh, miss,' said Millie's voice, 'they're coming . . . Mr. Jones just managed to find a place to park, and I've found a phone box where them vandals have been, only—'

'How is Teddie?' I asked quickly.

Millie lowered her voice. 'Very quiet, miss. Seems stunned-like. There was one of those reporters there when I come, said he was from a local paper and you should have heard what Teddie said about Ron's mates behaving so nasty to him—fairly let herself go, she did . . . I . . . I'll be that glad to be home, miss, and Teddie says I'm to thank you . . . about an hour, we'll be, Mr. Jones says . . . my Eric's lovely, miss, but I think he wonders where his daddy's got to . . .'

'All right, then, Millie. Everything's ready, I'm looking forward to seeing you all. Tell Teddie. Be sure to tell her. Good-bye.'

I replaced the receiver.

The house was looking unusually beautiful, to me, that morning. The colours of the old Eastern carpets glowed like dim gems in the sunlight, and the spines of my books were rich-tinted and warm. Every object in view had its load of memories, for me, like a fringe of silvery, invisible moss.

CHAPTER 28

IT WAS nearly twelve o'clock: I purposely did nothing ahead about our luncheon, because I knew that it would be better for Millie if she could at once set about that herself. The sun was still soft and bright and the birds sang in my poplars almost as if it were still summer, and I sat there and thought and thought of Ronnie Parker, and wondered how those strong opposing forces, his wife and his workmates, had managed, between them to make him *do it*. I wondered, at last, if there were some other reason as well.

I did just wonder.

My favourite place to sit does not look out over the road, and I was sitting by the window of the larger drawing-room, which does.

I had time, before they arrived, to realize what I had 'let myself in for'; and I confess that I had to swear at my sinking heart a good many times before it decided to accept the situation. If I hadn't had a strong feeling of happiness at the thought of seeing the little boy in his bath, and asleep in Jock's room—almost as if he had been Jock's son—I would have been dismayed indeed.

Ah! there was the car. I stood up; my first sight had been of something white as chalk at the window; Edna's stone face. Oh, what can I do to help, was my thought as I went through to the hall and experience answered, nothing. And one doesn't believe it when they say 'Time will help', and sometimes time doesn't.

Mr. Jones was helping Millie out, Mr. Jones was helping Edna with suitcases and a kind of woven affair with handles called, I know now, a carrycot or Moses basket. Edna looked noticeably tall and well-dressed, in a pale green fitted coat with buttons of gilt; she suggested a girl soldier. Millie had been crying.

I went down the path to meet them and swung back my tall iron gate. Edna came up rather quickly, looking as it were *through* me and at something beyond, and put out her hand, and I took it, and then she bent her tall head and kissed my cheek. I was so surprised and touched that tears rushed to my eyes, and for a second I could not speak.

'Thank you for having us; it's very kind; I'm afraid the papers may be a bit of a nuisance—but that won't last long,' she said, 'about a couple of days, I should think.' Her voice was quiet, but her tone, on the last words, was as if she had spat.

I nodded, and said, 'Excuse me, my dear—' and, smiling at Millie and taking a peep at the boy asleep in her arms, I went past her to Mr. Jones, who was setting a high-chair on the pavement. The pram was fastened to the car's roof.

'You've been so kind, Mr. Jones,' I said as I was paying him, 'you aren't used to your car being used as a van, I'm sorry.'

'I was glad to be of any help, madam, and there's no harm done. Thank you . . . I'll just get the pram off the top and I'll be off.'

But he wheeled the pram up the path and took the carrycot and the cases up to Jock's—their—room, before he did go off.

Edna seemed to see nothing; the one blind glance at the bedroom which she flung around her was merely courteous.

'Nice and sunny . . .' she said, then turned to me. 'I'll have to be off at once, I'm afraid, there's a lot to see to down there . . . they've . . . got . . . there'll have to . . . be an inquest. Granny can see to Eric, can't you, love?' coldly, to Millie.

Millie had told her, then.

Millie nodded vehemently, but kept her eyes down, rocking Eric gently to and fro.

'I may be late,' Teddie said, turning at the door, 'but if I'm going to be, I'll call you.' She almost ran down the stairs and out of the house.

Millie looked up as the front door slammed.

'Please excuse her, miss. She . . . it's been so awful . . . there was three of his mates' wives come round to—to apologize, like, first thing this morning, and she wouldn't see them.'

Apologize!

'I understand perfectly, Millie, and don't worry. I don't suppose she has had any lunch, but we mustn't fuss . . . now shall I hold Eric, or watch him, while you get ours? Or would you like me to try?'

Millie looked slightly shocked. 'Oh, no—miss—I know what we've got, and I can manage. You don't have to *watch* him while he's asleep, miss, we'll just lay him in the carrycot and leave the door ajar . . . oh, I do know we're out of potatoes . . . I'll just run round . . .'

I thought it would be good for her to just run round.

I did not practise, partly because I was too disturbed, and partly because I did not know whether the sounds, however distant, might not awaken Eric.

Before she slipped out, Millie came in again to speak to me.

'I do hope you'll excuse Teddie making rather free, miss . . . you see . . . she's so headstrong . . . and it's been such a shock . . .'

'It's all *right*, Millie, don't distress yourself. She's behaving as if she were a young cousin or a niece of mine . . . it's quite the easiest way . . . now run along, dear.'

She gave me the oddest imploring glance, and went.

In truth, Edna's absolute assurance had struck me. Not struck me as peculiar or offensive, but just struck me. I took up *The Times*, but after ten minutes with it I ceased to study a detailed account of the progress made in the law relating to abortion over the last century, with which the editor of their Women's Page had seen fit to brace her surely already braced readers, and crept upstairs to discover whether the complete silence in Eric's room had any sinister import.

There Millie caught me, having returned and crept upstairs herself. We looked at each other, and then we both silently laughed.

'I thought you said we needn't watch,' I whispered.

'Well, we needn't, miss . . . but the truth is I just come up to have a peep . . . isn't he lovely . . . I could eat him!'

She gazed down at the span-wide face turned sideways into the pillow; pale gold, with sweeping ray-like lashes, and an absurd nose which might turn into any shape.

'I . . . I know what you mean,' I said at last. And then the telephone bell rang, making me start violently.

'Not like you, jumping, miss,' said Millie, '. . . it's the shock . . . shall I answer it, miss?'

'Yes, please; if it should be a newspaper, I'll come.'

It was a newspaper; an evening one. They wanted to know what Miss Barrington thought of his fellow-workers' action in sending Ronald Parker to Coventry, and very cleverly put their questions were, as cleverly as any trained barrister could have put them in court. But the young man's skill was wasted. It was the voice of a gentleman but the tone was not.

I made no attempt to conceal what I felt but clearly repeated Edna's own words:

'Cowardly and un-English. I am in complete agreement with Mrs. Parker.'

He tried to get me to say more, seeing, I imagine, an eminently printable 'story' with a class-war angle; asked me if I had private means and owned my house, and what I thought of The Beatles, drug-taking and so on; he also asked my age. I told him that he must pursue his enquiries elsewhere, and rang off.

'Teddie told those reporters this morning, miss, that she was going to stay with her granny. Said I was your housekeeper, miss,' Millie said timidly when I had toiled upstairs again. Eric had awakened.

'That was sensible; if she had made a mystery out of it that would only have caused more fuss . . . why is he crying?'

'Wants his dinner, miss . . . it's all right . . . he's taken to the bottle, thank God . . . Teddie's milk went when that wicked Coventry business started; she had to put him on to Cow and Gate at once.'

I said nothing; I was feeling quite ill with suppressed anger.

Millie and I got our lunch at two, having spent two hours in preparing Eric's and then—I am afraid I must use the word—gloating over him while he drank it. Millie held him.

'Mustn't let Teddie know we took all this time,' she confided, wiping his milky chin. 'She wouldn't like it . . . come on then, windies up.'

I was then given a short lesson, with examples, about the important part played by the bringing up of surplus air from the child's stomach; the pain and restlessness it could cause when retarded; and the various devices used and positions assumed to bring about the desired result.

It was a new world, and I found it fascinating. I know that sounds laughable, but it must be remembered that, for the first time in my life, my mother-instinct was being fed. I know now that, had it ever been developed, it would have been very strong—perhaps too strong. And I was under the spell, too, of the red gold head and the clear, staring slate-blue eyes, and the occasional soft, low sounds of content he made, and his warmth.

Millie was neither patronizing nor did she lay down the law. We enjoyed the boy together, and I remember thinking, as she sat with him spread out reclining on her lap, that she looked happier than I had seen her look since she was seventeen; the ghost of her prettiness had glowed into life again, under the crown of her thick silver-gold hair.

The rest of the day passed quietly. Tessa telephoned me to say that a short interview with me had appeared on the front page of her evening paper, describing me as a typical unmarried English gentlewoman of the old school, in her early seventies.

'All that's as snide as it can be, of course,' said Tessa. 'Nowadays gentlewomen are *out*, and you might as well be under your cosy little six feet as in your early seventies. The old school isn't exactly a riot, either. Of course, I know there are some old crabs about, but—'

'Thank you,' I said.

'Don't be touchy, dear. I only thought you ought to *know* about it. What I was going to say was—it's damned clever, because they haven't said a word that isn't true—they've only played up everything that people just don't go for nowadays. *Reading between the lines.* That's what it is. *I* think there's a lot to be said for the old school myself.'

I was wondering whether Tessa thought of herself as one of its pupils.

'And I don't see,' she went on, warming, 'how he could say you were *typical*. He didn't see you, did he? No, I thought not . . . you might easily be eight feet high with bright purple hair . . . how are things going?'

I said that they were going . . . as they were going, and added that she must come round soon and see the child, and rang off. I was beginning to wonder how and where Edna was.

She did not telephone. She returned about midnight, still terribly white, and still with that odd, absent manner; I came into the kitchen, where Millie was trying to make her drink something hot. She was standing by the table.

'I don't want it, love, don't fuss . . . oh . . . good-evening,' to me, 'I'm afraid I'm very late—that is, it will seem late to you.' A ghostly smile. 'I've been with Ronnie's father. We . . . made each other worse, I think. About . . . those bastards. I had to calm him down, in the end, I don't want *him* killed in some punch-up as well . . . I don't *want* it!' turning savagely on Millie, who was hovering with a cup. 'Can't you make her leave me alone?' to me, almost imploringly.

'I could try, but I think she's right,' I said. 'I expect you've had nothing all day.'

'I didn't want to be sick. I feel sick all the time, just on the edge of being . . .'

'That's partly hunger. Of course, at your age you can go without food for as long as two or even three days, without serious results, but you'll have a lot of very painful things to see to, and if you're starving, they'll seem worse. You'd better have something. Here,' I took the cup from Millie, 'and I'll cut some bread and butter.'

I held it out to her. She hesitated for a moment, then suddenly sat down at the table, slumping, as if completely exhausted.

'All right,' she said steadily, 'Sorry, Millie, love,' and took the cup and sipped at it.

'Has Eric been all right?' she asked in a moment, when she had eaten a little, looking up at us both as it, for the first time, she saw us.

We assured her that he had been as good as gold, Millie adding that she had given him his ten o'clock feed. Edna nodded. Then she said:

'I've given up the lease of the house and I'm going to get rid of our stuff . . . a lot of it's on hire purchase, I'll have to see about that, of course . . . I'll go to bed, I think. Would . . . is it all right if I have a bath?' to me.

'Of course.' (I usually have my bath at night, and I was not sure whether the tank would run to two).

'Thank you. You've been very kind,' she said carelessly, and, as she turned away, 'Good-night. I'll be up in the morning to give you a hand, love,' to Millie. She went out of the room, dragging off her coat as she went.

'Very free, she makes,' observed Millie, as if to herself. 'I'm ever so sorry about your bath, miss, I'll have to speak to her.'

'Later on,' I said; I was surprised at the amount of irritation aroused in me by this alteration in my habits. 'We must go with a very easy rein for a week or so.'

I was wondering, as I went to wash in the little cloakroom downstairs, how much longer it might be than a week or so? My house felt to me invaded, changed, as if it were melting and being swept away.

CHAPTER 29

I RETURNED to the drawing-room, to sit over a book until the bathroom was free; the prosaic fact was that I had to get my toothbrush.

But I had not been there ten minutes when I heard a soft rush, as of someone coming down the stairs, and then the door opened and Edna came in, exuding what I can only call a sense of bathed-ness, wearing a crumpled dark blue dressing-gown of the length they call 'shortie', and with her head swathed in a turban she must have made out of one of my towels, a white one. Her pink feet were bare; they were beautiful, and that is more rare than a beautiful face.

'Excuse my having no slippers. I did pack them but I couldn't find them and I wanted to speak to you,' she began quickly, kneeling down, shivering violently, in front of my big gas fire. 'It's about me and Eric being here. Please can we not say anything about it for two weeks? I think that'll give me time to . . . to . . . think.'

'Of course,' I answered at once. I was relieved that she had set a term to their visit. 'I won't even ask you if you have any plans . . .' I broke off.

She was staring into the shimmering blues and scarlets of the fire. 'Do you know what those women did?' she began quietly, in a moment. 'They had a whip-round for me. One of them went round collecting. *Money*. She brought it to Ronnie's father's place.'

'Dreadful,' I murmured, 'how dreadful.'

She looked at me quickly, then away. 'Do you know what I did? I—'

'I should think you threw it at her,' I said, 'or just managed to stop yourself. I would. But people want to be kind, they are exceedingly stupid, and they have skins like crocodiles. One learns that.'

'I bought an envelope, very white and large, and I put all the money in it and I wrote their names on it, as neatly as I could, really beautifully, and I pushed it through her letterbox. That . . . was what—I did.' Her teeth were chattering.

'There's some whisky in the next room. I'll get you some.' I half got up from my chair.

'No—thank you all the same. I'm not cold—I don't know what it is. I'll go to bed now. I just wanted to tell you. Good-night.' Before I could say anything she had gone.

Every morning she went out, after she had helped Millie and given the child his food. She never grew any less white; and she never failed to look in on me and say 'Good-bye, I'm off,' with a faint smile. Millie confirmed my supposition that she was occupied with the necessary business following the boy's death, and the disposition of the furniture. One morning some days after their arrival, Millie came to me, weeping, and asked if she could have the afternoon off.

'It's the funeral, miss.'

'Of course, Millie. Will you take some flowers for me? You can get them this morning.'

'I—I—suppose—you couldn't . . . if *you* was to come, miss? You did . . . know him.'

'Who would look after Eric if I did?' I said sensibly, even managing a smile. The thought of the lugubriousness, the stares and the clichés and the questions appalled me. And the reporters, perhaps, though the 'story' had faded into small paragraphs on the back pages of the newspapers. I would not have sent flowers had I not thought that the omission would hurt Millie terribly.

'I daresay Mrs. Halliwell would have him. I could just pop in when I go for the flowers.' Millie's tone was eager; plans, arrangements, will always arouse her.

'No, we won't bother Mrs. Halliwell . . . get red carnations, Millie, a large bunch, and bring a card back and I'll write on it.'

'Oh, thank you, miss. Teddie'll like that.' Edna, I knew, would probably not notice.

'You don't want me to come, do you?' I said to her, later that morning.

'Oh, *no*,' she burst out uncontrollably. Then checked herself. 'No—no thank you. Sounds funny, but I wish I hadn't got to go myself.'

'I understand. But the only, absolutely the only thing to do is to go straight through with these occasions, as quietly as possible.'

'That's just what I feel . . . Only . . . sometimes . . . you want to opt out.'

'Then you mustn't. You'll feel worse afterwards.'

'I know. How did—did Millie tell you that Ronnie's favourite flowers were dark red carnations?' It was painful to see her forcing the question through her lips: I felt for, and with her, so strongly, so strongly. She might have been my own young self.

'No. He made me think of them, that was all.'

Then she turned away, and I did not speak to her again before they left, just before eleven.

It had occurred to me several times that Edna might be short of money, but Millie, when I questioned her, told me that she had been able to draw an advance on the boy's insurance claim, and that his father was paying for the funeral. I was sure that it had been Ronald who had suggested getting himself insured; *'Not what you might call moderate in her requirements, Teddie isn't.'* Nor prudent, either, I was certain.

When they had gone, I tip-toed upstairs—needlessly, for he always slept like a beautiful log—to inspect Eric. At last I had him to myself! perhaps for four or five hours! I forgot about his dead young father, and the event of that day, and everything except care in preparing his luncheon. The quiet, and the peace, and the little boy, were all delightful.

All went well until after we had eaten.

Then, while I was engaged in the wind-disposal ceremony, with him upright against my shoulder and his wet face against my cheek, that wretched telephone bell went.

It would only be Tessa, about some nonsense. But, suddenly recollecting the funeral and remembering Edna's face as she went out of the house, it occurred to me that I had better answer it. Something *might* have happened. So I went very carefully downstairs, patting Eric's back and murmuring absurdities as we went.

'Wilton Abbot wants you,' said the operator's voice, 'you're through, caller.'

'Hullo?'

'May I speak to Mrs. Miller, please?' said a heavy male voice, with a rural intonation.

'I am sorry, she isn't in. This is Miss Barrington . . .' Eric was wriggling and beginning to whimper '. . . can I give her a message? (there . . . there . . .)'

'Ah . . . if you could. It's her brother-in-law here. Phoning from the hospital. Her sister's been taken very bad. Wants to see her. If she'll come down. Soon as possible. There's a train at nine o'clock . . . I could meet 'er.'

'That's Mr. Summerfield, isn't it? I'll tell her,' I went on, somewhat distracted between the man's murmurs of 'That's right' and short, alarming yelps from Eric, '. . . I'm so sorry to hear . . . but Millie may be very tired when she comes in, Mr. Summerfield, she has gone to the funeral, you know. Her grand-daughter's husband's funeral.'

'I read about that. Bastards, excuse me,' said the heavy voice that had ploughed fields in it.

I assumed that he shared our views about the men who had sent Ronald to Coventry.

'Could you telephone again, Mr. Summerfield? about—say eight this evening? She is sure to be in then.'

'All right, I'll phone again. Tell her she's very bad.' The voice did not change at all. 'Very bad indeed, she is.'

'I'll tell her . . . (there . . . there . . .) Good-bye.'

He rang off, and I could turn my attention to Eric.

What a two hours that was. He roared and bellowed and writhed until I was in despair of calming him. Tears literally spurted from his eyes, he kicked convulsively, his face was purplish-red—oh dear. I was beginning to wonder whether I ought not perhaps to telephone Dr. MacRae (walk Eric round to Tessa I would *not*: her patronage would be intolerable) when two great gushes of wind burst from his mouth, and, instantly, the storm began to subside.

Slowly we paced up and down, he reposing exhausted against my shoulder, head down and eyes shut, and I finding solace in the gentle movement. Presently, he slept. I lowered him with the greatest caution into his basket, and covered him, and left him.

All I wanted, now . . . no, it was *not* tea. I wanted someone in whom to confide every detail of the last two hours. It was not an experience, I decided, that anyone should be asked to go through without the luxury of mulling it over afterwards with a sympathetic listener.

I could hear Frances saying, 'Why didn't you shove the little beast into his cot and let him yell it out? Or get some dope down him?'

No, Frances was not the confidante for this experience. I wished that Millie would come in—poor Millie. I suddenly remembered the news that was waiting for her.

They came in about five, both looking white and quiet. Edna went straight upstairs without a glance at anyone, and Millie, murmuring, 'I'll get us a cup of tea, if you'd like it, miss, though I have had one,' was moving off to the kitchen. I followed her:

'Millie, I hope Eric is all right . . .'

'Oh, miss!' She turned an even whiter face to me, 'he isn't ill, is he? Does he seem poorly?'

'Poorly! He's fast asleep and he ate all his lunch . . . it's I who am poorly!'

I gave her a vivid and, I felt, alarming account of the attack. At the end, she laughed, for the first time for several days.

'Oh, miss! Excuse me, but you . . . I can't help it . . . it was only wind, miss. I reckon you let him take his lunch too fast. Their poor little bellies, see . . .'

'Well, I *told* myself it was, but he seemed . . .'

'Some babies make more than others; it's ever so painful for them, poor little loves . . . oh, miss! the flowers! You never see anything like it! There was a whole room full of them, and all in the hall, too . . . and a great wreath from the directors and heads of the Works . . . all bronze chrysanths and gold ribbons . . .'

She lowered her voice, 'Teddie did put a card on their door, miss, saying "Flowers will not be accepted", but Ronnie's dad, he talked to her, and he had her crying, after a bit, and she took the notice down. And *everybody* sent, miss, simply everybody. All the shops, and everybody. And *crowds* there . . . there was television cameras and everything ... I couldn't help feeling it made it seem not so sad, if you know what I mean.'

I did not know what she meant. I wanted to say, 'There was a dead young man there, too, as well as the television cameras and the directors' wreath, wasn't there?' But I didn't.

Poor Millie. She sneaked off to her little parlour to turn on her television at news-time, and was rewarded, I afterwards heard, by seeing the funeral again through that ghoul's eye, and herself, 'and Teddie and Ronnie's dad, and all.' I shut myself into the drawing-room and Edna remained upstairs.

I was not going to let Millie fret herself into a fine state by three hours worrying about her sister, so it was not until after our supper (Edna came down to get her own on a tray, but only smiled silently and slightly at me) that I told her about the expected call.

CHAPTER 30

'IT NEVER rains but it pours, miss,' was what Millie said, on coming to me about ten minutes past eight. 'Poor Lizzie.'

I looked at her questioningly.

'I told Bob I couldn't go not tonight, miss; that train at nine, it doesn't get in till three in the morning, stopping every station, and I doubt if I'd catch it now ... I'm that tired ... it's giving you a lot of trouble, I know, miss,' she went on, looking wistfully, 'but ... I would like to go tomorrow and stay a bit, in case ... but how will you manage? The cooking and that ...'

'Edna will help me, no doubt. I expect she has finished with all the business side now?'

'I think so, miss. The truth is, I daren't say much to her. She fair frightens me.'

'She doesn't frighten me.' I checked the tactless remark that possibly I understood her better; Millie had more than enough to bear. 'We shall get on, I am sure. She shall take you down to Paddington in the morning.'

This was what was done, although there was actually an impatient, though subdued, exclamation from Edna when I spoke to her in the morning about escorting her grandmother; (Millie had been afraid to 'tackle' her). But the next instant she muttered 'Sorry,' and set about getting breakfast, telephoning the station and securing the services of one of the numerous cab-hire services which are continuously putting their speciously worded cards through my letterbox.

They went. Poor Millie, for days I seemed to have been having last glimpses of her sad face looking through the windows of departing cars, and it was a relief to go up to Jock's room and look at Eric.

I reflected, as I gazed down at him, how swiftly our separate breakfasts had been whirled on to their tables—but with every detail as usual—and the facts about the train ascertained, and even the capricious, chancy mini-cab, brought, in ten minutes, to our front door.

No wonder, I thought, that employers are anxious to secure the services of the young. One can talk about fidelity and honesty and experience as long as one likes: as usual, the brutal fact prevails. The young are four times as quick.

When Edna returned, she announced that she would cook for us while Millie was away.

'Oh, thank you. That will be very nice. And perhaps I may, in my turn, sometimes take Eric for a walk? That would be a help, wouldn't it?'

Then—oh, then—I saw what I had forgotten; the sudden break-up of her face into the delicious quick smile. But she did not answer, only turned away to the kitchen.

I could feel my expression growing haughty. She supposed that I was making the suggestion for my own enjoyment!

And what else was I doing? I smiled too, alone in the hall, and then I went to the kitchen door and put my head round.

'I am going to play some Handel . . . will that . . . ?'

She shook her head. 'I don't mind. It doesn't make any difference.'

No; it had not done with me, either. But certain scents, certain turns of phrase, had been unendurable . . . only, of course, I had endured them.

Millie telephoned in the evening to say that Lizzie was a little better, but the doctors thought 'the up-and-down' might go on for some time, and Lizzie wanted her to stay. The hospital was being ever so kind about visiting, and Bob said it was all right having her there, so might she stay on? I said of course, hoping that Bob's temporate expression of approval at her presence might be warmed, when uttered, by his tone and look; and went on to answer a dozen questions about her Eric and the cooking.

It was plain that Millie was homesick, or rather Eric-sick.

But I was finding it a relief to have her away. I have made it clear that she has always 'got on my nerves', to use an expression I dislike and am ashamed of—as I am ashamed of the fact. Edna did not get on my nerves. She had none of the mannerisms that grated on me in poor Millie.

The days began to drift past like a dream. It was a spell of golden weather; still dawns, misty sunlight, red sinkings of the sun into dulled blue and scarlet cloud, and then frost and stars.

'About where I eat,' said Edna to me before lunch on the first day, 'I read, now, when I eat, and I know you do when you're alone; Granny told me. So I'll be in the kitchen. All right?'

'That is right,' I answered, '"Kun? Payah Kun."'

'What's that?' she asked, lingering. 'Hindu or Arabic? It sounds like it.'

'No . . .' and I told her about the Eldest Magician in Kipling's story *The Crab That Played With The Sea*.

'My middle brother—the one whose room you're in—was so fond of Kipling,' I ended.

'Kipling. He was an Imperialist, wasn't he?' she said meditatively, looking down at the hall floor.

I tumbled into the trap without hesitation.

'My dear child! He was a magnificent *writer*! And at that time England was the greatest nation—' I stopped, because she was laughing.

'It's all right—they told us at school about the Imperialism but *I* just liked some of the stories—it's funny. They're sentimental, and prejudiced, and kind of made up—but they certainly have got something.'

'A little thing called genius,' I said tartly, 'and what else do you expect a story to be but "made-up"?' Then I withdrew, having relished the little clash.

So we ate our meals in mutual solitude. I read my glorious *Westward Ho!*; for the fourteenth or fifteenth time, I suppose; I do not *know* what she read; but I saw a number of what Harry would have called 'shockers' on the kitchen dresser; *The Valley of The Dolls* was the title of one; I turned over the pages in the silent kitchen, thinking, oh dear, oh dear, we shall have to do something about this, and then reminded myself that her tastes were no business of mine, and that she and the boy would be gone in another week.

She might have turned over the pages of *Westward Ho!* in the silent drawing-room, but I hardly thought so.

Millie's sister had rallied, though she was still in hospital, and the officials there gave no definite date for her return home.

But Millie had begged me, during one of the telephone calls she made every other day, that she herself might come back for a few days: Lizzie was 'temporary out of danger, and being taken ever such good care of, miss, and Bob's there and everything, and I do miss my Eric that bad, miss—course, I know he's all right with you and his mum, miss, but I *do* miss him . . . and it's all right about the fare, miss, I've got my savings . . .'

I refrained from assuring her that I would pay it; I don't believe in encouraging dependence in the working-classes. I said what I knew she wanted to hear.

'You come then, Millie dear. Get an early train.' And I added, 'I really do believe he misses you; he has a little way of looking round sometimes as if for someone who wasn't there.'

This was untrue, and it led to a delighted investigation of my lying invention by Millie.

Melting! The Snow-Woman was hardly recognizable; a mere lump of wet crystals on the grass.

The beautiful weather continued, and in the afternoon I took Eric for a short walk, up the slight incline to Tessa's cottage, while Edna was busy washing his clothes and her own.

Tessa is quite sickening over babies; she seems never to stop poking them and squeaking imbecilities over them yet at the same time pointing out, to whoever is in charge of them, how far less 'gorgeous' they are than her own grandchildren. Eric responded at first to these intimacies with pleasure and attention, then became solemn, and finally his fruit-like face assumed such an expression of weary boredom that even Tessa noticed it. I thought it to her credit that she laughed.

'Look at him—just like all the men—give 'em enough attention and they're bored stiff with you.'

'I should hardly have thought that that applied at eight months,' I observed. 'I think he's just sleepy,' and I went on to describe the morning's attack of wind.

Tessa of course was full of lore on this subject, some of it novel to me, and some coinciding with that imparted to me by Millie. At any moment, I knew, she would begin an analysis of Eric's inner disturbances based upon what the late Aldous Huxley has called 'The swamps of popular psychology', so I made my farewells (Eric made none) and wheeled him away; down the darkening, narrow old street, where the freshness of the autumn air lingered above the poisonous fumes poured out by the cars in the evening traffic rush; under the cold pink and purple sky; through the hellish unremitting noise of the accelerating or temporarily pausing engines.

Modern life is full of luxury, and discomfort, I thought, skirting the litter and dogs' ordure on the pavement. In London at least, daily existence for the ordinary person is becoming like that in the eighteenth century, even to us earless ones being splashed by the (horseless) carriages of the gentry.

Edna seemed relieved to see us back.

'I must stop myself getting silly over him being out after dark with anyone but me,' she said, gathering him up into her arms, '(nice cold face). It isn't that I don't trust you,' she added.

'Thank you,' I said.

'And I don't mean to be rude, either.'

'I know you don't, my dear. I understand. But it is only just dusk, and he is well wrapped up.'

She had made me some tea and put it in the back draw-ing-room: near the gas fire, because in late autumn the wind, blowing up from the enormous valley in which London smoulders, can chill the room as it presses, even lightly, against my window.

I sat, sipping gratefully, and reflecting with mingled remorse and dismay that Millie would be back tomorrow. My time with Eric and his mother had been the happiest I had known for years—yes, in spite of Ronald Parker's death, and Edna's face of settled grief that only changed when she compelled herself to make conversation with me.

I thought that she liked me; was, indeed, becoming fond of me. I would miss them both dreadfully when they went. I must ask her what her plans were (I thought, in fairness, I might do that without feeling that I was taking advantage of the hospitality I had shown them) and I would try, I wanted very much to try, to keep in touch with them; close touch, even a fortnightly visit.

The evening quietened. Eric was bathed, with a short visit from myself, and put to bed; Edna made my omelette, and brought it in to me, and then she lingered. She was dreadfully pale and had on her stone face, and I remember wondering whether anything had happened during the afternoon to make her grief more bitter to bear.

'I'm lonely in the kitchen sometimes,' she said quickly, 'just in the evenings. Can I come in and sit with you tonight . . . for a bit? I . . . it's bad tonight.'

I could see that she had extreme difficulty in making the admission.

'I should like that very much,' I answered. 'Let us eat our supper first, and read our books,' I held up Miss Warner's *Queechy*, which I was enjoying for the ninth or so time, in spite of some slight recurring irritation with the faultlessness of its heroine, 'and then . . . may I help you wash up?'

'I'm the world's wonder; I like washing-up,' she said, less flatly, 'gives me a bit of time to think . . . no, I'll do that, thanks, and then I'll come.'

I nodded and smiled and turned to the omelette (Edna's cook-ing was improving daily), and my book.

When she came in about an hour later she carried a tray with two glasses and a bottle.

'Are we going to drink brandy?' I asked, in surprise.

'Yes,' was all Edna answered, and put the tray down on my little table with its brass railing, and with a steady hand poured out two small glasses.

'"Kun"?' she said, with a smile, as she finished filling my own.

'"Payah Kun". But we could have had the pretty balloon ones; they are in the glass cupboard.'

'Are they?' But she sat down on the tuffet at the left-hand side of the gas fire, where I always keep the current numbers of *The Times* and *Punch*, with her glass in her hand, and stared steadily into its flames. And a silence fell.

'What shall we drink to?' I said, almost lightly, at last: I think that I feared some outburst and I shrank from it. I loved this child and I knew it now, but still I shrank.

She roused herself. 'Oh . . . just "cheers". We . . . might drink to . . . to . . . something else later.'

I admit that for an instant I did speculate whether she had had some brandy before she brought it in to me. Then I wondered if she had had some good news . . . yet her expression did not imply as much.

'Are we celebrating something?' I asked, 'You haven't got a job, have you, my dear? If you will forgive my expressing an opinion, I think that that would be unwise, while the boy is still so small.'

She turned to look at me. She was muffled in a thick cream jersey with a polo neck, which made her hair, for some reason, look even more gold. 'No, I haven't got a job . . . it's all right, I'd never leave Eric while he's little.' She turned back to the fire and there was another long silence.

CHAPTER 31

I AM so accustomed to being in the back drawing-room in solitude. On summer evenings I sit by the open windows and watch London sparkle into lights below the poplars in my garden; and in the winter I sit by the fire, with the curtains drawn against the outside world, and, for company, all those possessions fringed with their invisible fringe of silver memories of which I have already spoken. Books are piled on my little round table where the brandy now stood, and my piano is a friend, silent against the wall. I had just wondered if Edna's presence would irritate me.

But it did not. She fitted in as if she belonged. I did not feel any pressure from her young personality; it seemed natural for her to be there. The room was warm and very silent.

Quietly, her voice came into the silence.

'You don't know why I was called Edna, do you?' She did not look at me as she spoke.

'No, of course not—how . . .'

'There's no reason why—you should.'

'Millie told me that you don't like your name,' I said.

I was wondering whether there was to be an outburst of adolescent anger against the parents who had named her. I hoped not; partly because the warmth and quiet were soothing and I liked sitting there with her in silence, and partly because such an attack would seem weak and silly; disconcerting, too, when she had a real grief to endure.

'That wasn't true. I like it, all right—very much, in fact. Grannie is a bit of a liar, you know.'

'You must not say such things, Edna. They—weaken valuable relationships and they are disrespectful, too. Make up your own mind, of course, but keep your conclusions to yourself.'

Then she did look up.

'I like the truth,' she said, 'but I suppose weak people have to lie.'

'I suppose so. It's often their way of defending themselves. But I would never advise anyone young to begin doing it. Strengthen your character instead.'

'I think mine's strong enough—a bit too strong, if you ask me.' She glanced up, and smiled. 'But you aren't asking me.'

'Talk if you want to,' I said, as quietly as I knew how.

'That's what I came in to do, talk. May as well admit it. Mind you, I don't want to . . . at least, in some ways I do, and in some ways I don't.'

'A very usual experience. Fire away, as my brother Harry used to say.'

She was silent for a moment, while my gilt clock, with the figures of Peace and Plenty on it, ticked drowsily in the warmth and silence, and I heard the autumn wind rushing harmlessly past the curtained window. When she spoke at last, I was surprised at what she said.

'I'm leaving the working-class . . . for good,' she said decidedly. 'What those—what those men did to Ronnie finished me. I won't go on about it. It's no use. But I don't think . . . middle-class men . . . would have done it. That's why I'm opting out.'

'They do it as boys, at their Public Schools,' I felt compelled, in justice, to put in.

'Boys aren't men . . . there were chaps of forty and fifty among that lot . . . when I think about it I . . . I daren't tell you . . . what . . . what my thoughts are . . . I might one day. I can't now.'

'You must behave like a soldier's daughter,' was all I could find to say to her. 'Your grandmother tells me that your father was in the Regular Army.'

She answered after a pause, and after a strange little gasp, almost as if she had been holding her breath, 'He was in one of the regiments that held Calais and helped to hold up the Germans while the rest of the Army got away to the beaches. Dunkirk. You know. I must say it all seems a bit unreal to me. I was hardly born. Like something in a history-book.'

'It is something in the history-books. It's already a legend, but it's in the books as well. It *would* seem unreal to someone as young as you are; I can understand that, but your father's coinage is in you; I can feel it. Such qualities are inherited. If it's any comfort at all to you to know it, I think you've behaved with great bravery during the last weeks. I have . . . respected you very much.'

She turned to me suddenly, with a troubled expression. Where now was the face of stone?

'There's something I must tell you. That first day, with that business about the sofa . . . I stuck it on a good deal, you know. I stuck it on a *lot*.'

'You mean you were not so stupid and nervous as you appeared to be? I had guessed that, some time ago, Edna. It was excellent acting. But what I *cannot* understand, what has been puzzling me ever since I saw you that second time in the garden, with Eric, is the *change* in you. You were simply not the same girl. You still aren't. And *why*—this is another thing I have been meaning to ask you when I had an opportunity—*why* did you allow Mr. Crozier to bring you here, when you knew that your baby might be born at any minute . . . ?'

My voice tailed off, as she quickly leant forward and put both her elbows on my knees, cradling between her hands her face, pleading, and lit by its delightful smile.

'But you're glad I did, aren't you?' she asked coaxingly. 'Oh—I'd had one of my rows with Ronnie, about something, I forget what it was, and I'd just walked out . . . and I was feeling bloody-minded . . . you *are* glad? Say you're glad.'

'Certainly I am.' I pressed her hands between my own. 'But I should still like to know what Mr. Crozier's part was in it all, Edna. If you are going to be my honorary niece—'

'That's just it,' she burst out, and hurried on, gabbling so that I could hardly hear what she was saying—and of course I didn't at first take in its meaning—'I'm . . . that's why we came. We were going to tell you, but the baby started and we—Lionel and me, we lost our heads (it was almost the first time in my life I've ever been frightened). I *am* your niece—at least, I'm your great-niece. I'm your brother Edward's grand-daughter, darling.'

Such a silence followed. We sat absolutely still, she with her elbows on my knees and smiling yet, though less spontaneously now, up into my face, and I feeling the warmth in her two long young hands coming through to my old ones. We stared into one another's eyes, and we did not utter one word.

If anyone had told me that I should have had to listen to this revelation, I should have answered that I could not bear it—that the room would have turned black, that dizziness would overwhelm me, and that I should die. Nothing happened; nothing; I did not even grip her and whisper 'Is this true?' I knew that it was true; I simply knew it. Before a hundred tiny details had had time to slide into their right place, this truth had leapt into my heart, and I *knew* that it was true. The note in that 'darling' would have convinced me if I had doubted. But when I tried to speak, all that came out was a kind of wild croak.

She darted to the brandy. 'You're all right, love, you're all right, just hold on . . . here . . .' She slipped an arm behind my head and held the glass to my lips, but my chattering teeth would not let me drink. I pushed it aside, gasping.

'I'll turn the fire up,' she exclaimed, and darted across and put it on to its full strength. 'Is that better? Just hang on—I'm here—I'll take care of you. It's all *right*, love. Just hang on.'

'I'm . . . all . . . right . . .' I gasped, and added (I suppose in an attempt to get back my control), 'was . . . that . . . why . . . you . . . got . . . the . . . brandy . . .' I broke off, shuddering violently.

She held the glass to me again, nodding, as I sipped.

'Now you're not to die,' she commanded, standing tall and firm over me, and I could feel the authority coming out from her, while her expression was all concern and love, 'I know you've got a heart and all sorts of things, but you're not to die. You understand?' She grasped at my hand and actually shook it. 'Everything's going to be all right. *You're not to die.*'

'Don't . . . bully . . . me . . . try . . . to . . . bully me . . .' I managed to get out. 'Let . . . me . . . get my breath. Edward's—oh, my darling. My darling girl.'

I was weeping. She took me into her arms as if I were her child and held me close, as I held her, with a sensation of unutterable comfort.

'I am so sorry, Aunt Maude,' she said when I was at last a little quieter, 'It must have been the kind of shock I simply can't imagine. I'm—I *am* so *very* sorry.'

I shook my head feebly. Speak I could not.

She sat down again on the tuffet at my feet. But she did not take my hand, and I remember thinking that she understood me as well as I did her; at that moment, all I wanted was to become myself once more; to be at my own helm, so to speak.

'I really meant to talk to you about Ronnie,' she began in a moment, speaking low, 'I'm . . . getting to the state when I can't bear it any longer . . . feeling like this, I mean. You see . . . are you all right? or do *you* want to go on talking about the . . . other thing?'

I actually found my face-muscles moving into the faintest of smiles. The question was so young. But I shook my head. 'Tell me,' I whispered. It was my first infant lesson in mother-love.

'I used to nag at him,' she went on, in a new tone, 'well, not exactly nag, but I was fierce with him—I can be fierce, you know—and I—I used to—to go on at him, every night when he came in after—after a day in that place—and—and—I didn't blame him or call him—a—a coward, of course, but I blamed the others, and I swore at them and told him to hold out, even if it went on for years—I said it—it—*would* be cowardly if he left there and—tried to get another job—and—and—'

I thought it wisest to let her confess, and I continued somehow to control my own raging desire to know what had happened fifty years ago while she did. I knew that had it been I who had been kneeling there staring into the scarlet and blue flames and stammering out my guilt, I would have flung off a comforting hand. So I neither spoke nor moved; indeed, I felt almost incapable of doing either.

'I'm—hard,' she ended, almost in a whisper, 'and—I've always wanted to get away from—his—class. I hate them—stupid, sentimental, cruel. I can be cruel, but it isn't their kind of cruelty. I *hate* them.'

'But your mother's people,' I croaked, 'her class—and your grandmother's—are also loving and loyal. Your grandmother has a softness and kindness and a long-sufferingness that I have never had. Those are the Christian virtues, Edna. You and I have the pagan ones.' I almost whispered the words, with a tremendous effort.

She glanced up quickly.

'I wanted to stay on at school and get to a university,' she hurried on, 'but Mum's cousin, who brought me up, wanted me to leave and get a job, and I *could* have gone to—to some people I knew for help, but—I was just proud. I knew it all. And I was—I'd loved Ronnie since we were at Brierley Road Junior together, and he'd loved me, and I knew if I got a job and we saved, we could get married. So that's what—we did. But I've always wanted to *know* things, everything. He didn't. I'll love him until the day I die, but *he* didn't want to know things. And it used to make me angry. I'm—not a very nice girl, Aunt Maude.' She smiled across at me bitterly.

'Did he know about your . . . grandfather? Give me a little more brandy, dear, will you.' My voice was more under control, now.

'Oh, God, yes. That was—one of the troubles.' She poured a teaspoonful or so into my glass. 'He was so *jealous*. He was always afraid I would go off to my grandfather's people and he'd get—left behind somehow.'

'I wish . . .' I murmured, 'he was a sweet boy . . .'

'And he's dead, isn't he,' she said hardly, 'and now I've told you and—no, I don't think you *do* think I'm a hard little bitch, do you?'

I shook my head. 'Strong, not hard. And certainly not . . . you see, you're very like me. Well, I suppose that's natural.'

'The fact is,' she said, in a conclusive tone, and turning away from her absent inspection of the fire with an air of decision, 'you and I love each other. You're—the kind of mother I've always wanted.'

We took a long look, I smiling faintly, she very grave.

'And you'll stay here with me, and let me look after you and Eric and Millie, won't you?' I said at last, and then I did put out my hand, and she took it and let it lie in hers. But—

'I must get a job,' she said instantly. 'Later on, when Eric's older. I won't let you keep us.'

'Very well, a job, then. And Millie and I will look after him,' I added, wishing (perhaps *I* am not a very nice old woman) that I were to have that task to myself. 'Some training, perhaps?'

'I'd love that,' she said, and I could actually see the healthy relish for life beginning to stir faintly in her again, bubbling up in the light of her eyes and the turn of her head. 'I could be a Girl Friday . . .'

It was fascinating, I thought, the mixture in her of Edward's over-riding intellectual curiosity—oh, how familiar that was to me—and her use of clichés and the concepts belonging to what Mr. J.B. Priestley has called 'the admass'.

'There is so much to be done,' I said weakly, 'no, dear, no more brandy . . . there's another thing I *must* know, Edna—did Lionel . . . and . . . his sister . . . keep in touch with Millie, for all those years, more than half a century?'

'Of course they did! Particularly Lionel. I used to get sweets from New York, and dolls from Paris, and lovely presents at Christmas and my birthday. You know Lionel seems so . . . well, not particularly a *soft* person, wouldn't you say? He told me one day that your family was the only one he'd ever had, and how much he looked up to—to my great-uncles when they were all young. Sort of *hero-worshipped* them, he said.'

'Dear Lionel,' I murmured. 'Oh, the relief of being just a silly old fool at last!'

'What?'

'It's all right, dear. But just one more thing—*why* didn't they—Millie, and Lionel and Mrs. Gelfors—Frances—*tell me*? My life would have been so different. I wish—I wish so very much—that they had.'

At the thought, my voice sank almost into inaudibility.

I felt that I was nearly at the end of my tether—which I had always assumed to be a good long one. But I had to know. The story, with its roots back in a past that had been everything to me, must be made plain to me in every detail.

I remembered as if it had happened yesterday the struggle I had had with myself during that last leave of Edward's towards the end of the autumn of 1918.

I had been in the country, nursing, in a large house belonging to some friends of my parents, and the wounded had been pouring in . . . how I had longed and longed to go to London! Just for a week, just for a night, to see Edward! But he had understood why I stayed at my post, and did not go.

And during that leave, his last, he and Millie . . . if I had been there, I *must* have guessed what was happening.

But I had not been there. I had done my duty.

'How did . . . they, Lionel and Frances, come into it . . . at all?' I almost whispered.

'When Grannie found she was pregnant she wrote to Miss Crozier (as she was calling herself again) because she was *desperate* (Great-Aunt Lizzie was quite poor, you know and couldn't help much). She didn't know *why*, Granny told me, but she'd always felt that Miss Crozier—Mrs. Gelfors—wouldn't *tell*. And she did come across: she sent Grannie money, and when I went down to Wales to Mum's cousin she helped, and when Dad was about eighteen, Lionel helped him to get into a tank regiment. They always kept in touch with Grannie, you see, and with me.'

Yes, I remembered now; Frances would have been working in some Ministry in London; already a war widow, she had resumed her maiden name.

'The second generation in the Army,' I murmured disconnectedly, 'though your grandfather, of course, was a volunteer.'

'Yes, and I want Eric to be the third,' Edna said calmly.

How like she was to me. How like! Had I not argued with Harry for hours, throughout months, persuading him whose temperament was naturally pacific and scholarly, though not pacifist, to give his age as more than it was, and to enlist there and then?

In those days, I don't think I believed that anyone was ever *killed* in a war. We who were born before 1914, you must understand, did not take war for granted.

'Won't you leave him to make his own mind up about that?' I said almost inaudibly. I felt too weak to move, too weak to think; I could only feel—she is of my own blood, she and the boy have Edward's blood in them.

'If you train up a boy to the idea that he's going to be a soldier, he gets used to it,' she was saying. 'Love, you're feeling better, aren't you?'

'Well—not really, dear, no. As you said, it's really impossible for you to understand what a shock this has been.'

What was tearing at me was the fact of their—Millie's, Frances's, Lionel's—half-century of silence. They had condemned me—us, for my parents were involved of course as well—to years and years of the equivalent of 'the dry pan and the gradual fire'. *Why* had they not trusted in our love for Edward?

'Why didn't they tell me?' I burst out at last.

'*Because*, darling,' Edna's tone had just the slightest touch of natural niecely impatience, 'you were so—frozen up and inhibited and shut-in and all the rest of it, they thought it would kill you to know, coming on the top of—everything else.'

So I had myself to blame for my fifty years of starvation. Not that it mattered now. Nothing seemed to matter now.

'Of course, in those days,' she went on, kindly, 'people were brought up to make such a *fuss* about that sort of thing.'

I was silent, leaning back in my chair, with my heart still leaping erratically. Yes, it was true. Even now, even in the midst of my sacred joy in the fact that Edward's blood had not been wasted in the soil of France but flowed on in two living creatures more beautiful and more lasting than poppies, I thought *She was our kitchenmaid*. The bonds of class, for my generation, are as bonds of steel.

'He was going to marry her if he'd lived, you know,' said Edna, as if reading my thoughts. 'I've seen a letter he wrote her, calling her "my adored wife", and saying they would marry if he came out of the battle alive.'

'Mauberge,' I murmured; 'not one of the well-known ones.'

'Was that it?—oh, there's Eric—I forgot his feed! I'll just fly up and "do" him. Now don't you die, love, while I'm gone, I won't be fifteen minutes. I mean it; you're *not* to.' She towered over me, tall and strong and young.

'Do bring him down, Edna,' I pleaded weakly. 'I do so want to see him now that I know.'

'All right, I will. It's against all the rules, but he doesn't get a new great-great aunt every night in the week.' She flew out of the room.

I was glad to be alone, yet I longed for them to come back. I think that my greatest comfort, at that moment, was the thought of that as yet unseen letter of Edward's. His expressed intention was, of course, sacred to me.

And presently the door was pushed gently open, and round it came the two sovereign-gold heads. In silence, smiling, Edna put the sleepily smiling boy into my arms.

The mid-seventies are still an age at which people are likely to die, in spite of the fashionable assumption that we shall all go on for ever. Frances went, suddenly, in the summer of that year.

Sometimes I read again the letter that she wrote to me in reply to mine thanking her for what she had done for me, and I smile with pain and affection over its most Frances-like conclusion: *'And for God's sake don't make a fuss about it now, it was all a hundred years ago anyway. Hooray, the old Snow-Woman's gone for good.'*

Yes, she has gone, and for good. I trust that God deals with Frances's loyal and difficult spirit, in one of those unimaginable countries to which I am drawing near.

Lizzie, with whom Millie found shelter when she left us with her story of a forthcoming marriage, died not long after my Frances, and was mourned, needless to say rather mawkishly, by her sister.

It is Millie, too, who keeps Ronald Parker's memory as green as the remorseless pressure of healthy living will allow it to remain: Eric has been taught to kiss a picture of 'Daddy in Heaven'. This he does with precisely the same expression as he kisses his toy panda and with much, I should imagine, the same feelings. But it is always good to learn to kiss something.

Millie *does* continue to irritate me. She looks ten years younger, and I really think she has ceased to be afraid of me, though I must confess that my sisterly feelings were sorely tried on the day that she faltered out that she 'couldn't never manage Maude, but I might manage "Maudie", miss, it seems friendlier-like.'

So, occasionally, I answer to 'Maudie'. No doubt it is good for me to be chastened.

Tessa Halliwell is really intolerably patronizing about Eric, perpetually hinting that her own grandchildren are handsomer, larger and cleverer, but we see a good deal of her; Eric, with the incalculability of children, is devoted to her.

As the years have gone by, Ronald's name has almost ceased to be heard in our house, except when Millie murmurs it to Eric. This is right; this is as it should be; it is also almost unbearably sad.

But Christians (oh, yes, Christianity has come into my life, of late, and I am fighting every step of the way!) were never told that life was not unbearably sad, only that out of the sadness a richness and a glory grow—if not here, then in one of—the unimaginable countries.

And now once more that 'tempting season' of which Edward used to talk to me is here, and the flowers are out in our garden, and on this warm, sunny morning Mr. Grayshott, who has become rather tiresomely besotted with Eric—even to the slight putting out of joint of the black nose of Meggy—is 'making fingers' at him over the hedge, while our little boy plays with his miniature cars on the grass.

On Saturdays, Edna does not go down into London to the secretarial post at which she is rather alarmingly efficient, and, to me, *certainly* alarmingly highly paid. But as much of the money goes on lectures and seminars and courses and tutorials and private lessons and books that it is a relief to me that a wholesome proportion of the remainder goes on Eric—and on clothes.

I am sitting at my favourite window in the back drawing-room, alternately looking at London in its summer haze and at Eric busy on the lawn, when her brilliant head comes round the door.

'Hugh telephoned, darling. We're lunching in town. "Kun"? (Is that right?)' smiling.

I have met Hugh, who is thirty-two years old and in love with Edna.

'"Payah kun" (that is right),' I answer, smiling too; and indeed—oh, indeed, it is.

THE END

FURROWED MIDDLEBROW

Printed in Great Britain
by Amazon